D.G. HEATH MYSTERY COLLECTION

A Person of Interest

Accent

Vortex

VOL. II

Publishing services by Hamaca Press
www.hamacapress.com

Design: Lee Steele

ISBN: 978-0-9911444-8-8

A Person of Interest

READERS' COMMENTS
on *A PERSON OF INTEREST*

Lots of twists and turns. I didn't see the end coming. But I love surprises. —*Kaaren C.*

You hooked me in the first chapter and didn't let go. Beverly Hills and the movie industry have always been full of intrigue, and the courtroom drama played well. You nailed the details. —*Joseph T.*

I read the first *Mystery Collection* and wanted more. Volume II answered my wish. Don't stop now. —*Susan P.*

From start to finish, well done. —*M.H. Clarke*

A brilliant plot. The clues and details all woven together for a grand closure. The characters played their parts well—even the Colombo-type detective. Mystery with a touch of humor. Bravo! — *Gloria O.*

I was there at the scene of the crime like a fly on the wall. I sat behind the defendant in that courtroom, staring darts at the prosecutor. And I cried at the final goodbye. —*Laura S.*

Chapter One

Margaret Gordon's body went limp as she finally stopped struggling. Life was no longer an option. She was dead. Marc removed the pillow from her face and stared at her open eyes, frozen in terror. Liz, Margaret's daughter, standing on the opposite side of the bed, reached across and gently closed her mother's eyelids, as she studied Mark's face.

"What's wrong with you? You look like you're about to faint. Haven't you ever seen a dead body before?" she mocked.

Marc Garret had been a hospice nurse for seven years, and none of his patients had ever died while in his care, but Margaret Carson Gordon was not his patient. She was the victim of her daughter's greed, envy, and hate. With millions riding on Liz's planned murder-suicide, Marc's nerves caused him to shake as he peeled off the surgical gloves he was wearing to prevent leaving any fingerprints on the pillowcase.

He wiped the beaded sweat from his brow with the cuff of his long-sleeved shirt. "I need a drink," he said, reaching for a glass next to the bottle of Scotch on the bedside table.

Liz slapped his hand. "Don't touch that, you idiot. You'll get fingerprints all over it. Let's go downstairs to the bar—I think we can both use a shot or two before the night is over." Liz Carson, cool and calm on the surface, stared at her mother's dead body, her thin lips stretched across her face in a wicked smiled. Revenge is sweet, she thought.

Not a word was spoken as they sat at the bar in the library. Marc could see that Liz was deep in concentration, her brow furrowed in a scowl. Was she having second thoughts about killing her own mother? He poured another drink and moved to a comfortable leather chair by the fireplace. Harboring his own doubts and guilt in silence, he stared into the flickering flames of the gas logs. How had she managed to convince him to murder her mother? Did he really love her that much, or was it his chance to be a millionaire? The alcohol soothed Marc's nerves and his shakes slowly began to vanish.

It was now almost midnight. Liz nodded. "It's time to finish the job. You need to get William's dad upstairs. With his Alzheimer's memory loss and confused state of mind, he won't know what's going on, but bring him to Mom's room. We have to be sure his fingerprints are found in the room and on the pillowcase before his accidental fall down the stairs. Can you handle that?"

"It shouldn't be a problem getting him upstairs," Marc stated. "But what if the fall doesn't kill him?"

"Don't worry," Liz assured. "If he survives the push down the stairs, he'll most likely die of his disease before they can bring him to trial for the murder of his second wife. In his will, Mom was to inherit half of his twenty-million-dollar estate; but if she dies before he does, it comes to me as her only heir."

Liz paused at the base of the stairs with a devilish grin. "However, there's a chance we could have it all, if we fuel the fire by casting suspicion in William's direction." Her mind had been working as she perched on the bar stool. "After all, he's a mystery writer. Who better to come up with a plan to kill them both and claim the fortune?"

"I'm not sure I follow you," Marc said as he tried to comprehend her diabolical thought process.

Liz was steps ahead of him. "You and I will have verifiable alibis. Tonight, you felt like you were coming down with the flu, and Mom told you to take the night off and go home after you had put the old man to bed. That put you out of the house with her permission. Four other dinner guests, the cook and I, all heard her say she could handle things. I left immediately after dinner to spend the night with Margo at her condo in Palm Springs."

Marc listened carefully as Liz explained her plan to make sure her half-brother would be indicted for a double murder. "William is alone at the cabin in the Tehachapi Mountains—a short two-and-a-half-hour drive from Beverly Hills. Plenty of time to drive back, kill both of them, and make it look like a murder/suicide then return to the cabin without being seen by anyone. He knows the security code and has a key to the house."

Marc shook his head in disagreement. "No one's going to believe that William would kill his father. He's like a tick on an old dog. He depends on his dad and loves him. I should know, because he's refused to put him in a nursing home and was furious when the doctors even suggested it."

Liz laughed. "I overheard him arranging a meeting with the lawyers to draw some funds out of the trust. He's in need of money, and who would have a better motive for wanting to acquire his fortune sooner, rather than later? Unfortunately, he forgot about me, as he often does."

Marc started to say something, but Liz broke his train of thought. "You didn't see William at dinner tonight, did you? Shall

I tell you why? He had an argument with his dad in the library this morning. I heard him ask for a large sum of money. Michael shouted at him to get out of the house and said he wasn't giving any more money to charities. He didn't even know he was talking to his own son. William bumped into me on the way out and said he was going to the mountains to cool off. So, you see—all the dominos are tumbling in the right direction."

Liz leaned into Marc. Putting her hand behind his head, she gave him a lingering lover's kiss. "Let's finish this job and call it a night. Carmen will be here at seven in the morning to fix breakfast and I need to be in Palm Springs when she calls with the news."

Chapter
Two

Liz waited in her mother's bedroom for Marc to get Michael Gordon out of bed and up the stairs. She was not having any regrets. On the contrary, she was remembering the abuse and struggle her mother had forced upon her as a child. This was her revenge.

Margaret, now lying dead in the bed while Liz gloated, had been a part-time actress who managed to snag producer Michael Gordon on the rebound, after his first wife had died in a mysterious accident. It didn't take her long to become the lady of the house, and a grand duchess if ever there was one. As an actress, she knew how to play the part of a Hollywood producer's wife.

Liz recalled her childhood years, when her mom was constantly on the move to find work. Margaret, or Maggie, as she was called by her drinking buddies, had emerald green eyes, wavy blonde hair and the figure of Playboy model. She was a good-looker, all right, but lacked the talent to become a star of any caliber.

As the child of a movie-gypsy extra, Liz spent her young life in turmoil, moving from place to place, changing schools, living in cramped apartments and single-wide trailers in remote set—locations, never in one place long enough to make friends and lead a normal life. She had been raised by babysitters, movie friends, and "aunts" and "uncles"—who she knew weren't really her relatives. Maggie had been an only child and a bitter woman, whose own mother had disowned her at the age of eighteen. She never married Liz's father because she couldn't be sure who he was.

~

Marc entered the room with Michael and guided him to the side of the bed. The pillow still rested over Margaret's face. Michael looked confused as he grabbed the pillow to remove it and let out a howl in shock when he saw the blood running from her nose. He grabbed her shoulders and shook her body trying to wake her. Liz and Marc left the room as he became violent, smashing the Scotch bottle on the night table and knocking over the bedside lamp. Her plan was working, as she listened to the sounds of destruction coming from the bedroom and smiled with glee. It was more than she had hoped for.

Then suddenly, all was quiet. The bedroom door opened and Michael stumbled out. He didn't see Marc and Liz, huddled against the wall, as he staggered to the top of the stairs and reached for the railing. Just then, Liz rushed towards him with a final push, not waiting for Marc to finish the job.

Losing his balance, Michael tumbled head-over-heels to the marble floor at the base of the stairs, his head twisted at an awkward angle and his blue eyes open in a blank stare. The fall had proved fatal, as she had hoped.

Liz and Marc returned to Margaret's bedroom—it was in shambles. Dresser drawers had been emptied and their contents thrown about the room. The wall safe in the closet stood open. Liz knew it would be. She had already removed her mother's valuable jewels while waiting for Marc to appear with Michael. Once again, she had planned ahead.

She reached for Marc's hand. "Don't touch anything. Not even the light switch. It's time we separate and leave this place. Call here in the morning and pretend you still don't feel well. Make sure no one sees you. Take the fire escape at your apartment like we planned. I'll handle the police once I arrive back from Palm Springs. I'm sure Carmen will make the necessary call to William."

Marc had parked his car a block away when he returned to the mansion. Liz had parked in the driveway of a vacant house on the corner and walked over. "You leave first," she said. "I need to reset the alarm. And don't worry, everything's going to be fine."

~

Meanwhile, all was quiet at the mountain cabin as author William Gordon sat alone by the fireplace. Mesmerized by the flames and the aroma of burning oak, he was deep in thought. This time, he hadn't come here to write. He needed time to consider the changes, soon to happen, that would affect his life. His concerns, however, were not for himself, but for his father.

William's mother had died years ago in a tragic auto accident as she rounded a hairpin curve on the mountain road leading to the cabin. Clair Gordon was an excellent driver, and always cautious when rounding that curve in the narrow road, but the brakes had failed and she was not able to stop as she descended the steep incline.

The jeep exploded when it smashed on the jagged rocks at the bottom of the ravine. Fire-charred, and twisted metal and broken glass were all that remained by the time the rescue units were able to reach the scene. Clair had suffered a broken neck when thrown from the vehicle. Michael Gordon, William's father, had married his second wife, Margaret Carson, a year later.

Seven years ago, Michael Gordon, at fifty, had been diagnosed with the onset of Alzheimer's. His doctors said the disease, when contracted at such a young age, is known to develop at a more rapid pace than it does in much older people.

His current condition was now in the advanced stages. Memory loss was evident when he could no longer add two and two. A year later, he couldn't remember who he was or where he was. Family members, friends, and business associates were total strangers except in fleeting moments of recognition.

At times, Michael was extremely violent and destructive, becoming a danger to others and even himself. For his own safety, he had been moved into a downstairs bedroom at his Benedict Canyon Drive mansion in Beverly Hills, where he lived with his wife, her daughter, his son, and a fulltime male nurse and caregiver.

William loved his dad, who was both father and friend to him. It was now only a matter of months before Alzheimer's would claim Michael's life and William would become heir to a fortune, but he would give it up in a minute if it would save his dad's life.

He had arranged a meeting with the family lawyers the next day to discuss putting his dad in a nursing home for his final days. Marc, his caregiver, had given notice that he was taking a new position in Arizona and would be leaving at the end of the month. William knew the care for her husband would be too much for his stepmother to handle alone. His heart was heavy and his mind muddled with decisions to be made as he fell asleep in the chair by the fire.

Chapter Three

Her cell phone was ringing the following morning as she reached for the bedside table to retrieve it. With blurry, red eyes from lack of sleep, she squinted through fake eyelashes. "Who the hell is calling me at this ungodly hour of the morning?" she said into the phone, through cracked lips caused by the dry air in the desert.

"Ms. Lizzy, it's Carmen. You must come home. It's terrible. I don't know what to do."

She sat up in bed and smiled. "Carmen, you're not making any sense. Calm down and tell me what's wrong."

Carmen started to sob. "They're dead—both of them!" she exclaimed.

"Who's dead Carmen? I don't understand." She thought to herself, I should have been the actress instead of Mom.

"Mr. Gordon and your mother are dead. I find them this morning when I arrive to work."

"Oh my god!" She exclaimed in mocked horror. "Did you call

911?"

"Sí...they are on the way, but I don't think it will help. They are both cold as ice. I'm sure emergency can't help."

"Can you tell what happened? Was the alarm still on? Did someone break in?" She wanted to know how the scene looked to Carmen.

"The alarm was still on and the doors were locked. Mrs. Gordon is in her bedroom and Mr. Gordon is at the bottom of the stairs. I'm so frightened. I don't know what happened."

"I'll leave as soon as I'm dressed. Stay calm, and call William. Don't touch anything."

"I called Mr. William and he comes soon. Please. Hurry."

~

Emergency vehicles and police cars were parked in the drive and along the street in front of the house when Liz arrived. Neighbors were gathered on their lawns and in the doorways of their elegant homes, gawking at the activity on their normally tranquil street. Even the press had arrived before she did. The scene could not have been set any better by a movie director. Cameras flashed and reporters shouted questions as she exited her car and rushed to the main entrance before disappearing into the mansion.

Michael Gordon's body was already in a body bag on a stretcher. She stood aside as the EMT's carried him out to a waiting vehicle. Carmen and a man approached her. "Ms. Carson, I'm Detective Barrett with the Homicide Division of the Beverly Hills Police Department." He flashed his badge. "I understand you just arrived from Palm Springs."

"Yes, that's true." She glanced at the maid. "Carmen, can you get me some water, I need to sit down." With tears in her eyes and an anguished expression on her face, she was playing her part like a pro. "Will you join me in the library, detective? We can talk there." She led the way. "Has William arrived yet?" she asked in a curious tone.

"He's upstairs with Detective Grant. He was pretty shaken when he arrived."

"I'm sure he would be after the row he had with Michael yesterday." She took a seat on the camel-colored soft leather sofa in front of a massive carved stone fireplace.

"Excuse me, I don't understand—was there some kind of confrontation?"

"I suppose you could call it that. Michael yelled at William and ordered him out of the house when he asked for some money. I'm sure he's feeling remorseful for upsetting him—and now he won't have a chance to apologize."

"I see." Detective Barrett sat in a leather chair opposite her as he wrote in his notepad.

"Detective, can you tell me how my mother died?" she paused, taking a handkerchief from her purse to dab her eyes as Carmen entered the library with a glass of water. "Carmen didn't mention it on the phone when she called and I was in such shock, I forgot to ask."

"Oh Ms. Lizzy, I'm so sorry."

"No, no, Carmen, it's not your fault. You were in a state of shock as well."

Detective Barrett cleared his throat. "I believe the cause of death was asphyxiation, but we will know for sure when we get the coroner's autopsy report."

"Is an autopsy necessary?"

"Always, when there is any suspicion of a homicide," he confirmed.

"I don't understand why anyone would want to kill my mother. She was such a loving wife and doted on Michael hand and foot. She didn't want to put him in a care facility like William was planning to do. We were such good friends, she was more than a mother to me. I miss her already." She dabbed the fake tears from her eyes once again.

Detective Barrett waited. "I understand you were here for a dinner party last night. Can you fill me in on the details and tell me who else was at the party?"

Liz heaved a sigh and sniffed. "We were celebrating mom's birthday. There were eight people. All close friends; mom and Michael, Dr. Thompson, Michael's doctor, and his wife Grace, movie director Greg Farrell and his wife Linda, myself and Marc Garret, Michael's live-in male nurse and care-giver."

"And where would this Mr. Garret be this morning? Shouldn't he be here?" Barrett asked.

Carmen answered before Liz opened her mouth. "Mr. Garret went home sick last night, to his own apartment after he put Mr. Gordon to bed. Mrs. Gordon told him she could take care of Mr. Gordon and didn't want him to catch anything Marc might have."

Barrett tapped his pencil on his notepad giving thought to Carmen's statement. "Has Mr. Garret been notified of his patient's death?"

Carmen shook her head. "I called and left a message, but he hasn't called back."

"I'll need his address and phone number," Barrett said, "and the same information for everyone here last night." Carmen volunteered to retrieve the information and left the room. "Why wasn't William here?" he asked.

"That's not hard to answer." Liz said as she made her way to the bar and poured herself a Scotch on the rocks. "He wasn't invited. William and Mom didn't get on that well. He resented that she had taken his mother's place. It's as simple as that." She raised her glass to toast her brilliant statement.

Barrett sensed there was no love lost between Liz Carson and her half-brother. "I can tell you're taking this very hard and I think you've given me a lot to go on for now." He stood and tucked the notepad in his coat pocket. "I appreciate your answers and we'll be back in touch with more questions as soon as we have time to check on things." He moved toward the door.

"Oh, detective." Liz was not ready for him to leave just yet. "I asked Carmen, when she called this morning, if the alarm system was on when she arrived." She studied the drink in her hand.

"Yes. She already told us it was, and that the doors were locked. It appears to be a murder/suicide, but we can't make any judgments until all the facts are considered. You have my condolences. I'll find my way out."

Chapter Four

Detective Grant sat in a chair in the bedroom upstairs, facing William, who appeared to have finally gotten control of his emotions. "Mr. Gordon, do you mind if I call you William?"

"Not at all, formality doesn't matter that much at times like this."

Grant continued, "I know this is a difficult time for you, but we need to ask some questions as soon as possible when there is the probability of a murder involved."

"Probability! That's a strange word to use in this case. As a mystery writer, I wouldn't hesitate to tell you straight out that a murder has definitely happened here!" he shouted.

"I'm sorry, sir. I know you're upset with the loss of your father right now, but it's important for us to know if you might have any idea how these two deaths may have happened or what may have led to this situation." He waited for a response.

"You want to know if I believe my mentally ill father, in the final stages of Alzheimer's, would, in a violent rage, murder his second wife and then commit suicide when he realized what he had done?" He shook his head. "I can't answer that. I wasn't here. I don't know what provoked the attack on Margaret Carson—or even if my father was involved in her murder." Grant, without speaking, nodded his head in agreement.

William continued, "Her room looked as if someone was trying to find something. The safe was open and some jewels are missing. Perhaps it was a robbery in progress—she woke up, and they killed her. Dad could have wandered into the bedroom at the wrong time and they shoved him down the stairs to make it look like he killed himself, or he stumbled and fell as he left the crime scene."

Detective Grant looked amused. "I can certainly tell you're a mystery writer, sir. You've got it all figured out."

Furious with himself, William stood and looked him straight in the eye. "I haven't figured out a goddamn thing, detective. That's your job. Now if you don't mind, I want to be alone."

"Just one more question if I may: Where were you last night between the hours of 11 p.m. and 3 this morning?" His pencil was poised for the answer.

"I was upset yesterday. I had some decisions to make, so I drove to our cabin in the Tehachapi Mountains."

"Were you alone all evening? You don't have to answer that if you have any reason not to, but we will be checking."

"Of course I was alone. The cabin is very remote, and for your information, I haven't anything to hide."

"One last question and I will scoot out of here: Did anyone see you at the cabin or on the road to the cabin?"

"No. I drove straight to the cabin and didn't leave until I got the call this morning from Carmen. Now I must ask you to leave; I have phone calls to make and arrangements to take care of." He looked out the upstairs window as the last body was loaded into the back of the EMT's vehicle. Reporters were scattered everywhere. TV trucks were filming for the afternoon news and correspondents were poised in front of the cameras. It was a field day for the hungry media, and he knew it wasn't over. It had just begun.

He wondered where Liz was hiding. Not that he really cared. A bad penny will turn up when you least expect it, and Liz was a corroded penny if ever there was one.

Detective Grant left the bedroom as William stepped into the walk-in closet and changed into his jogging clothes, slipped into his running shoes and laced them quickly. He needed fresh air, and to get away from the mansion and the media circus on Benedict Canyon Drive.

As he descended from the upper level, Liz Carson was standing on the grey-and-white marble tile at the base of the stairs, waiting for him, with a look of vindication on her face, and a fresh Scotch in her hand.

"Where are you off to?" she said, her speech slurring as she stared at him through eyes that had difficulty focusing.

"I'm going for a run, if it's any of your business." His statement was curt as he shoved passed her.

"Well, don't plan on going far," she said in a raised voice, "You may be the son and heir, but you're still a suspect, you know."

He stopped and turned back, "What the hell are you talking about? You're drunk and it's not even noon, but that's no surprise," he sneered.

Liz squared her shoulders and glared at him, "My mother has been murdered and the police are going to investigate everyone who was in this house, or who might have had a motive; and you, Mr. Big Shot Mystery Writer, are a person of interest."

"You don't know what you're saying." He turned again and headed to the door.

"I know more than you think I do," she paused, "But have a nice jog along the beach, while you still can. Enjoy the fresh air. It won't smell the same in a cell. Ta-ta, Sherlock." Liz waved over her head as she returned to the bar in the library.

The news media, camera men and TV reporters surged to meet him as he exited the house, shouting questions as he rushed to his black Mercedes SUV and slowly maneuvered through the crowd to escape the ambulance-chasing hoard. Once he was out of Beverly Hills and speeding along the coast highway, he eased his white-knuckle hold on the steering wheel; he breathed a sigh as he approached Malibu.

He had lowered the car windows so he could smell the salt air and feel the ocean breeze on his face as he listened to the waves rolling in and crashing on the beach, releasing their calming effect on the stress that encased him like a vise.

William hadn't eaten since noon yesterday at the cabin. With all the stress he was under, he hadn't given a thought about food until now, as he pulled into Maria's Tacos-To-Go stand, on Highway101, to fill that empty spot in his growling stomach.

At thirty-two, William resembled his dead father when he was the same age. Six feet tall, with sandy hair and turquoise-blue eyes, he looked the image of a Cambridge graduate and a pampered movie-producer's son.

It was true. His father had spoiled him—at least until Margaret Carson married his dad a year after his own mother had died. It was all Margaret's fault. Even though she and William were not close, they seemed to get along fine at first. However, tension developed when she encouraged his father to stop writing William a check every time he had a financial problem.

Instead, she suggested giving him an annual allowance. "William's an excellent writer," she had said. "If only he would settle down and stop being such a playboy, he could make a good living and become a more independent and responsible person."

That was the point of separation between William and Margaret as friends. Michael Gordon stopped writing checks for William's extravagant spending and put him on an allowance of one-hundred thousand dollars a year—paid annually on his birthday. Unfortunately, the funds did not cover all the expenses of his flamboyant lifestyle and posh living, partying, gambling, and travel.

Jogging down the beach from the taco stand, William reflected on the trivial argument he'd had with his father the previous morning. He realized that Michael didn't even know who he was. Alzheimer's disease whittles away at a person's mind. They forget who they are and who you are. They frequently believe that people are lying to them, trying to steal their money and take advantage of them. They become suspicious, irrational and abusive with the slightest provocation.

The doctor had told them to expect these changes in Michael's behavior. But when you love someone so much, it's hard to understand that they are no longer in control of their own mind and actions. Often patients are like a two-year-old child throwing tantrums, but with the strength of an adult, and the ability to injure themselves and others.

William knew in his heart that his father could never murder anyone. There had to be another answer for the two deaths at the mansion, and he needed to find it.

Chapter
Five

Back at the crime scene on Benedict Canyon Drive, the media had vanished as quickly as it had arrived, leaving the neighborhood tranquil once again. But inside the house was another story.

Carmen had been busy cleaning after the police and homicide forensic teams had departed. She cried as she changed the bed sheets and picked up Margaret's clothing, refolded and placed them in the drawers of the Bombay chest. The furniture had been covered in fingerprint dust, and the antique Oriental rug, dirtied with powder-like footprints, was shoved half way under the bed.

She pulled the rug from beneath the bed to clean it and something sparkling caught her eye. Reaching down to retrieve it, Carmen held her breath as she moved to sit on the chaise lounge at the foot of the bed and closely inspect the object in her hand. It was a diamond earring that had belonged to William's mother, Clair Gordon.

Over the past seven years, Margaret Gordon had managed to

become the keeper of the family jewels. The safe in her walk-in closet now stood open and empty. Carmen had cleaned the combination lock and the surface of the safe that was dusted for prints. There was no indication it had been broken into.

She thought to herself: whoever took the jewels had to know the combination, but Ms. Margaret and Mr. Michael were both dead, so who could it be? The house was locked securely and there was no sign of forced entry.

Carmen slipped the earring into her apron pocket. She would need to remember to tell the nice policeman who gave her his card.

"What are you doing sitting there? Get this place cleaned up and fix my dinner. I haven't eaten today and I'm starved." Carmen had jumped when Liz Carson entered the room and shouted at her. She knew her job here would soon be over.

"Yes, Ms. Lizzy. Will Mr. William be here for dinner?"

"Frankly, I don't believe he will—and I could care even less," she said. Turning on her heels and retreating through the doorway, she headed downstairs to the library bar.

Liz closed the library door, crossed to the bar, and made another Scotch on the rocks. She fumbled in her purse for the cheap, prepaid throw-away cell phone and called Marc Garret. He answered on the first ring.

"What?" he said.

"Why haven't you called? I haven't heard from you all day." Liz asked.

"You said I should lay low. I didn't know I was supposed to call," he said meekly. "Is everything going as planned?"

"Even better. If William isn't arrested for murder by the end of this week, I'll be surprised. Did you cover yourself like I instructed?" Liz lit another cigarette and took a sip of her Scotch, waiting for his response.

"I'm sure I'm on the apartment's security video tapes. When I got here after dinner, the widow-woman, Mrs. Baker, arrived at the same time with some packages and I helped her get in the door. I left and returned by the fire escape—so no one saw me in the hallway or elevator. The old woman brought me some chicken soup for lunch today, after I told her I was catching a cold and planned to be home all day. I'm sure she'll vouch that I was here all night and all day, but I haven't heard anything from the cops."

Liz smiled. "Don't worry. You will. Be sure to stick to the story and don't forget to mention old Mrs. Baker; and get rid of your phone before they show-up. I'll pick up a couple more tomorrow. Carmen told the cops that she left a message on your personal cell phone, but call her later and let her know you received the call. It'll be all over the TV this afternoon. And stay calm. We're in the clear." She disconnected the call.

"Who's in the clear?" William sounded as he stood in the doorway to the library.

Liz almost dropped the phone when she heard his voice. "I was talking with Margo in Palm Springs. She's already heard the news on TV and wanted to know if she should come up and offer her support. She wanted to be sure the media had left, so I told her they had and we were in the clear." Liz was a practiced liar.

She paused to catch her breath. Downing the last of the Scotch in her glass, she slammed it on the bar and stood to leave the room. "Are you staying for dinner? If so, you'll need to tell Carmen. I'm going to shower and change." She brushed past William and exited the library.

William moved to the bar, put ice in a glass and reached for the bourbon, then stopped his shaking hand. No, he thought, I won't do it. I stopped drinking a year ago, and I'm not going to start again. Instead, he took out his phone and called his lawyer, who is also a recovering alcoholic.

Shawn Harris, of Morton, Harris, and Bernstein, Attorneys at

Law, had grown up with William, and both had graduated from Cambridge. As college frat buddies, they used to do a lot of drinking together, but were now support partners in Alcoholics Anonymous.

Shawn checked the caller ID when his phone buzzed, "William, buddy! I heard the news and..."

"Save it, man. I need your support." That was their AA signal for help.

"I'm here for you anytime. Where do you want to meet?" Shawn said.

William was quick. "Your office. I can be there in twenty minutes. Are you still at work?"

It was almost six o'clock, and most of the legal staff had gone home for the day. "I'm the only one left in the office. I'll wait for you and let the floor guard know to expect you. Have you eaten this evening?" Shawn knew that food always helped.

"No. I haven't had time today."

Shawn's voice was calming. "Don't worry, man, I'll order something in. See you in fifteen—and repeat after me...I'll be OK."

William knew the drill—"I'll be OK. And thanks. Ciao." He was already out the front door as the setting sun began to cast a pink glow in the sky and the black starlings found their roosts in the dense foliage of the carob trees that lined the street.

Chapter
Six

William made good time. It was still early for a Friday night and the traffic was light on the boulevard. Shawn's offices were located on the fourteenth floor at 9200 Sunset. Boulevard—a posh, steel-and-glass, contemporary high-rise, overlooking Beverly Hills and the Sunset Strip near Doheny Road. William was met by Carl, the guard, as he stepped off the elevator. "Mr. Harris is expecting you, Mr. Gordon. Just sign here, please." He pointed to the clip board on the desk and buzzed Shawn on the intercom to announce William's arrival.

"Thanks, Carl." William scribbled his name quickly. "Don't get up. I know the way."

Shawn met him at his office door. "Get in here. You look like something the cat drug in. When did you last shave?" Shawn always looked like he had just stepped off the page of a fashion magazine. His prematurely gray, wavy auburn hair and his David Niven pencil mustache gave him a movie star appearance. At six-foot-two, his taunt, muscular frame was proof that he worked out at the gym.

William stroked the stubble on his face. He hadn't shaved since he returned from the writers' conference in San Francisco on Tuesday. It was now Friday.

"Guess I do look like a bum. Is that food I smell?" His mouth began to water.

Shawn smiled. "I've never known you to turn down Mediterranean cuisine, so I had them send some food down from Nava upstairs. It's on the table in the conference room. Come on, we can talk while we eat. Food stimulates the brain, as we used to say at Cambridge. And by the way, I want to know everything—all the details. You've had a rough day from what I've seen on TV. I assume that's what you need to get off your chest." Shawn always cut to the chase so he could put the puzzle together with his unbelievable photographic memory.

William sat at the table while Shawn poured them both a mineral water. "Ok, bro...I'm all ears." William began to eat. He didn't realize how hungry he was until now. His taco at the beach hadn't lasted long. Shawn was patient. He knew William would talk when he was ready and he watched his friend with interest.

William finally sat back in his chair, stared across the table at his friend and confessed. "I'm frightened, man." He paused for a breath, then continued. "I believe the police think I had something to do with Margaret's death. He then explained the events of the day and his meeting with Detective Grant.

Shawn studied him with a lawyer's gaze—his body language—his voice—his emotions and facial expressions. "William, you are no murderer."

"You know that—and I know it," William said. "But the police told Liz that I'm a person of interest, and that means I'm a suspect."

Shawn shook his head. "Don't go jumping to conclusions. It's still early in the investigation. I'll sign on as your legal representative on one condition—we'll take this one step at a time. The media seems to believe that your father lost control in his medical state and smothered Margaret, then fell down the stairs, accidentally killing himself. An accident—maybe—but suicide has not been ruled out."

"I just don't believe that's how it happened. I can't say why, but I don't. I woke in the middle of the night at the cabin when I heard my father's voice call my name. But he wasn't there—I was alone. The same thing happened when my mom was killed in that car accident—she called my name."

Shawn was already making notes. "I'll call Martin Grant first thing in the morning and see what I can learn. He's kind of a Colombo-type character—bit of a strange duck, but I've worked with him before. What was the other detective's name?"

"Barrett, I think. He questioned Liz and must have told her that I was a suspect. She's the one who told me."

"William," Shawn said, "once I let the police know I'm your legal counsel, which I must do if I request any information about the case, it may cast more suspicion on you. However, it pays to be a step ahead, and for the record, this is pro bono. I don't want any argument."

"I can't let you do that," William exclaimed.

"You can't stop me." Shawn smiled. William nodded his agreement.

~

The following morning Detectives Barrett and Grant had been busy narrowing down the persons of interest in the murder investigation. They drank black coffee and munched on donuts as they compared notes, sitting across from each other at a scarred wooden desk, in the small cubical they called their office. "What have you got on the list of suspects?" Grant asked.

Barrett shoved his written report across the desk. "I checked on Liz

Carson's whereabouts last night. Her friend, Margo, in Palm Springs, verified she was at her condo and sound asleep when she returned from a wedding party. So I put her on the back burner for now."

Detective Grant shuffled through the report. "What about this nurse caregiver? What's his name...Marc Garret? Any leads on his story?"

Dave Barrett held up his hand as he finished a bite of chocolate-glazed donut and took a sip of coffee. "I paid a call to his apartment, but no one came to the door. So while I was there I met with Scott Cooper, the building manager. They have security cameras in the lobby and on each floor. He's going to send us copies of the footage during the timeframe of the crime and through noon today.

"The hospice firm Garret works for gave me his description and a photo. I'm sure he'll show up eventually. I ran his information through the criminal ID channels but nothing popped up, so he must be clean. No record—not even a parking ticket unpaid. That's unusual for a man in his early thirties."

Grant appeared to be deep in thought. "They're all innocent until proven guilty. But I'm going to bet it was William."

"So share. What do you know that I don't?" Barrett said.

"You know all the facts, but just don't want to accept them." He thumbed through the report. "You interviewed Liz, who was a fount of information about William. His blow-up with his dad about money—his ill feelings about his step-mother taking his mother's place—his absence at the birthday dinner and his disappearance to the mountain cabin until yesterday morning, and a fortune to inherit." Grant was painting the portrait of a man with several motives.

He continued, "You read the report on my interview with him. He doesn't have a verified alibi. He said he saw no one, from the time he arrived at the cabin until he left the following morning. He became defensive and averted answering my questions. In an off-handed way, he dismissed me, telling me to leave. Said we were the ones who needed to find the answers—it wasn't his job, he had other things to take care of. Now I ask you—does that sound like a grieving son?"

Barrett smiled and shook his head. "He's right, you know. It's our job to find the killer, but it would be nice if he would cooperate with the investigation. However, I'll take you up on that bet—I don't think William would kill anyone. Call it a hunch or a premonition, but I didn't see murder in his eyes."

"Fine," Grant agreed, "let's make it ten bucks and lunch at Musso and Frank's. Now, who's next on the list?" he asked as he dumped the empty donut box in the trash.

"Well, there's Doc Thompson and his wife or the movie director Farrell and his wife," Barrett said.

"I'll take Doc Thompson; you're much better with those movie types." Grant confessed.

Barrett chuckled. "What makes you say that?"

"You're more the leading-man type. At least my wife thinks so. But then look who she settled for."

"Tell Beth I appreciate the compliment, but I'm sure she wasn't referring to the movies," he said.

"Hey—we forgot about the cook, Carmen Martinez." Grant said.

"Don't worry, Carmen isn't going anywhere, I told her I'd be back today with more questions. Meanwhile, we better find a stronger suspect or the media is going to crucify William without a trial. Did you see the morning papers? Someone's been leaking information, and I have a good idea who it is. Did we get the coroner's pathology report on Michael Gordon?"

"It was hard to say if he broke his neck before the heart attack or the heart attack caused him to fall, breaking his neck. Either way, I think we can rule out murder," Grant said.

"Don't be too quick to judge. Forensic reports aren't in yet," Barrett reminded him.

Chapter Seven

Liz sat at the dining room table eating breakfast and reading the newspaper accounts of the crime on Benedict Canyon Drive. Her reporter friends were making good use of all the information she had emailed to them. Like a spider, she was weaving her web around William as a prime suspect with malice toward her mother, his financial problems, and the burden of his father who was no longer there mentally.

Of course the media touted his flamboyant life-style of travel, gambling, parties and drugs—which was old news, but nonetheless made their editorials worthy of gossip in every beauty shop, restaurant and club in Beverly Hills. *The public are like hungry mice,* she thought; *throw them some cheese and watch them devour it.* Liz was pleased with herself.

The doorbell rang as Carmen appeared in the kitchen doorway with a silver coffee pot in her hand. They glanced at each other. Liz didn't move. It rang again. "Well, aren't you going to answer that?"

she demanded.

Carmen quickly sat the pot on the sideboard and hurried to the front door. It was Detective Barrett. "Good morning, Mrs. Martinez. I wonder if now would be a good time to ask you a few more questions?"

Liz appeared in the entry. "Oh my god...not more questions! Can't you see how distraught poor Carmen is? Is it really necessary right now?"

"In a homicide case, it's best to question people while their memory of the events is still fresh in their minds—so yes, it is," he said.

Barrett followed her into the main room. "I would like to speak with Carmen alone, but I also have a few questions for you as well."

"Then you may as well join me at the dining table. Carmen just brought a fresh pot of coffee from the kitchen. I assume you drink coffee, detective."

Liz poured him a cup of coffee without waiting for his answer. "Cream or sugar?" she said with her back to him as he registered the suspicious reaction on her face in the mirror.

"Black, please." Barrett retrieved his notepad from his jacket pocket. "Have you, by any chance, been in touch with Marc Garret since the dinner party? I went by his apartment yesterday, but he didn't answer the door."

Liz was cautious with her answer, "I'm sure there's a logical explanation, detective. Perhaps he was at the doctor's or picking up medication for whatever made him ill. I don't keep up with his comings and goings. But to answer your question—no I haven't heard from him." He noticed she did not look directly at him as she stirred her coffee.

He continued. "Do you recall what time your friend Margo returned to her condo where you spent the night after leaving the party here at the mansion?"

"Honestly, detective, I was sound asleep when she returned. I have no idea what time it was. I didn't wake up until I received the call from Carmen."

"May I ask, what was the purpose of your trip to Palm Springs?"

Liz had rehearsed her answer for this question. "Margo and I had planned to do some shopping, have lunch and go to a movie, but my phone call changed all of that. Is what I do in my spare time that important?" She stood to leave the room.

"Perhaps—perhaps not," he added.

"On that revelation, I will leave you alone with Carmen—unless you wish to follow me as I run my errands this morning."

Being the gentleman that he was, he stood by the huge mahogany table in the dining room, with its matching crystal chandeliers, as she exited the luxurious setting.

Detective Barrett tapped on the door to the kitchen and entered, finding Carmen sitting quietly at a small table next to the window, polishing silver and waiting for him. "May I come in?"

"Please, detective," she waved her hand indicating an empty chair at the table, "but I don't know what else I can tell you." He glanced around the spotless kitchen, everything in its place as it should be. Carmen was an excellent employee.

"Don't worry Carmen, these are just simple questions that might help us create a better picture of what took place the night of, and the day after, the crime. For instance—How long have you worked for the Gordon family?"

"I've been Mr. Gordon's housekeeper and cook almost eighteen years," she said proudly.

Dave Barrett smiled, "That tells me you're a valued employee. Do you recall what time the dinner party ended the night before last?"

"It was ten o'clock. Mr. Garret wasn't feeling well, and asked Mrs. Gordon if he could be excused to go home. She told him to put Mr. Gordon to bed and then he could go. That's when the doctor got a call from the hospital and had to leave. Mr. Farrell and his wife were parked behind the doctor in the drive, so they left too. Ms. Lizzy left at 10:30 p.m. I finished cleaning the kitchen and left at about 11:30."

Detective Barrett studied Carmen as she continued polishing the silverware, taking a nervous glance at him as she answered the questions. He sensed Carmen knew something that she was hiding and was confident he would discover her secret—if he was patient.

"You said yesterday that you set the alarm when you left and it was still on the next morning when you arrived to work. Correct?"

Carmen nodded. "Yes, and all the doors were still locked. I come and go through the back. Mrs. Gordon locked the front door after Ms. Lizzy left for Palm Springs."

"How many people have keys to the house?"

Carmen stopped polishing to think. "Mrs. Gordon, Ms. Lizzy, Mr. William, and myself. Mr. Gordon's key hangs by the back door, but he didn't use it anymore. Bless his heart, he couldn't remember what it was for."

Barrett glanced at the back door. There was no key hanging on the empty nail. "It appears the key is missing," he said.

Carmen was shocked. "But it was there. It's been hanging there for the past seven years. Someone must have taken it."

"And the security alarm code," he asked, "does everyone know that as well?"

"Yes sir, we all know that except Mr. Gordon, God rest his soul, he couldn't add two and two. Numbers confused him so."

Detective Barrett moved on to his next question. "I believe you cleaned Mrs. Gordon's bedroom after the forensic team had finished their work. I'm sure it was a mess, but the evidence we find is always important to help solve the crime. I'm sure you would let me know if you found anything unusual. Now and then the forensic team might miss something very important."

He noticed her hands began to shake and her large brown eyes had a look of fear. She placed the polishing cloth on the table and cleared her voice. "I was going to call you, but wanted to wait until today. I found an earring next to the wall on the rug under the bed. It was part of an antique set that belonged to Ms. Clair, Mr. Gordon's first wife."

She reached into the pocket of her soiled white apron, retrieved it and handed it to the detective. "I kept it safe in my pocket so I wouldn't forget where I put it."

Barrett turned the earring in his hand, studying it closely, "This has to be part of the jewels stolen from the safe. Whoever dropped it must have been in a hurry to get away, or was very careless. This could be the clue we need, Carmen, and I appreciate your honesty."

"Then I'm not in trouble, even with the missing key?" she said with a sigh.

"On the contrary," he smiled, "you may be a star witness."

Chapter Eight

Doctor Thompson was not in his office when Detective Grant arrived unannounced. His assistant said he was calling on his patients at the nursing home in Malibu.

Grant handed her a card. "Ask him to give me a call when he returns. I need to see him regarding his former patient, Mr. Gordon."

She stared in surprise. "Oh—poor Mr. Gordon. We were devastated to learn of his accident."

"Well, that's just it. We're not so sure it was an accident. That's why I need to speak with Dr. Thompson."

"I'll have him call the minute he contacts me," she said, still in shock.

As he left the office, he chuckled to himself, "That should give the old fart a few more gray hairs on his head." His psychic intuition told him the good doctor's assistant was hiding something. But he would address that later.

His next stop was a visit with movie director Greg Farrell.

Detective Barrett had other fish to fry, so Grant was left to interview both the doctor and the director. Just his luck.

He had phoned ahead and caught Farrell at the Beverly Hills Golf Club, where he had just finished a morning round of golf. They arranged to meet in the art deco Polo Lounge at the Beverly Hills Hotel.

Grant found the director seated in one of the outdoor booths, surrounded by flowers and green foliage under the mushroom-like concrete canopies. The maître d' was expecting him and directed him to the table.

"Will you have something to drink, detective?" Greg Farrell offered as he gave Grant the once-over from head to toe—noticing his rumpled appearance in a brown suit that looked as though he had slept in it and his wrinkled blue shirt with open collar and loosely knotted tie.

"No thanks. I'm on duty," he commented as he slid into the booth. "But I appreciate you fitting me into your busy schedule. You movie people are always in a rush. I just wanted to get your view of the events on the night of the murder at the Gordon's residence. I understand you were a guest at the dinner party that evening."

Farrell had finished his lunch as was on his second martini. "I was a close friend of Mrs. Gordon's and Michael's physician. It was her birthday, and my wife, Linda, and I attended the party. Other than that, there isn't much to tell. Dr. Thompson had a call from the hospital. We were parked behind him, so we left at the same time. However, the party was breaking up anyway. Michael's caregiver was ill and left after he put Michael to bed."

Grant nodded. "I see. Well, that sounds pretty much like the other accounts. Do you remember what time that was?" He scribbled some notes on his small notepad.

"I believe it was around ten o'clock."

Out of the blue, Grant took a stab with his next question; "How well did you know Margaret Gordon—being as how she was an actress and all?"

"Like I said, we were friends for years. I dated Margaret when she was an acting extra. As a matter of fact, I introduced her to Michael and Clair, and, vice-versa, they introduced me to my current wife, Linda."

"I see, quite a cozy little group." Grant mumbled as he stopped writing in his notepad.

"No, I don't think you do see, detective," Farrell said defensively. "Michael was a mess after his first wife Clair, died in an auto accident. Clair and Margaret had become close friends. She was with her on that fateful day at the cabin and would have been in the car with her, but was ill. Clair was heading into town to get some medicine for Margaret when the accident happened. Michael and William were out hunting.

"Margaret was a strong woman, and Michael needed a strong hand to help him through those troubled times. She had a head on her shoulders and after their marriage, she took charge of his home and his social life. Everything she did was for Michael. Even her daughter was jealous."

This last statement caught Grant by surprise, but not off-guard; as his inquisitive face registered with Greg Farrell, causing the Farrell to suspect he may have said too much.

"I have some appointments shortly, detective. If there's nothing further, I must rush."

"One more question, if I may. How long did you and Mr. Gordon work together as producer and director?"

"Since our first mystery thriller, *The Silent Scream* in 1998. We've produced nine movies since then. But how does that relate to the crime, detective?"

"Oh—it doesn't. That's just a trivia question for my kids. They love the movies. I thank you for your time, Mr. Farrell. I'll find my way out."

Grant reached for the cell phone vibrating in his coat pocket as he left the hotel. He recognized the caller ID. "Yo, buddy, what's up?"

"I just finished with Carmen and Liz. There's a new piece of evidence I'll share with you later. The chief just called and the search warrant for Gordon's office is ready. I'll swing by and pick it up. His office was sealed yesterday morning, so nothing's been touched inside. Meet me on the sixth floor of the Chase Bank building, corner of Wilshire Boulevard and Beverly Drive."

"I have some interesting information myself," Grant announced. "Let's grab a bite to eat at 280, next to Tiffany, It's close by."

"What's wrong? Didn't the donuts fill that empty spot you carry around all day?"

"Very funny...ha-ha!" He disconnected.

Chapter
Nine

Meanwhile, the media were having a heyday with the incrimi-
nating evidence that Liz had made available for them. They
were demanding that the district attorney's office subpoena
William as the prime suspect in the murder of Margaret Gordon
and possibly his own father.

Their editorials were filled with suspicions. William had access
to the house. He knew the security code, and was aware of his
father's mental condition, with Alzheimer's and fits of verbal and
physical abuse during periods of dementia. William had never
accepted Margaret in place of his mother, and was furious when
she suggested that Michael stop writing checks for his extravagant
lifestyle—and insisted he be placed on an annual allowance. Plus
the fact that he stood to inherit a fortune.

It was also noted that he was the only person with access to the
house who didn't have a verified alibi. It was his word against theirs.
There was no proof of his whereabouts on the night of the crime.

Liz's malicious statements, planted with several reporters, were now making newspaper headlines, "Best-Selling Mystery Writer Prime Suspect in Murder Case" and "Mystery Author Gordon / Suspected of Murder."

The DA's prosecutor, Paul Patterson, had no choice but to assemble a grand jury and pursue an indictment with the evidence at hand. Time was ticking by and the fear that William could leave the country was a cause for concern. The Beverly Hills police chief couldn't keep this one on the shelf much longer. A grand jury was assembled quickly. It didn't take long to submit the circumstantial evidence, which lead to an indictment. Speedy justice was demanded, and a trial date was set.

Drug dealers, pimps, robbers, and prostitutes could take weeks even months to process through the legal system. But when crime reached its nasty tendrils into the social-elite of Beverly Hills and the movie industry, it demanded immediate attention. The feathers of the A-group had been ruffled and needed to be smoothed. Evil would be put in its place, but never totally forgotten. And most likely, someone would write a book or make a movie out of it.

Shawn Harris contacted William with the news, as he was not required to be present at the grand jury hearing. "I have good news and bad news," he said, sitting across the desk from William.

His white knuckles clutching the armrests of the chair, William stiffened. "Give me the bad news first," he said.

"There is going to be a trial," Shawn said. William closed his eyes as he sat in silence, breathing slowly. Shawn continued, "Without more evidence to refute the picture the prosecution presented, I wasn't able to get a dismissal. But we still have time to search for more facts. The trial won't start until the end of next month."

"The good news is that you will not have to go to jail. You are innocent until proven guilty. However, you are under house arrest and will be allowed to stay at my place. I knew you wouldn't want to be in the same house with Liz, so I made arrangements with the judge and the prosecutor Paul Patterson. It'll give us the opportunity to work day and night on our trial presentation.

"We'll drop by the mansion when Liz isn't there and pick up whatever you need. Carmen can let us know when that's convenient." William hadn't said a word as he sat with his hands folded under his chin, deep in prayer or thought.

Shawn sensed that he was composing his strength. The mind of a mystery writer would come in handy as they began to weave a tighter case to prove his innocence. Shawn had already contacted the detectives who were assigned the case. He had worked with Dave Barrett on two previous cases and knew that Martin Grant had a psychic sense for discovering details—not to mention his elephant-like memory.

Shawn would not leave a stone unturned. If there was a snake hiding there, he would find it. He had arranged to meet with the detectives, but first he wanted to study the evidence without the diatribe from the press. Shawn believed, as did many others, that William was not guilty of murder, and he would not allow the media lynch mob to gather at the base of the hanging tree.

He sent a private investigator to the remote area of the Tehachapi Mountains, armed with a photo of William in search of anyone who may have seen him on the evening of the crime. In the meantime, he decided to pay a visit to Carmen. Perhaps she knew more than she had told the detectives.

Shawn put the word out among his secretive sources, street informants and shop owners in Beverly Hills, to be on the lookout for any information that might be helpful, and to scour the neighborhood where the crime had been committed. The police may have missed something, and often there are people who see or hear things that they don't tell the cops, because they don't want to get involved.

William was pleased that Shawn was onboard and seemed to

know what to do. He was frightened with the possibility of going to prison for a murder he didn't commit, but Shawn kept reminding him. "Beyond a reasonable doubt, William—beyond a reasonable doubt."

"I hear you," he said, "but there are innocent people who have been sent to prison with less evidence than they have put together on me."

"I can't argue that point, but in your case it won't work," he smiled.

"Why not?" William asked as they sat at the dinner table with Sandra, Shawn's wife.

Sandra quickly chimed in. "Because they didn't have Shawn as their defense attorney, my friend." They all three chuckled.

Shawn leaned over and gave her a kiss on the cheek. "My cheerleader wife. Where would I be without you?"

She patted his hand, which was holding hers. "Probably still working as a law clerk in some obscure courtroom in West Virginia," she laughed. And now I will leave you with that terrible thought. I have a book to read and you two have work to discuss." Sandra was from an old moneyed family in California. Her Irish father had invested well in real estate and had owned almost half of downtown Santa Barbara, which she inherited on his death.

Her green eyes and flaming red hair, reminiscent of Rita Hayworth in *Sadie Thompson*, were a clear statement of her Irish heritage. "Look for leprechauns to find the truth—they hide in the strangest places," she said, disappearing through the dining room doorway.

William gave Shawn a questioning glance. "It's the luck of the Irish, William. We've just been given the inside scoop, and she's never steered me wrong."

"You're telling me that riddle is a guiding light to point the way?"

"Precisely, my friend, if you know the source from whence it came like I do. Now, let's get to work. We have a busy day tomorrow.

Chapter
Ten

It was 8:50 a.m. on Friday, four weeks later. Among the fourteen jurors selected after an extensive vetting, five were men and nine were women. While some of them had read about the case, they were all confident they could review the evidence without any preconceived beliefs, offering a fair judgment to both sides.

Judge Tyler Wilson had explained to all fourteen jurors that at the end of the trial, twelve members of the jury would be selected and the other two would serve as alternates, in case someone should become ill.

Reporters were seated in the front row of the wood-paneled courtroom, buzzing with anticipation, waiting anxiously for the spectacle to begin. The court stenographer, a young woman in her late twenties with limp, mousey-brown hair, a beak nose and thick glasses, was seated at her desk to the right.

The defendant, William Gordon, flanked by his attorney Shawn Harris and Harris's paralegal aid, entered through the tall doors at the rear of the courtroom. The chief prosecutor, Paul Patterson, a veteran of fifteen years, was already seated at the state's table.

William was dressed in a conservative navy suit, white shirt with button-down collar and a burgundy and silver striped tie. He wore a black arm-band on his right arm. Shawn had suggested the arm-band would telegraph sympathy to the jury and remind them he was still in mourning for the loss of his father and stepmother.

The prosecutor, Paul Patterson, in his mid-sixties, with a mane of brilliant white hair, sat erect, reflecting his military bearing and arrogant attitude even while seated. His snobbish appearance was totally opposite that of his colleague at the defense table, as he shook hands and greeted people seated behind him. Patterson's legal team of three, perhaps in their thirties, sat to his right as he impatiently drummed on the table with his manicured fingernails.

Two uniformed officers stood at opposite ends of the room. Liz Carson sat in the front row directly behind the prosecutor, while Marc Garret was seated to the back of the room full of curiosity seekers, which was not surprising due to the notoriety of the case.

At precisely 9 a.m. , the court clerk announced, "All rise—this court in now in session." Judge Wilson entered from his chambers and took his place on the bench.

"Good morning, counsel. The court will proceed to hear the case of the State of California verses William Lawrence Gordon. Are you ready with your opening statements?"

"Yes, Your Honor," they replied in unison.

The judge addressed the officer standing by the door to the jury room, "You may bring in the jury."

Once the jury was seated, the judge explained to them that they were about to hear the opening statements of the attorneys, and that what they would hear was argument and not evidence. "Since the prosecutor has the burden of proof in a criminal case, he will proceed first with his statement."

Paul Patterson stood erect and confident as he approached the jury box. "Thank you, Your Honor," he said, nodding to the judge. "Good morning ladies and gentlemen. My name is Paul Patterson. I am the chief prosecutor in this case for the State of California. I will introduce to you during the course of this trial, witnesses and evidence for the proof of guilt against the defendant, William Lawrence Gordon."

Patterson read from the indictment as is the custom. "On or about February 10 of this year, the defendant, William Gordon, did knowingly and willingly cause the death of his stepmother, Margaret Carson Gordon and perhaps the death of his own father, whose cause of death is still in question." He paused for effect, as a collective gasp was heard throughout the courtroom. "This, ladies and gentlemen, is a trial of premeditated murder, spurred by hatred and greed."

He continued in a less dramatic voice, "William Gordon is a well-known, bestselling writer of mystery. He is the only child of Michael and Clair Gordon. The state will admit that their marriage and family life was a happy one, until the tragic accident that took the life of Clair Gordon. A year later Michael Gordon married Margaret Carson."

William's head turned as he scanned the courtroom, his eyes falling on Liz Carson, a vindictive, thin-lipped smile plastered on her face, confident she would be the sole heir to the Gordon estate. To the back he caught a glimpse of Marc, his father's caregiver, hunkering in the corner as he tried to become invisible, perhaps ashamed he was not there to offer his help on the night of the crime. The attorney's statement was still in progress.

"Evidence will show this is where things began to change. Seven years ago, Michael Gordon, at the young age of 50, began to display early signs of dementia. Forgetfulness and irritability were not part of his prior character and demeanor. After extensive neurological testing, he was diagnosed with an early onset of Alzheimer's.

"It's a medical fact that contracting this debilitating disease at such a young age causes it to spread at a more rapid pace. Studies have proven a person's life expectancy to be between seven and ten years in such cases.

"Michael Gordon's health tragically deteriorated until he was no longer able to function without twenty-four-hour assistance. His second wife, Margaret, made sure he was properly cared for at home. His son, William, moved back home to be near his father and to oversee his care. Why? Because he did not trust his stepmother."

William's thoughts were flashing through his mind. The attorney was right—he didn't trust his stepmother. He had always harbored the idea that Margaret had something to do with the death of his mother. A belief he had never expressed to anyone. Once he had moved back home, he quickly learned what a manipulating woman she could be. Even her own daughter didn't escape her grasp. Margaret ruled with an iron hand. Patterson was still droning on with his dramatic flair as William's mind returned to the courtroom.

Patterson was in his element. "William had not been fond of his stepmother ever since she convinced his father to stop paying for his extravagant living expenses, and instead give him an annual allowance of $100,000. In essence, she cut the purse strings for his drugs, gambling, drinking, and playboy lifestyle eight years ago. He also resented the friendship Margaret Carson had formed with his own mother, Clair, prior to her death.

"You will hear, ladies and gentlemen, that prior to Margaret Gordon's death, Michael Gordon had made her the heir to half his fortune and estate. I will introduce witnesses who confirm that William Gordon had an argument about money with his father on the morning of the crime, and he was not in attendance at Margaret's birthday dinner that evening."

William was shaken. How had the attorney learned about his

financial secrets? How did he know he resented his mother's friend-ship with Margaret Carson? As he glanced right, he noticed Liz was staring at him with that look of satisfaction on her face. She was the only one who knew about his argument with Michael that morn-ing. He realized, without doubt, she was just like her vindictive and calculating mother.

Shawn tapped him on the shoulder. "It's all speculation and hearsay," he whispered.

Patterson continued with his show and tell. "You will also hear that Michael Gordon was put to bed early by his caregiver and his doctor, who gave him a sedative to help him sleep. The caregiver, who usually stays in an adjoining room on the lower level, had taken ill and, with the permission of Margaret Gordon, left for the evening to stay at his own apartment until the next day.

"A witness will testify that the doctor received an emergency call from the hospital and the rest of the party guests left by 10 p.m. Liz Gordon, Margaret Gordon's daughter and William's stepsister, left to spend the evening and following day with a friend in Palm Springs." The prosecutor paced slowly in front of the jury box, mak-ing eye contact with each juror as he passed, to be sure he had their attention—trying to read their body language and facial reactions to his opening statement.

"Ladies and gentlemen, the housekeeper and cook for the Gordons was the last person to leave the house that evening. Your will hear from her very lips what she found on her return to the house the following morning—when she discovered Michael Gordon's body, lying dead at the bottom of the stairs.

"You will hear that she screamed as she entered the bedroom of Margaret Gordon, whose body was lying stiff and cold on the bed—the room in shambles, as if a tornado had passed through it. The woman was in a state of shock when she called 911."

Paul Patterson could feel the tension in the courtroom as he continued his delivery. "Ladies and gentlemen, the coroner's report indicated Margaret Gordon had died of asphyxiation. Her body was taken to the pathological forensic laboratories for further testing. Michael Gordon suffered a heart attack and a broken neck from his fall down the stairs. It is not yet determined which happened first. But either way—he, too, was dead."

Patterson stopped at the state's table and took a sip of water. He was milking his little drama for all it was worth. "Distinguished members of the jury—I wish to point out that William Gordon has yet to confirm his alibi on the night of the crime.

"William also has a key to the house. He knows the security code and can enter and exit freely, without setting off the alarm." He paused to be sure they had time to memorize those statements. "I also intend to prove that he knew the combination to the safe in the master bedroom closet where all the jewelry, now missing, was stored. And that he planned to make this look like a crime of a burglary gone wrong.

"I would like to add that the police, after a thorough inspection of the premises, found no indication of forced entry. No broken windows or locks that would suggest a break-in." He glanced in William's direction.

"Ladies and gentlemen, I have presented to you an outline of the state's case against William Lawrence Gordon. I suggest to you, that when all of the evidence is presented, you will—beyond a reasonable doubt—find the defendant guilty as charged." Dramatically he pointed to William, seated beside Shawn at the defendants table.

"There sits the man that I will prove to you is the murderer of Margaret Carson Gordon."

Patterson returned to his chair.

Chapter Eleven

The courtroom hummed with subdued voices. Judge Wilson tapped his gavel to bring the court back to order. "Is the defense counsel prepared with their opening statement?"

Shawn stood. "Yes, Your Honor, the defense is ready."

"Then you may proceed," he said.

Patterson watched as Shawn confidently strode across the courtroom and faced the jury. "Ladies and gentlemen," he smiled, "if the evidence you have just heard from this prominent and powerful prosecutor is as cut-and-dried as he proclaims, then there is no need for further deliberation. Find Mr. William Gordon guilty and we can all go home." A wave of shock wove its way through the courtroom. Heads were turning, as the sound of susurration filled the air.

"However," he continued, "what you didn't hear in the prosecutor's statement was the love and devotion that a faithful son had for his father over the past thirty-six years. William's heart sank when he learned of his father's diagnosis with Alzheimer's. He moved back home to be with him. Of course he welcomed assistance from the caregiver and Margaret Gordon.

"The truth is undeniable that for the past six years he watched his father's health decline, as his physical, mental and emotional condition deteriorated—but William was there for him. He refused to listen when the doctors recommended putting Michael in a nursing home, where strangers would take care of him. He knew that was not what his father would do, as they say, if the shoe were on the other foot. No, William would not agree with Margaret or anyone else on that account."

Shawn paused to pace himself. He wanted to give the jurors time to contemplate the love and devotion of an honorable son. "You will hear how Michael became physically and emotionally abusive to William, which is understandable when people forget and become suspicious of everyone they once knew and loved. Margaret and Liz had become victims of Michael's abuse as well. Please keep that in mind.

"I call your attention to the fact, that the prosecution cannot produce one witness who will testify that he, or she, witnessed what happened in the Gordon mansion on the night of the crime. They have nothing but circumstantial evidence and a vivid imagination.

"You will hear that there were five keys to the Gordon's home, but only four have been accounted for. You will also learn that there is no way to know for sure how many people had access to the security code. I suggest the possibility that someone entered the home with a key, turned off the alarm and was caught in the act of robbery, prompting the murder of Margaret Gordon and possibly causing the death of Michael Gordon, before resetting the alarm and locking the door behind as they left."

He held out his hands in offering and shook his head. "It's an assumption that's as easy to believe as that of the prosecution."

Shawn turned and smiled at William, then turned again to the jury, "I would like to leave you with one more thought in closing. William is not the only person who stands to inherit from the death of his father and stepmother. His half-sister, Liz Carson, is also named as heir to half the twenty-million-dollar estate if her mother should die before her, which indeed has happened.

"There will be more evidence presented as the trial proceeds. It is, of course, up to the state to prove guilt beyond a reasonable doubt. William does not have to prove his innocence, but we will do our best to present a clear picture and connect all of the dots to solve this crime. I thank you for your time and understanding and I look forward to speaking to you again in summation at the end of this trial. Remember, you must weigh the scales of justice and allow intelligence and conscience to be your guide."

He turned to the judge and added, "Thank you, Your Honor."

Judge Wilson rapped his gavel. "The court will take a fifteen-minute recess, after which, Mr. Prosecutor, you may call your first witness."

Reporters rushed out the back doors to phone their stories in to the newspapers. Cell phones are not allowed in the courtroom. Paul Patterson was not used to being put in his place by such a young attorney. He was in conference with his paralegal aids and didn't notice that a police officer had approached Shawn at the defense table and Shawn had followed him out of the room.

William's mind was in another zone. He was still trying to remember if he had told Shawn everything. Detective Barrett tapped him on the shoulder. "Hang in there, buddy. It sounds like you've got yourself a smart lawyer."

"Strange to hear that coming from you. Didn't you tell Liz that I was a person of interest—a prime suspect?"

Detective Barrett smiled. "Maybe I did—but it got the results I wanted. As my old man used to say, there's more than one way to skin a cat."

William folded his arms and breathed a sigh, "So, what's that supposed to mean?"

Dave leaned forward and winked, "The investigation isn't over. We're still beating the bushes. No telling what'll turn up. But right now, I have to go jewelry shopping. Tell Shawn I'll be in touch."

Dave Barrett was on a mission to canvas the exclusive jewelry stores in Beverly Hills with his photo of the antique earring found by Carmen. He believed that the person who had stolen the Gordons' jewels, would try to have the earring copied once they were aware it was missing, and he wanted to alert the local jewelers to be on the lookout for the antique piece.

While searching Michael Gordon's office, the only information the detectives found were some personal files that could be of interest and deserved further review. Meanwhile, Barrett had contacted Sargent Willis of the Palm Springs police department. He was aware that they use traffic surveillance cameras to monitor the flow and speed of vehicles on the desert roads; especially late at night when people are more apt to speed through the quiet neighborhoods with fewer cars to hamper their progress.

Shawn suggested checking the traffic cameras on the outside chance they might learn more about Liz's visit to her friend's condo at the Club Condominiums on West Racquet Club Road. His wife Sandra had mentioned that the driving time to Palm Springs wasn't much different than the driving time to the Tehachapi Mountains. Sandra was a detective's wife and always saw things from a different point of view. She didn't always accept what appeared as facts.

Chapter Twelve

The court recess was over and the trial was back in session. Judge Wilson took his seat and rapped his gavel. "This court is now reconvened." He nodded to the prosecutor. "You may call your first witness, council."

"Thank you, Your Honor. If it please the court, I call Abraham Goldman." Mr. Goldman is the lawyer for Michael Gordon's estate. At the request of the prosecution, he explained that after the death of his first wife, Michael Gordon had revised his will, designating his son and second wife Margaret Gordon as equal co-heirs to his estate, except that the house and its contents would remain with his wife, Margaret. He also granted Margaret his power of attorney to make any legal, financial, or medical decisions for him should he become incapacitated.

Questioned further, Goldman testified that without the home and its contents, the estate's current value was just over twenty million dollars. He noted that two additional bequests were made in the will for Mr. Marc Garrett and Mrs. Carmen Martinez, in the amount of five hundred thousand dollars. Mr. Goldman did not know if either person was aware of this bequest prior to Mr. Gordon's death.

"Thank you, Mr. Goldman. No further questions."

"Does counsel wish to cross-examine the witness?" the judge asked Shawn.

"Yes, Your Honor." He approached the lawyer. "Mr. Goldman, was there any mention of Ms. Elizabeth Carson in Mr. Gordon's will?"

Goldman cleared his throat as he quickly glanced at the prosecutor. "Yes, there was. He stated in the will that Elizabeth Carson was to receive her mother's share of the inheritance upon her mother's death."

"No further questions, Your Honor."

Next, Patterson called Officer Derek Jacobs to the stand. Officer Jacobs was summoned from the anteroom. "Please state your name and occupation for the records."

"Officer Derek Jacobs of the Beverly Hills Police Department." Officer Jacobs was the first to arrive for the 911 call at the Benedict Canyon residence on the morning of February 10.

At age thirty-six, he was a ten-year veteran on the force. His six-foot tight muscular frame filled his crisply starched uniform with its knife-like pleats. His short-cut, sandy hair looked like peach fuzz, complimenting an intelligent face with piercing hazel eyes and a square jaw, creating a commanding appearance.

In answer to the prosecutor's question, he explained he had been on patrol in the canyon area on the morning of February 10. At 7:10 a.m., he was dispatched to respond to the emergency call from Michael Gordon's home on Benedict Canyon Drive. The dispatcher had informed him that, arriving at the residence, Carmen, the housekeeper, had found the bodies of Mr. and Mrs. Gordon inside the locked house, and that homicide detectives had also been notified and were en route.

"Had you ever been to that home before?" Patterson asked.

"Yes. Once before, at about four in the morning. I was dispatched on a 911 call regarding some domestic violence."

"And what was the situation you encountered on arrival?"

Officer Jacobs checked his notes. "Mr. Gordon's caregiver, a Mr. Garret, was having difficulty controlling Mr. Gordon, who had become violent and was damaging property and threatening members of the household, as the dispatcher had informed me."

"Who met you at the door to the residence?"

"On that date, I was met by a woman who claimed to be Mr. Gordon's wife."

"That would be Margaret Gordon." Patterson clarified for the jury. "So what did you do next?"

"I held Mr. Gordon so the caregiver could administer a sedative. I asked if they wanted me to call an ambulance, but they agreed it wasn't necessary. We carried Mr. Gordon to his bedroom downstairs and I waited until the caretaker assured me Mr. Gordon was asleep. I asked if Mrs. Gordon wished to file a complaint of abuse, but she said no. Then I left."

Patterson, in his pinstriped, double-breasted, Giorgio Armani suit, white-on-white Italian cotton shirt and candy-striped, Hermes silk tie, looked like a fashion plate out of Vanity Fair magazine. In his baritone voice, as smooth as his glossy manicured fingernails, he continued. "I want to direct your attention back to February 10. Can you tell the jury what happened when you arrived at the home on that morning?"

Jacobs shifted in his chair to face the jury. "I was met by the housekeeper, whose name I recall is Carmen. She told me that Mr. Gordon was dead. I followed her from the entry into the main room, where his body lay on the marble floor at the base of the staircase.

"She then said that Mrs. Gordon was also dead and pointed

upstairs. She had found her body in the master bedroom on the second level. I asked if she would make some coffee, giving her something to do to help calm her down and keep her from further disrupting the area of the crime scene."

"What did you do next, officer?" Patterson glanced at the jury to be sure they hadn't dozed off in the stale air of the warm courtroom.

"I checked the bedroom upstairs and found Mrs. Gordon's body in bed. There appeared to have been a struggle in the room and white feathers from a ripped pillow floated in the air as I cautiously moved toward the open closet door."

"Carefully describe for the jury the scene you encountered," Patterson requested.

Jacobs flashed back in his mind, remembering the smell of death, by then, several hours old, the copper metallic odor of drying blood, the stench of feces and urine on the bed sheets, and the horror on the face of the dead woman. Contents and the drawers of a Bombay chest were tossed about the room, as if someone had been searching for something. He noticed, without entering, the safe in the closet was open and appeared empty.

"I believe the homicide detectives will be able to describe the crime scene more accurately, Counsel."

"I understand, officer, and we will hear from them later today. "But what were your further observations of the scene described in your report?"

"Based on my EMT certification as a trained police officer, I concluded, from all appearances, that Mrs. Gordon had been suffocated. There was dried blood from her nose still on her upper lip and blood was smeared on a ripped pillowcase lying on the floor."

"What did you do next, officer?"

"I returned to Mr. Gordon's body at the base of the stairs. His head was turned at an angle that indicated his neck was broken."

"Was anyone else in the house when you arrived?"

"No. Only the housekeeper, who confirmed the security alarm was still on and the doors were securely locked on her arrival. I asked the housekeeper for the name and phone number of the family doctor and called to give him the news.

"She informed me she had already contacted William Gordon and Liz Carson, the remaining members of the immediate family, and that they were on their way from the mountains and Palm Springs. The homicide detectives arrived at that time and I filled them in on my observations, then left them in charge."

Patterson cleared his voice. "No further questions, Your Honor."

Judge Wilson nodded to Shawn at the defense table, indicating it was his turn. Shawn gathered his thoughts for a moment, picked up his notes and approached the witness. "Officer Jacobs, you testified that you were dispatched to the Gordon residence on a separate occasion prior to February 10. Do you recall exactly when that was?"

Jacobs checked his notes again. "Yes, it was before Christmas on December 20 at 4 a.m."

"I understood you to say that no charges were filed in that domestic violence report. Is that correct?"

Jacobs thought for a second. He needed to be careful with his answer. Paul Patterson was on his feet quickly. "Objection, Your Honor! That incident has no bearing on the case being tried."

"Overruled," the judge said. "If you'll remember, Counsel, it was you who brought that report to the attention of the court in the first place." He nodded to Jacobs. "You may answer the counsel's question officer."

"That is correct," he said. Shawn was calm and cool. Patience was one of his many virtues in seeking a more direct response.

"As with most domestic violence cases, officer, I'm sure your report included any observation of abusive behavior, damage to valuable household items and, of course, your assessment of the situation. Is that correct?"

Jacobs glanced in the prosecutor's direction again, as if awaiting instructions, but Patterson avoided his eyes as the hum of reporters' whispers buzzed softly in the room. "Yes, all of that information is required, Counsel."

"Therefore, your report of this incident must have described the scene inside the home upon your arrival and the physical condition of the victims. So without reading the entire report, officer, will you tell the jury in your own words what you saw? And remember, you are under oath."

Patterson was in a state of fury as perspiration glistened on his high forehead, "Objection, Your Honor, I...

Judge Wilson cut him short with the bang of his gavel. "Overruled, Mr. Patterson. The witness will answer Counsel's question." Wilson was having none of the prosecutor's pompous behavior.

"I observed broken glass and pieces of pottery on the floor. Some damage had been done to some of the furniture during the scuffle. Chairs were overturned, a small table had been shattered and a painting was damaged."

Shawn acknowledged his answer with a nod. "You have a good memory officer. Again I question—did you notice any signs of physical abuse to either Mrs. Gordon or her daughter?"

He looked Shawn in the eyes. "Yes. Mrs. Gordon appeared to have injuries to her face and her daughter's wrists were bruised and red. However, they were given the opportunity to file a complaint and chose not to do so."

"As you have stated." Shawn paused before continuing. "Did you notice any tension between Mrs. Gordon and her daughter?"

"No, sir. I did not."

"So the main disturbance was between Mr. and Mrs. Gordon?" Shawn clarified.

"That was how it appeared to me."

Patterson's feathers were ruffled. "Your Honor, I really must object. Where is defense going with this wandering line of questioning?"

The judge motioned to both, "Counsels, you will approach the bench please?"

The judge leaned forward and whispered to them, "Would the defense care to explain where he is going on this?"

Shawn was quick to respond. "Your Honor, I simply wish the jury to know of any discord between Michael Gordon, his wife and his stepdaughter—that could easily lead to other issues and possible motive for injury later."

"Very well. Are the answers you've received sufficient?"

"They are, Your Honor," Shawn said.

The gavel sounded. "Overruled. You may continue, Counsel."

"Just one more question, officer. Was there anyone else in the house on this particular occasion besides the wife, the daughter, the caregiver, and Mr. Gordon?"

"No sir. There were only four people in the house at that hour of the morning. They told me that Mr. Gordon's son, William, was in New York at a book-signing event."

"Thank you, officer. You may step down. No further questions."

Judge Wilson asked the prosecutor if he was ready with his next witness. Patterson stood as he spoke. "Our next witness is Dr. Lee Thompson, Your Honor, who has been unavoidably detained in surgery. As it is almost noon I would like to request a recess until after lunch. He should be available by then."

Wilson glanced at the defense table. "If the Counsel for the defense has no objections, I will so order the recess."

Shawn nodded. "The defense concurs, Your Honor."

"Ladies and gentlemen of the jury, the court will recess until 2:15 p.m. The bailiff will escort you to the jury lunchroom." He banged his gavel. "Court is adjourned."

Chapter Thirteen

Shawn and William opted to have lunch at THE Blvd in the Beverly Wilshire Four Seasons Hotel. After placing their order for two Caesar salads and iced teas, William began the conversation. "When you were called out of the courtroom this morning, what was that all about?"

Shawn scratched his chin and grinned. "Let me put it this way—things are looking up in our favor. My people, scouting in the mountains, have come up with some witnesses that could substantiate your alibi. I hesitate to say more until we have their written, notarized deposition as evidence. But whether you were aware or not, your presence was noticed."

William breathed a sigh of relief. "Remember," Shawn teased, "I said it was never too soon to start our own investigation."

"Oh, speaking of investigations," William said, "Detective Barrett said to have you give him a call. He was sitting behind us in the courtroom when you had to leave—said their investigation is still happening—whatever that means."

Shawn leaned back in his chair. "That means we're in good hands, my friend. In the hands of an expert."

"Has there been any news on the forensic reports? They're certainly taking their time." William said.

"We don't want a rush job. Taking their time means they are doing a thorough job, and they are one of the most through forensic teams in California."

THE Blvd restaurant is a sophisticated dining spot in the heart of Beverly Hills, with its floor-to-ceiling windows overlooking the one-and-only Rodeo Drive. Soft tones of gray, white, and charcoal, complemented by satin wood paneling, stainless-steel light fixtures, and soft jazz playing in the background tended to lull diners into a relaxed state of mind.

Their salads and iced teas were delivered and they ate quickly—each lost in his own space and thoughts. There would be time later to rehash the testimony and happenings in court.

Shawn broke the calm. "It was a stroke of luck Judge Wilson got our case. He's one of the most liberal judges in town, and I've heard he's always fair on behalf of the defense. He interprets the law with an open mind. We have a good chance for a mistrial with the prosecution's lack of hard evidence." Flagging the waiter, Shawn paid the check. "It's time we headed back to the courtroom."

At 2:15 p.m., the trial resumed. Without looking at the prosecutor as he moved papers around on his desk, Judge Jacobs barked, "You may call your second witness, Counsel."

Patterson sensed the judge wanted to move the questioning along. Dr. Thompson was sworn in and seated quickly. His professional appearance, in his Emile Ziggleo silver, sharkskin suit, apricot silk shirt with matching silk pocket square and candy-striped charcoal-and-apricot Armani tie, was that of a doctor with expensive taste and wealthy patients. His frameless glasses hanging from a golden chain about his neck completed his fashion statement when he placed them on his beak-like nose and raised his chin to look down at Patterson.

"Dr. Thompson, I believe you are the medical physician for the Gordon family, and have been for over fifteen years—is that correct?"

"Yes sir, that is correct," he answered with a snooty attitude, feeling his reputation was in question.

"Can you tell us when Michael Gordon was diagnosed with Alzheimer's?"

"Michael was diagnosed with the early stages eight years ago, by myself and two other physicians in neurology." He wanted to point out that it wasn't just his diagnosis alone. "The family was informed at that time that the disease could spread quickly in someone as young as Michael, who was then fifty." This was a lead-in question for Patterson.

"So, eight years later, is it safe to say, that Michael Gordon was in the final stages of Alzheimer's as recent as December last year?"

The good doctor was careful not to answer yes or no. "In my opinion, I would say his condition had progressed close to the final stages around that time."

Patterson approached the jury box, standing with his back to the witness, "Dr. Thompson, would you, in your esteemed professional opinion, say that a person in the advanced stages of Alzheimer's would be capable of murder?"

Thompson knew this question would be asked and had a prepared response. "In the specific case of Michael Gordon, I would have to say, although he might react in a violent and abusive manner, he would not have committed an act of murder intentionally." His key word was *intentionally*. "His behavioral pattern was one of forgetfulness, mistrust, and suspicion, but never malicious."

The prosecutor watched the reaction of the jury; to be sure they understood his purpose for asking that question. He did not want them to think that Michael Gordon was capable of murdering his own wife. "Thank you, doctor. No further questions."

The judge motioned to Shawn for cross-examination. He was on his feet and approached the witness stand. "I just have a few questions, Your Honor. I realize it is getting late in the day."

Judge Wilson nodded. "Take your time, Counselor."

"Dr. Thompson, I thank you for being here today and would like to know if, during the past fifteen years of your personal relationship as a friend of the Gordon family, have you ever had the opportunity to notice any discord between any members of the family?"

"Objection, Your Honor!" roared Patterson.

"Objection overruled, Counsel. The question is not about patient/doctor private information. You may answer the question, doctor." Shawn noted that the judge was being fair. He had never worked with Judge Wilson in the past. Sandra would say, it was the "luck of the Irish."

The direction the defense was leading was obvious to the doctor. "On a few occasions, I detected animosity and disagreement on certain subjects. I assume you are referring to their decisions regarding the treatment of my patient?"

"You are correct, doctor. That was my intent," Shawn acknowledged, "specifically with regards to putting him in a nursing home facility."

The doctor looked at the prosecutor, who was staring at him over his half-spectacles, before answering. "It was the desire of Mrs. Gordon, in her capacity as his legal guardian, to place her husband in a facility where he would receive proper care and medical attention during the final stages of the disease. William did not agree with her decision and refused to allow his father to be committed."

"Thank you, doctor. I have no further questions, Your Honor." The judge glanced at the clock in the back of the courtroom.

"Due to the late hour and the weekend to follow, the court will recess until Monday morning at nine. The jury will follow the instructions of the court as explained by the bailiff; transportation to the hotel's been arranged." He banged his gavel and declared, "Court is now adjourned."

Shawn looked at his cell phone to check if he had received any messages while the court was in session. He read a text from Detective Dave Barrett. The forensic reports were in. He would drop them off at Shawn's office by 6 p.m. He tapped William's shoulder, "Come on. We have work to do, and I promised Sandra we'd take her out to Tom Bergin's for fish and chips tonight."

Back at his office, William and Shawn met with Shawn's private investigator, Dan White, regarding the research he had done in the Tehachapi's, where the Gordons' mountain cabin is located.

It appears that two hunters were camping not far from the cabin and noticed a Black Mercedes SUV parked at the cabin on the night of the crime. They would be willing to testify at the trial, that the automobile was there all night. They saw and heard it leave the following morning. Shawn would call Dan as a witness for the defense when the trial resumed next week.

Barrett had dropped off the lab reports that offered even more interesting information. Shoe prints, of a specific type of shoe worn mostly by medical personnel, were found on the rug next to the bed in the master suite and fingerprints were barely visible on the eyelids of the deceased Margaret Gordon. The prints found on the pillow used to smother Mrs. Gordon, however, were Michael Gordon's.

On the left shoulder of the bathrobe worn by Michael Gordon, they had found a fingernail chip with bright green polish and some smeared finger prints which they were attempting to enhance for a clearer picture.

In Shawn's mind he was beginning to connect the dots. There

were now more questions that needed to be asked, but he would not rush to conclusions. He knew there was more to come. His mother had always taught him: "Answers come to those with the patience to wait." He would wait. It was time to pick up Sandra and head to Fairfax for some downtime delicious food, and entertainment at Tom Bergin's.

"Will you tell Sandra about all the new information we have?" asked William.

"Not yet, but she will probably sense it. We're respectful of each other's space and she can read me like the runes in a wine glass. She swears she must have some Irish gypsy blood in her. Sandra's the reason I stopped drinking. Said she wouldn't marry me unless I did."

"Wow! She must have some potent magic," William teased.

"She does," said Shawn, turning out the lights and closing his office door as they headed for the elevator.

"Goodnight, Carl." He waved to the floor guard.

"Have a good evening, Mr. Harris. You too, Mr. Gordon." He waved as the elevator door slid shut.

Chapter Fourteen

Detectives Barrett and Grant were back on the job Saturday morning after reviewing the pathology findings and the forensic reports on the Gordon case. Grant had been called as a witness on another trial and was catching up on the Gordon case.

A secretary in the division tossed some papers on the desk between them. "This fax just came in for you. Mmmm...donuts again?" she said grabbing the chocolate one with coconut. "Mind if I have one?"

Grant huffed, "Looks like you already do. Now make yourself invisible and let us work."

"My, my...you must've gotten up on the wrong side of the bed this morning."

"If you must know, sweetheart, I haven't been to bed for 24 hours. So put that in your donut and eat it." He was about to continue his little speech, but she turned and scurried off.

Barrett's phone buzzed. He looked at the caller ID. "This might be important evidence, so hold those nasty thoughts." He answered, "Sergeant Willis, my friend—what's the news?"

Sergeant Willis, of the Palm Springs Police Department, had checked the video tapes from the traffic cameras on the night of February 10, as Barrett had requested. "Your hunch was right. You must have ESP or something.

"There was a camera van set up on West Racquet Club Road on February 10—one of those designated with a speed sign that you can't read until it's too late. At 3:10 a.m., a black BMW with the licensed plate LIZ-ONE was captured on film, registering 59 miles per hour in a 35 mile-per-hour zone.

"Due to our backlog in high season, the ticket was just issued this morning and should be on the way to a Liz Gordon on Benedict Canyon Drive in Beverly Hills. I'll send you a copy of the tape by special courier today."

"You're an angel in disguise Sergeant. I appreciate your diligent efforts."

"Hey," Willis said, "you're the one with the inquisitive mind. I just did the followed up."

"Thanks a million." Barrett disconnected the call and phoned Shawn without putting the phone down, while Grant stuffed another donut in his mouth and closed his tired red eyes. He could wait for the news; right now, all he wanted to do was sleep. Shawn was not yet in his office, so Dave left a message for him to call back.

It was Saturday morning and the jewelry stores on Rodeo wouldn't be open until 10 a.m. He felt positive that he was on to something with the missing earring. If anyone is planning to fence the jewelry, the diamond necklace and erring set wouldn't garner the highest amount of cash with a missing earring. And it would be difficult to sell a single antique diamond earring on the black market.

Dave nudged Martin with his foot, "Wake up, old man. Go home and get some sleep. I'll bring you up to speed tomorrow, before the trial starts again on Monday. You look like shit and the chief won't like that. It would look bad for the department."

Grant left the office as Dave began to organize the reports, marking the ones he would need copies of for Shawn. Monday would come soon enough and it would be their turn on the witness stand. He knew the prosecution was out to prove William guilty of murder. But he had a few cards up his sleeve that were yet to be played, and a poker face to hide behind.

Barrett was about to leave the office for lunch when an officer dropped in. "Hey there Eddie, what's up?"

Eddie was a young recruit, just a few years out of the Police Academy—six feet tall, skinny as a bean pole with sandy hair and blue eyes. Dressed in his crisp uniform and smiling from ear to ear, at twenty-nine, he was the perfect image for a police officer recruiting poster.

In his soft voice and shy manner, he didn't waste time with formalities. "You're working on that Gordon case, aren't you?"

Barrett gave him an inquisitive glance, hesitating for a moment. "That's correct. Why, have you got something to share with me?"

"May I sit down?" he asked. Dave motioned to the only other chair in the room.

Eddie wasn't sure how to begin. "I may be stepping out of line with this, but here goes. Early this week, I was on security patrol with Dan Peters up Benedict Canyon Drive when we got a 911 call. We arrested a man for breaking and entering one of the houses. The owners had been on a two-month vacation and returned home to find him in their guesthouse above the garage."

Dave was curious, "I see. So where is this story leading," he asked.

"Well…I'm gettin' to that. You see, he says he was in that guesthouse on the evening of the crime at the Gordon's house. His state defense attorney says he wants to plea bargain and get out on parole. Seems he saw someone leaving the Gordon house around one in the morning on the date in question. He watched them get into a car parked in the driveway of the house he was in down the street and would swear they were driving a black BMW."

Barrett leaned forward, his elbows braced on the desk, his chin resting on his knuckles. "Did he see the license plate?"

"He said it was a personalized plate with the first three letters L-I-Z. The rest was hidden by a bush as the car drove off."

"You say this guy was arrested for breaking and entering. Is he a homeless person? Was he living in this home while the owners were away?"

Eddie chuckled. "He's harmless enough but does have a bit of a record for theft, vagrancy, disturbing the peace, and public indecency. The owners were pissed because he had broken the locks, damaged some furnishings, emptied their storage cupboards and drank over six cases of their quality wines. You might say he made himself right at home."

Dave was shaking his head trying not to laugh. "Doesn't sound like a reliable witness that the jury will believe—and I'm sure the prosecution would tear him apart with that record...the interesting thing is, I believe him."

"Yeah? And why is that?" Eddie asked.

"Because there's not been any mention in the media about a license plate or the make and model of an automobile. We just received that info this morning. There wouldn't have been any way he could have known—unless he actually saw it with his own eyes. I hope he can identify his cars in the dark. He may have to."

"The house was on the corner next to a street light," Eddie said.

"All the better to see you, my dear, said the wolf." Dave laughed at his own quote.

"I'll contact the defense attorney and let him deal with this guy.

What did you say his name was?"

"Jason Ross, better known as Jiggs among his friends," Eddie said.

"Shit! I know that guy. Hangs around all over town. Well, I'll be damned."

Chapter Fifteen

Detective Barrett had been able to call in a few favors and got a search warrant for the apartment of Marc Garret by Sunday morning. He and Grant presented it to the building manager along with their ID's and were escorted to the third-floor unit. They knocked on the door, but no one answer. The manager, Scott Cooper, proceeded to allow them entry.

They were looking specifically for two things: a certain type of shoe worn by medical personnel and any clothing that might have stains which could be blood. They found neither.

"What days of the week does the city pick up trash from the building?" It was a long shot, but they were there, so Grant decided to give it a try.

"Monday, Wednesday, and Friday," said the manager as he relocked the door to the condo.

"What time?" Grant pressed.

"Around four in the afternoon. Dumpsters are in the parking

garage below. Why, is there a problem with the garbage?"

"There could be if I say there is," Grant growled. "How many dumpsters are there?"

"Three big ones," Scott grumbled, with a look of concern.

Grant turned to Barrett, "Feel like getting down and dirty?"

Dave smiled, holding up his latex gloved hands, "Why not? It's been a while since I waded in trash."

The manager looked at them sideways and shook his head, "Follow me, nut-heads." He led them to the elevator and punched PL for Parking Level. This was obviously not his day. "You have to clean up your mess afterwards. The trash people won't do it." They both grinned.

"What kind of transportation does Mr. Garret have?" Dave asked.

"A Rolls-Royce," Scott said. Catching the look of surprise on their faces, he began to chuckle to himself.

"Ha-ha," Grant smirked as the elevator came to an abrupt stop.

Parking garages have a distinct odor of gasoline, hot engines, motor oils, and other fluids all mixed together, but this one added the smell of decaying foods and miscellaneous combined trash in its three large dumpsters.

"He drives a silver Mustang," said Scott as the elevator door opened to the parking garage and they were assaulted by the unique aroma of two-day-old trash from thirty-seven apartment units. "There it is over there." He tilted his head to the right.

"What's his car doing here if he's not home?" Barrett asked.

The manager was quick to answer. "His girlfriend picked him up early this morning."

"So why did you have us knock on the door before you opened it, if you knew he wasn't home?" Barrett quizzed.

"In case he came back and I didn't see him," squealed the manager, shrugging his shoulders. "I can keep up with everyone's comings and goings around here."

Grant gave him a suspicious glance. "Yeah, right. I'm sure there isn't much you miss."

They walked towards the car. "Didn't that search warrant include his vehicle?" he asked Barrett.

"Why, I believe your right, Watson. How fortunate for us." Grant mimicked with a British accent.

"I don't suppose you have a key to the trunk of his car by any chance?" Dave asked.

Scott shrugged his shoulders once again. "You guys are real comedians. You should be on TV."

Grant smiled as he spoke, "Not to worry—I have a universal key that fits any car trunk. He pulled an apparatus from his pocket." The manager's jaw dropped.

Barrett quickly turned Mr. Cooper around, escorted him back to the elevator and punched the up button. "Thank you for your assistance, Mr. Cooper. We'll show ourselves out."

Barrett returned to Grant as he worked his magic on the trunk lock. "You've gotta be crazy, you idiot. The chief will demote you for that if he finds out."

Martin gave him an exasperating look. "So, who's going to spill the beans? We'll say, I just tapped on the trunk and it popped open. Now give me a hand and push down." Indeed, the trunk did pop open and their eyes rested on the evidence they were seeking.

"Well, well, well...what have we here?" Dave said, holding a pair of men's shoes in his latex-gloved hand.

"Looks like we hit the jackpot," Grant said as he held up a stained shirt with the distinct copper odor of dried blood, a cheap throwaway cell phone, wrapped inside the shirt, dropped into the trunk.

"I believe our date with the trash will have to wait," Barrett said. "We'd better get this evidence over to forensics now."

"Gee, that sucks," Grant whined. "Just when I was starting to have some fun."

"You're weird," Barrett laughed as they closed the trunk with a click, gently locking it again.

"If the lab results are what I think they will be, I'll put out an APB to pick him up, but we'll have to wait and see," Dave said.

"You won't have to look far. He's been sitting at the back of the courtroom since the trial started last Friday. Must be pretty sure of himself, if you ask me," Grant exclaimed.

"Looks like you may lose that bet we made," Dave reminded him.

"The trial isn't over yet, Sherlock, but you may be right." They walked up the auto ramp into the fresh air and bright sunlight—saved from having to get down and dirty.

Chapter Sixteen

Sunday flew by and suddenly it was Monday morning; the clock in the courtroom showed 8:30 a.m.—thirty minutes before the gavel would sound and the circus would begin.

Sunday had been a busy day at the Harris house. Shawn and William met with detectives Barrett and Grant and went over their findings and reports. Shawn was putting together his witness list and composing his questions carefully. He knew the prosecution would be calling Carmen, the housekeeper, the director, Mr. Farrell, Liz Carson, and Marc Garret.

Shawn would, of course, have a few questions for each of them. However, he planned to recall Mr. Garret and Liz Carson after his defense witnesses gave testimony. The timing had to be primed and the order of recall was the key. The detectives had done their job and it was now up to him to draw together the strands of the spider's web and catch them at their own game of murder. He was ready.

The defendant and his counsel checked the courtroom to be

sure no one was missing. Liz, dressed in an emerald-green silk Anne Klein suit, was seated again on the front row, behind the prosecutor's table, her fingernails matched the color of her attire and her subtle light green eye-shadow and dark eyeliner gave her face a Chinese-dragon-like appearance.

"Do you think she'll blow smoke out her nose and belch fire through those pink-colored lips before the trial is over today?" William whispered to Shawn.

Shawn studied her movements. "She's confident because she doesn't suspect we know. I'm not sure what she will do or say when the truth is revealed, but you can rest assured it will be a worthy performance. However, the one person I'm counting on is Marc Garret. It's like I'm a director and screenplay writer and they are the characters. I have to guide their performance to make the movie end the way I've written it."

"Court is now in session. All rise for Judge Tyler Wilson." The judge mounted the bench.

"Good morning, Counsel. The court will proceed in the case of State v. William Lawrence Gordon. Prosecution may call their next witness."

"Thank you, Your Honor." Patterson cleared his throat. "I call to the stand Carmen Martinez." As Carmen was led in, a police officer delivered a note to Shawn. He smiled as he read the content and tucked it in his jacket pocket.

Carmen was sworn in and seated. "Mrs. Martinez, would you state your profession and place of employment for the court, please?"

"I'm the housekeeper and cook for the Gordon family on Benedict Canyon Drive in Beverly Hills."

"And you've been employed with the Gordon's over eighteen years, is that correct?"

"Yes, sir," she whispered.

"Mrs. Martinez, you will have to speak up so the jury can hear you," said the judge.

"Yes, sir," she said in a louder voice.

"During this period of time, have you noticed any ill feelings between Mr. William Gordon and Mrs. Michael Gordon?"

"I don't gossip about my employers," she said nervously.

"I'm not asking you to gossip, Mrs. Martinez. I'm asking you to tell the truth under oath, regarding your personal observations while in the Gordon household." Patterson said impatiently. "Did William Gordon and his stepmother ever have disagreements, arguments, or abusive language between each other? And remember, you are under oath to tell the truth."

She glanced at William. "Well, they didn't always get along, if that's what you mean."

"Did he have issues or arguments with his stepsister or father?"

Carmen's nerves were on edge. "Ms. Lizzy and Mr. William didn't get on with each other, but that was mostly about the care of Mr. Michael."

"I see. Perhaps you could tell us what they disagreed about?" Patterson coached.

Carmen wrung her hands together. "Mrs. Gordon and Ms. Lizzy wanted to put Mr. Michael in a nursing home and Mr. William wouldn't allow that to happen."

"So, as I understand your statement, you're telling me that Mr. William refused to follow the advice of Mr. Gordon's doctors, against the wishes of his legal guardian."

"I don't know about that. I just know he wasn't going to let Mr. Michael go to no nursing home. He said it was the kiss of death."

"Thank you, Mrs. Martinez. No further questions, Your Honor."

"Does the defense wish to cross-examine?" the judge asked.

"Not at this time, Your Honor. We wish to reserve that opportunity for later."

"Then the prosecution may call their next witness."

Chapter Seventeen

"The prosecution calls Detective Martin Grant to the stand, Your Honor."

Grant hadn't planned to be a witness for the prosecution, so he looked confused as he took the witness stand.

"Mr. Grant, I believe you're one of the homicide detectives who investigated the murder of Mrs. Gordon, are you not?"

"True," he said.

"In your report, you stated that William Gordon was not very cooperative when being questioned regarding the death of Mrs. Gordon. Is that correct?"

Grant was reluctant to answer. "You will answer Counsel's question, detective," the judge said.

"True, but..."

"And did you not report that the defendant asked you to leave? That he dismissed you because he had other important things to do?"

"Yes, but..."

"And did you also report that he showed little or no remorse for the death of Mrs. Gordon?"

"I did, but…"

"No further questions, Your Honor." Patterson was patting himself on the back for that little bit of maneuvering. He gave a conquering-hero smile of success to the jury as he returned to his seat.

Judge Wilson nodded to Shawn. "Counsel?"

"Counsel will reserve to recall the witness later, Your Honor." Patterson was giving away his game plan and although he was not amused, Shawn had his own hidden secrets in store for the final count. Patterson was now wondering what the defense's next move would be.

"Counsel for the prosecution will call their next witness."

Patterson hesitated, trying to figure out this new twist in not questioning, but he was determined to stick to his outline. His voice was softer now, not as confident and robust. "Counsel calls Mr. Marc Garret."

Marc Garret waited in the witness holding area in the outer hall. He entered from the back of the courtroom and made his way down the center aisle to take his oath.

He was dressed in a tailored black sport coat and tight gray pants, topped by a soft, creamy silk shirt with open collar unbuttoned half way down his chest, showing off the strong muscular figure needed in his profession. His wavy dark hair gave him an Italian gigolo appearance as his heavy aftershave followed him in a cloud, causing some of the reporters to cough and fan themselves as he passed.

Garret appeared nervous as he was sworn in. As he took his place in the witness box, beads of perspiration formed on his forehead. Patterson wanted to confirm Marc's alibi to the jury and eliminate him as a suspect.

"Mr. Garret, please state for the jury your occupation, and most recent employment."

"I'm a trained physical therapist and a registered nurse. I've been employed by Mrs. Gordon for the past three years as a live-in caregiver for her husband, Mr. Michael Gordon."

"Can you describe for the court your recollection of events on the evening of Mrs. Gordon's birthday party, at their home on Benedict Canyon Drive?"

Garret tilted his head back and gazed at the chandelier in the ceiling of the courtroom, as if deep in thought. Shawn shook his head at the poor acting attempt as he watched the jurors faces, catching a few smirks and a couple of eye rolls. He could tell these people were not easily fooled.

"Mrs. Gordon had a dinner party for eight people. I usually sat with the family to assist Mr. Gordon with his eating. He didn't remember how to use the utensils because the disease had destroyed that part of his memory.

"I felt ill earlier in the day, but it got worse that evening and I asked Mrs. Gordon if I could be excused to go to my apartment for the night. I put Mr. Gordon to bed and the doctor gave him a sedative to help him rest for the night. The doc received a call from the hospital and several of us left at the same time." He paused for a sip of water and to mop the sweat from his brow.

"I helped the widow, Mrs. Baker, in with some packages on arrival at the apartments and went to bed after taking some medication. I was home most of the following day when I received a message from Carmen on my cell phone about Mr. Gordon's death. I didn't think the family would be in need of my services and I was still feeling queasy that morning. I knew Ms. Carson would call if she needed me."

"Thank you, Mr. Garret. One more question about Mr. Gordon, if I may. You said the doctor gave him a sedative to help him sleep.

Would he have been able to awake on his own during the night?"

Garret nodded. "It was a mild sedative, and if disturbed during the night, he would have been able to physically move around, but in a dreamlike state of mind, and would of course not be cognizant of what he was doing. He could become violent, but only if someone or something upset him."

"I appreciate your candid and knowledgeable answers, Mr. Garret. No further questions, Your Honor."

"Your witness, Counsel." He nodded to Shawn.

"Thank you, Your Honor," he acknowledged as he approached the witness.

"Mr. Garret. During the time you worked for Mr. and Mrs. Gordon did you have a close relationship with Mrs. Gordon?"

"I'm not sure I understand your question, sir. I was close with every member of the family. I even agreed with Mr. William to keep his father at home as long as was possible." Shawn could tell that he didn't want to answer the question directly, so he made another approach.

"Did you personally ever have a reason to visit Mrs. Gordon in her bedroom?"

"I never visited Mrs. Gordon in her bedroom and had no reason to do so."

Patterson was on his feet. "Objection, Your Honor, Counsel's line of questioning is irrelevant."

The gavel sounded. "Objection sustained, Counsel. The defense will approach the bench."

Shawn stepped up to confer with the judge. "Where are you going with this, Counsel?"

"It is my intent to expose a possible motive with Mr. Garret as a person of interest in this case."

"And do you have substantial evidence to introduce your theory?"

"We have, Your Honor. But I would like to hold that evidence until I recall the witness for further questioning." Judge Wilson nodded his approval.

Shawn stepped down from the bench. "No further questions at this time, Your Honor."

Chapter Eighteen

"The court will take a twenty-minute recess. I will see both counsels in my chambers." Judge Wilson sounded the gavel.

The dark, wood-paneled walls of the judge's chambers, with subtle sunlight streaming in from louvered shutters at the windows, created a soft glow of warmth on the massive wall of books behind a huge mahogany desk. Two chocolate-brown leather chairs faced the desk. "Have a seat, gentlemen," he said, as he sat on the stately throne behind the desk.

"Defense counsel has some new evidence he will be presenting that the prosecution should be made aware of." He glanced at Shawn. "Counsel, if you please."

Shawn handed the judge a stack of reports and began to explain. "In the course of the investigation, the forensic team discovered footprints they determined were from a specific type of shoe worn by most medical personnel.

A search warrant was issued and a pair of these shoes was

found, along with a shirt stained with blood and a throwaway cell phone. These will be presented as evidence for the defense. And William Gordon's alibi will be confirmed." Shawn was hesitant to offer much more to the prosecutor until he was back in court.

Patterson was muddled. "I don't know where all this evidence is leading, but it will be interesting to learn. I have no objections for any new evidence to be presented," he huffed like an old rooster. "I'm confident we will be able to refute the source."

The judge looked amused. "Thank you, gentlemen. There's still time for some coffee before we reconvene. Review the new evidence and prepare yourselves."

The court was back in session and the reporters were all a-twitter as the judge call the room to order. "If the prosecution is prepared to continue, you may call your next witness."

"We are prepared. If it please the court, the prosecution calls movie director, Mr. Greg Farrell, to the stand."

Mr. Farrell, decked out in his Hugo Boss double-breasted charcoal suit, pastel-pink shirt and bold striped tie, made his way from the back of the room. Looking quite dapper with a pink pocket-silk sprouting out of his breast pocket, he adjusted his shirt sleeves to show the flashy gold-and-diamond cufflinks.

Patterson was impressed and assumed the jury was as well. "Mr. Farrell. I understand you and Mrs. Gordon were old friends, is that correct?"

"Yes. I knew Margaret before she married Michael Gordon. As a matter of fact, I introduced her to Michael and Clair less than a year before Clair's tragic accident. After that, she and Michael became close friends and eventually married a year later."

"Can you describe Mrs. Gordon's demeanor and character during her life with Michael Gordon?" Patterson hoped to show Margaret as a saint—a person of love and devotion for a husband whose abilities to function normally were rapidly deteriorating.

"Margaret became Michael's right arm after Clair's death. She was a strong woman who took charge of his household and guided him through tough times of depression. She managed everything, even his social life—which made his grief recovery much quicker, until he was diagnosed with Alzheimer's."

"So...we can safely believe that they had a happy life as husband and wife?" This was a leading question for Mr. Farrell's further response.

"Of course they led a happy life. With the exception of having to deal with William, there never seemed to be any other issues of discontent."

Patterson was pleased with Farrell's rehearsed answer. "Ah...so there were problems with her stepson, William?"

"Yes. Margaret had Michael put William on an annual allowance instead of writing checks for his lavish lifestyle. She felt he needed to learn the value of money and the hard work it takes to get it. Needless to say, William wasn't pleased with this arrangement. He also wasn't happy when Michael changed his will, leaving Margaret fifty percent of his estate. William believed she had taken advantage of Michael's mental condition."

Shawn had listened carefully but chose not to interrupt Farrell's testimony until it was his turn to question.

"I believe you have given us an accurate description of the situation. No further questions." He faced the jury and nodded with his satisfaction of the testimony.

"Will the defense cross-examine?" Judge Wilson asked.

Shawn stood at the defense table, his notes spread before him. "Mr. Farrell, I read here in the investigation report with Mr. Grant at the Polo Club, that you dated Mrs. Gordon prior to her marriage with Mr. Gordon. Is that correct?"

"Yes, as I said, Margaret worked as a movie extra and we dated off and on for about a year, before I met my present wife, Linda."

"In some private papers found in Mr. Gordon's office, you referred to Margaret Carson as a 'gold digger,' is that true?" Shawn asked.

Suddenly, Greg Farrell lost his dignity. "I don't recall using those exact words. I may have said she was a 'go-getter'—but only in jest."

Shawn handed Farrell a paper. "Do you recognize this as your personal stationery, Mr. Farrell?"

"Yes, it is, but…"

"Would you read the paragraph marked in red for the jury, please?"

Farrell's voice was cracking, "Maggie's a gold digger and a terrible actress, but she makes up for the lack of those qualities in more ways than one. She's just what the doctor ordered and you could use another trophy."

"Is that your signature at the bottom?"

"Yes, but I can explain."

"I submit these papers from Mr. Gordon's office as evidence, Your Honor, to prove the statement I just made to be true. No further questions." He wanted to discredit the witness's testimony to the jury. Patterson was fuming. His face turned red at this verbal slap from the defense. How had his team missed this evidence?

The judge handed the papers to the bailiff. "You will enter these as evidence." Without looking at Patterson, he stated, "The prosecution may call their next witness."

Patterson stood, looking down at his paperwork. "The prosecution rest, Your Honor." The wind had been knocked out of his sails.

Judge Wilson turned to Shawn. "Is the defense prepared to call their first witness?"

"We are, Your Honor. I would like to call Mr. Daniel White." Mr. White approached the witness stand and was sworn in. Patterson shuffled papers to see who this witness was.

"Mr. White, will you face the jury, tell them your name, what it is that you do for a living and why you are here." Shawn was ready to start the ball rolling.

"My name is Daniel White. I'm a licensed private investigator and former Los Angeles police officer. I was hired by Mr. Harris to look into Mr. William Gordon's whereabouts on the night of February 10."

Shawn handed another set of papers to the judge. "I would like to enter into evidence, the written investigation of Mr. White. He will now give his statement under oath. Please continue, Mr. White."

The judge scanned the report and handed it to the bailiff, who in turn handed a copy to the prosecutor.

"I made a visit to the ranger station in the area of the Tehachapi Mountains near the Gordon's cabin. All hunters are required to register at the ranger station before hunting." Patterson studied the faces of his paralegals, searching for an answer. However, it was obvious they knew nothing about hunting, as they shrugged their shoulders in response.

White continued. "A couple of hunters, Toby Davis and Cody Watson, had set up a small campsite about a mile down the road from the Gordon's cabin. On arrival, they had registered their hunting license and pertinent information at the area ranger station, requesting a three-day hunt permit. Returning to their camp in the early evening, they noticed a black Mercedes SUV parked at the cabin and saw smoke coming from the chimney. They knew someone was there but decided not to bother anyone and headed down the road to their tent.

"Their camp was hidden in the pine and fir trees not more than 150 feet off the winding road, but close enough that they would have heard any traffic and noticed any headlights during the night.

"Davis and Watson swore the vehicle never left the cabin until early the next morning. They didn't see William that evening, but no cars passed during the night. Cody was cooking breakfast on a small butane camp stove, when they heard and saw the Mercedes leave early the next morning.

"The signed and notarized depositions of Davis and Watson are herewith submitted as part of my full report. From the pictures of Mr. Gordon that had been in the papers, Mr. Watson, who had been standing close to the road, identified him as the driver in the Mercedes."

Shawn was trying his best to maintain his dignified composure, while inside he was bursting at the seams to scream...YES! William had his eyes on Liz and the prosecutor. Patterson looked bewildered and Liz, with her open mouth, looked like a pink fly catcher. He grinned.

"Thank you, Mr. White. No further questions." Shawn beamed.

Slowly the judge turned to the prosecution. "Counsel wished to cross?"

Patterson shook his head. The picture was not looking good. "No questions, Your Honor."

Wilson leaned back in his chair and folded his arms across his chest. "Defense may call their next witness."

Chapter Nineteen

"**Y**our Honor, I would like to call Sergeant Willis, if it please the court."

Sergeant Willis marched down the center of the room, showing off his starched uniform and polished badge. He carried with him the look of a veteran police officer, even though his chubby weight indicated he now had a less active job on the force.

"Sergeant Willis, will you please tell us what your present position is on the police force?"

"I'm with the Palm Springs Police Department and I'm in charge of traffic surveillance."

Shawn wanted to be sure the jury understood what that meant. "Can you be more specific regarding the duties of your office?"

Willis chuckled. "We issue tickets for speeding. We set up traffic surveillance vehicles with cameras to slow traffic in various locations where people tend to drive too fast, especially at night when there isn't a lot of traffic to slow them down."

Shawn was watching Liz Carson's reactions. "Can you tell us if you had any speeding activity on the night of February 10? And if so, where and what time that violation occurred?

Willis was on form. "We had a vehicle set up on West Racquet Club Road after midnight. There's always a lot of speeders on that road late in the evening and early in the morning after the bars close. But we set the warning sign up about twenty feet before the camera can record a photo violation.

"On the morning of February 11 at 3:15 a.m., a black BMW with the personalized license plate LIZ-ONE was captured on camera going 59 miles per hour in a 35 mile-per-hour zone. We have such a heavy backlog of violations it takes a couple of weeks to get the tickets mailed out."

"Can you tell the court who the owner of this vehicle is and whose photograph was on the camera shot?"

"Sure, it was Ms. Elizabeth Carson on Benedict Canyon Drive, and she's sitting right there." He pointed to Liz.

"No further questions, Your Honor?"

Patterson stood without being asked and approached the jury. "It has already been established that Ms. Carson was in Palm Springs on the evening of the murder and this is again unmistakable proof that she was in that area. I would like to thank the defense for establishing further evidence. I have no questions for the witness."

"You may step down," the judge instructed Sergeant Willis. We will now break for lunch and reconvene at 2 p.m. I'll see the Counsels I my chambers." He pounded the gavel once. The jury knew the routine by now and the counsels followed the judge to his office.

"Gentlemen," he said, where are we going with this case?" He looked at Shawn. "Are you going to declare a mistrial?"

Shawn cleared his throat. "No, Your Honor." Patterson's ears perked up as he began to pay attention to the defense.

"There's still more evidence to come, at which time we believe we will be able to reveal who committed these murders." Shawn announced.

The judge paused in contemplation. "Does the prosecution have any objections?"

"None at all. I should like to see the defense pull the proverbial rabbit out of the hat and amuse us all if he can." Patterson said with a smirk on his face.

Judge Wilson studied Shawn. "Can we wrap this up today or will it be tomorrow?"

"That depends on any delays by the prosecution, Your Honor. We are ready to move forward." Patterson folded his arms and stood his ground as he glanced at Shawn.

"I won't throw any monkey wrenches in your little play, Counselor, but this better be worth the ticket price and my time."

"Well gentlemen...shall we break for lunch before we return to the theater?" Wilson quipped. You could have heard a pin drop in the silent stand-off as they rose from their chairs and departed the judge's chambers.

~

During the lunch break Shawn and William headed for a local pub where they had arranged to meet detectives Barrett and Grant. "Wow! That was some fancy footwork in court today. You sure put old Patterson in his place, and wait till you hear what we have up our sleeves. Tell him Dave."

"First. Remember the antique diamond earring that Carmen found on the rug? Well. We got this call from Harry Winston's on Rodeo Drive. Seems there was a lady in just the other day looking to have someone make her a copy of that earring. Said she had lost it in at a club in New York while on vacation. But the sales clerk said it was the woman in the photo we left with them." He paused. "But that's not all."

Shawn and William were holding their breath. Fortune was smiling on them. They now had a lead in the theft of the jewelry. What other good news could these two men have for them?

"We've located some information on the nail chip that forensics found clinging to Michael Gordon's robe. The color is called Shamrock. Most of the salons in Beverly Hills carry it, as does the one that Liz Carson goes to. She was in the other day to have her nails repaired and done in the same color to match her green outfit for the trial."

Shawn scanned the report and grinned. "Luck of the Irish. Sandra knew what she was talking about at dinner that first night. I've never doubted a word she says—she's always been right. The leprechauns are on our side. You guys are tops in my book."

"Oh yeah...one more thing to pull the knot even tighter," said Grant.

"I don't dare ask for more, but what other surprises have you got up your sleeve? I'm all ears," Shawn said.

"Remember the shoeprints on the rug by the victim's bed? Here's the forensic report on that. I'm sure the prosecutor has a copy by now, since the lab just delivered it to the court clerk this morning."

Shawn noticed the underlined section of the report. "Well, well...looks like we just got a "Get out of jail free" card. I'm going to see where this leads. We may have the answers to a double murder."

William was shocked into silence. His suspicions were justified and he breathed a sigh of relief. He looked at his watch. "It's show time!"

Chapter Twenty

The courtroom was buzzing with activity as the jurors filed into the jury box. The prosecution team, with an air of agitation, huddled around their table, conferring in whispered tones. The detectives, Barrett and Grant, had arrived separately and taken their places in the front row, behind the defense table. It appeared more security had been added, with an extra police officer on each side of the room.

Reporters were head-to-head in muted conversations. Liz Carson sensed something she had not planned was about to take place. Marc Garret hid once again in his corner to the back of the room, chewing on his fingernails. He didn't like the smell of defeat and feared what laid ahead.

Shawn and William arrived together, striding with confidence down the center aisle. Placing his briefcase on the defense table, Shawn removed the recent documents he had received and shuffled them in the order he planned to follow.

The trial was reconvened at 2 p.m. "All rise for the honorable Judge Tyler Wilson," announced the bailiff. As the sound of people standing rippled across the room, Judge Wilson entered carrying a stack of documents, his black-framed reading glasses now perched on his Roman-like nose.

"The court is now in session." He gave the gavel a firm rap. "The defense will call their next witness." He offered no information to the jury about the new evidence to be presented. He would leave that to the defense. Although he was considered a liberal judge, he would not tolerate any undue emotional outburst in his court, but nonetheless had ordered the extra security for good measure.

"If it please the court, I would like to call Detective Martin Grant as the next witness."

Grant had already sworn to tell the truth. In his freshly pressed suit and tie he had lost his Detective Colombo appearance as he awaited questioning. "Will you please state, once again, your name and employment?"

Grant smiled at the jury. "Detective Martin S. Grant, Beverly Hills Police Department, Homicide Division."

"And how long have you been assigned to the Homicide Division?"

"I've been with the force for fifteen years and with homicide for five," he answered.

"During the course of your investigations, regarding the death of Margaret Gordon in this case, I'm sure you have worked closely with the forensic team in search of important evidence. Is that correct?" Shawn asked.

He faced the jury with a confident smile again. "Our forensic laboratories are the best in the state. We can depend on their expert findings in any case. If there is a clue, they'll find it—no matter how small." He was milking his moment of fame as he glanced at Detective Barrett, who subtly made a sign of slicing his throat and rolling his eyes.

"Would you say that the forensic reports handed to the judge and counsels here in this courtroom today are based on evidence discovered at the scene of the crime on Benedict Canyon Drive on February 10?"

"Yes, sir. I concur with that statement and their findings."

"Thank you, officer. No further questions, Your Honor."

"Cross-examine for the prosecution, counselor?"

Patterson waved his hand in dismissal. He had already questioned the detective. "The witness may be excused," said the judge.

Shawn was ready for his next witness. "Your Honor, I call Detective Dave Barrett to the stand." Dave took his place in the spotlight of events, ready to verify further findings in their investigation.

"Detective Barrett, I believe you are also a homicide investigator in the Beverly Hills Police Department, is that correct?"

"That is correct," he nodded.

"You recently made a startling discovery in the course of your investigation into this particular case. Would you face the jury and tell us, in your own words, how this came about and what your findings were?"

Detective Barrett took a sip of water and cleared his throat. He turned to address the jury. "Due to evidence provided by the people at the forensic labs, we were given cause to request a search warrant. The evidence, found on the rug next to Mrs. Gordon's bed, was the shoe print—of a shoe worn generally by people who work in the medical profession, such as caregivers and nurses. It's a special type of shoe with a distinct design on the sole."

Sitting in the back corner, sweat began to drench Marc's fancy apparel as he nervously stroked his neck, and his left knee bounced at a rapid pace as his eyes darted hopelessly with fear.

Barrett continued. "We made a search of Marc Garret's apartment, but didn't find anything. However, after searching his vehicle, parked in the lower garage level, we found a pair of the shoes we were looking for, and forensics determined they were an exact match to the prints found on the bedroom rug."

Shawn was pacing himself to allow the jury time to put the pieces of evidence together. Would they think that Marc was having an affair with Margaret Gordon? Perhaps they're wondering if he was stealing the jewelry and got caught in the act. But there was more to unveil as he played on. "I seem to recall in your report that there was additional evidence that you found in the trunk of Mr. Garret's vehicle. Would you tell the court what else was found?"

Dave Barrett watched as Marc squirmed in his seat. "There was a shirt spattered with what smelled like and appeared to be blood, wrapped around a throwaway cell phone. Forensics determined the blood matched that of the deceased Margaret Gordon."

Marc tried to make a run for the exit, causing a flurry of commotion, but he was stopped by the police officers and taken out. Everyone was talking at once as the judge calmly sounded his gavel three times. "Order in the court!" Judge Wilson shouted, bringing the people back under his command. "I'll have no more outbursts in this courtroom. Take your seats. This trial is not over." He nodded to Shawn, "You may continue, Counsel."

"Thank you, Your Honor. I have no further questions for the detective at this time."

"Counsel? Do you wish to cross?"

Patterson stood. "Indeed, Your Honor. Detective Barrett, can you tell the court how you obtained entrance to the vehicle belonging to Mr. Garret?"

"Sorry, Counsel, that is a secret of the trade that I'm not at liberty to discuss."

"So...you were breaking and entering under penalty of the law, which forbids you to do so."

"No, sir. We didn't break anything. We gave a push on the trunk and it popped open. The vehicle was covered by the search warrant issued at the request of the homicide division."

"How very convenient for you. No further questions." He returned to the table and continued to read the reports.

"Thank you, detective, you may step down." Judge Wilson held his hands out to Shawn as if offering him a gift. "You have the floor, Counsel."

Shawn was set for the next scene of drama to be performed. "I call to the witness stand Ms. Elizabeth Carson." A unified gasp echoed through the rows of reporters and spectators. What was the defense counsel doing? Liz is sitting on the side of the prosecution. It had been rumored she would not testify at the trial.

Patterson had not called on her for testimony. But for the defense to call a hostile witness to testify had the courtroom on edge, including the prosecution. "Your Honor, my client has not had time to prepare any testimony for this case. I request a postponement until we have had time to review her position."

Rap went the gavel. "Postponement denied. The witness will take the stand."

Defiant to the end, Liz moved to the witness box and was sworn in. The judge ordered the bailiff to read her Miranda Rights after she was seated. As her lawyer was there to represent her, he wanted to be sure she was legally aware of her position.

"Counsel may proceed with his questioning."

Chapter Twenty-One

Shawn sensed that Liz Carson was on pins and needles. She did her best to appear confident and calm, even as her thoughts seared her brain like branding irons. *How much does he know? What evidence has he discovered? What's going to happen to Marc? Will he cave under pressure? They have to believe me. Was he really screwing my mother and me? How did I miss that detail?*

In the meantime, Shawn was putting his notes in order, letting her stew. She would be more apt to make mistakes with her answers and her emotional senses would be exposed. He stood before the witness stand, calm and collected. "Will you please state your full name for the court records?"

"Elizabeth Carson," she blurted in defiance.

"No middle initial?" he asked

"None," she replied.

"Wasn't Carson your mother's maiden name?" Shawn asked as he observed her reaction.

"Yes, it was. My mother wasn't married when I was born, but who gives a fiddler's fuck about that matter?" She was getting impatient.

"I merely wish to establish the fact that you never had a father figure to relate to. That you were an illegitimate child of a movie extra, who didn't know who the father was." He could see the anger in her face, but she refused to give him the satisfaction of denial. Her lips pinched in silence.

"Objection, Your Honor! Counsel is badgering the witness." If looks could kill, Liz, staring daggers at Patterson, would have had him dead on the courtroom floor.

"Objection sustained. Counsel will refrain from comments of such a personal nature. The jury will disregard that last statement. Please continue."

"Did you murder your mother?" Shawn demanded, causing a burst of astonishment to roll through the courtroom like waves on a beach. Caught off guard, Patterson was speechless. His jaw dropped, but no sound came from his lips.

"What a ridiculous question!" Liz shouted back sarcastically.

"Let me rephrase that, if I may. Do you know who suffocated your mother to death on the evening of February 10?" Shawn stood his ground. Liz hesitated in silence. *Would this be her only opportunity to suggest that it had to be Marc? Would it work? Would she be implying she had suspicions and had changed her tune about William?*

Liz's brain was sparking on a short fuse. "You will answer Counsel's question, Ms. Carson." The judge ordered.

"I don't know. I wasn't there. I was in Palm Springs. It's been confirmed that the house was locked and the alarm was set. I don't know who would want to kill my mother or for that matter, who killed Michael Gordon."

Shawn allowed her answer to hang in the air. "So...are you suggesting that Michael Gordon was murdered?"

"I don't know. I already told you, I wasn't there. I'm merely quoting the newspapers," she said nervously.

"What time did you leave the house after the party was over?" he continued.

"As I recall, it was close to 10 p.m. The party was over. Marc was sick, Michael had been put to bed, Dr. Thompson had to leave on a call and the Farrell's left at the same time."

"And how far did you go?" he asked.

"I'm sorry. I don't understand your question. I left for Palm Springs and you've already proven that I was there with your stupid traffic cameras. What is it you don't understand?"

Shawn was sliding on thin ice. He knew the prosecution would do their best to discredit the vagrant, homeless man as a witness in court, so he presented the judge with a signed deposition from the police department. "Five hours is a lot of time to drive from Beverly Hills to Palm Springs. My wife and I made the drive two nights ago in less than two and-a-half hours. So I wondered where you were between the hours of 10 p.m. and 3:15 a.m."

Liz had a sinking sickening feeling in her stomach. She felt like a mouse cornered by a large, hungry cat. Her defenses were falling and Shawn sensed she was about to break.

Speaking in a slow and clear voice, Shawn added, "It was brought to our attention that a person, staying in the house on the corner of the block where the Gordon house is located, was sitting in a window seat around midnight." He paused to allow the time of midnight to register with the jury.

"He saw a person leave the Gordon's house and walk to a car, parked in the drive of the house where he was staying. Mr. Jarred Ross glanced out the window overlooking the drive and saw a black BMW as it backed out of the driveway of that house. Although he wasn't able to see all of the license plate, he was able to read the first three letters of a personalized plate. The letters were LIZ."

"Objection, Your Honor! Who is this Jarred Ross? Is he a reliable source? Why wasn't he called into court a witness?"

"If it please the court, Your Honor, Mr. Ross is currently detained and was not able to make an appearance here, but he was questioned by the police with Counsel present. The information on the license plate, and the make and model of the car, was not common knowledge and had not been released to the media when he made his statement. There was no way he could have known that information if he had not been an eyewitness."

"Objection overruled." Wilson gave his gavel a tap. "The bailiff will enter this deposition as evidence. You may continue, Mr. Harris."

"Ms. Carson, the homicide detectives also found a key in the trunk of Mr. Garret's car when they searched it. It matched the house keys for the Gordon residence. Do you know how it came to be in his possession?"

Liz knew she was going to have a difficult time crawling out of the quicksand mire she was slipping into.

"I haven't a clue." The less she said the better. Perspiration was starting to circle on her green silk Anne Klein suit as she reached for the glass of water.

"Then allow me to suggest the answer. Marc Garret took Michael Gordon's key that had hung by the back door for the past six years. He wanted to make the crime appear to be a robbery gone wrong. But that wasn't your plan, was it? You wanted to see William in prison for murder so you could inherit the entire estate for yourself."

Reporters began to stir, not wanting to miss a word of Shawn's version of the events. Liz felt the courtroom getting hotter and the smell of her own sweat made her feel nauseous. *He can't do this to me. Why do I feel like I'm balanced on a high-wire? One small slip and it's over. I won't let it happen.*

"Objection, Your Honor! Counsel's attempting to lead the witness.

"Objection over ruled. Counsel may continue." Patterson was furious.

Shawn continued, "You were angry with your mother for waiting so long. You knew you would never be rid of her even after Michael's death—she would still be in control of your life and the purse strings. You had been abused and ignored all your life by someone that Michael considered a saint. You decided it was time to end Saint Margaret's hold on you. It was the money you were after because you never had her love.

"Marc was an easy target. You used him to fulfill your goals, and when you found out he was sleeping with your mother, it made it that much easier. He was no longer your lover, but your tool."

"You're insane!" she shouted. "You can't prove any of those accusations."

Chapter
Twenty-Two

S hawn was prepared for her rejection of the facts. "You made a recent visit to Harry Winston's jewelry store on Rodeo Drive, with an antique earring you wanted to have copied. The sales clerk and store manager recognized your photo when we showed it to them. You must have dropped the matching earring, stolen from the closet safe in your haste to leave the house. Carmen found it the following evening while cleaning the bedroom."

The prosecutor was on his feet again. "I must protest, Your Honor. Counsel for the defense is wandering around la-la-land with his wild imagination, accusations, and speculations. He has no proof. It sounds like he has been reading his client's mystery stories."

"He's wrong, Your Honor." Shawn shook the papers he held in his hand in Patterson's face. "The proof is right here in these reports, which your legal team is combing through at that table even as we speak."

Judge Wilson nodded his head. "These documents arrived during the lunch break and perhaps I've had more time to review them than you have, Counsel. With that being said, I will allow the defense to continue. Your protest has been noted for the records."

Liz's heart was racing and her hands shook. This trial was not going as she had planned. *What was wrong with the prosecutor? This shouldn't be allowed.* The judge was obviously not in her corner. It was clear he favored the defense. Her mind was in a muddle and she couldn't think straight.

A police officer approached the defense table with more documents. Shawn handed a copy to the judge and a copy to the prosecutor as he began to read. "Your honor, Marc Garret has just confessed to the murder of Margaret Carson Gordon on the evening of February 10. His states that his accomplice was none other than Elizabeth Carson, the deceased's own daughter. According to his confession, the murder was orchestrated by Liz Carson in her attempt to gain control of the Gordon estate by placing the blame on William Gordon.

"I further submit that Ms. Carson here was personally responsible for the death of Michael Gordon. According to the lab report just completed, forensics found a broken nail chip caught on the left shoulder of his terry robe. The nail polish on that chip matches the color on the witness's nails today, which she recently had repaired at her regular salon. We have ordered DNA test to be performed."

The tiger was out of the cage. Her claws gripped the polished wood railing on the witness box. "You think you're so smart, don't you?" Liz growled in a low voice. "You've got it all figured out... but you don't even know the half of it. You never knew my mother. You can't imagine what a bitch I had to live with all my life, being handed down and passed around for everyone's pleasure."

Patterson was on his feet quickly. "Ms. Carson, please, you don't know what you're saying."

She flicked her middle finger in his direction as if swatting away a fly. "Fuck off Counsel! I know it's time the truth was told. Margaret

Carson was a gold-digging whore who set her sights on the richest men she could find in the movie industry. She weaseled her way through Greg Farrell to meet Michael Gordon and his goody-two-shoes wife, Clair. They became close friends until the opportunity arrived for her to arrange Clair's accidental death."

There was a collective gasp heard from the front of the courtroom to the back. Reporters were scribbling, their pencils scraping on paper and the air danced with lightning-like electrical vibes in the tension surrounding the witness stand.

Liz continued, "I had to show my stupid mother how to find and cut the brake line on the jeep. I helped her plan the death of Clair Gordon so she could take her place," she said with lips curling in a sadistic smile as she stared at William.

He was so stunned he couldn't move; his knuckles turned white as he clutched the arms of the chair where he sat, frozen in silence. He had no words and no feelings for this pathetic creature, as vehemence spewed from the mouth of this Medusa.

Liz was out for revenge as she continued to enlighten the court with her diabolical desires. "It was Saint Margaret's time to go. She'd served her purpose and hung on longer than needed. Marc suffocated her while I watched. Wretched worm that he is—he thinks he's God's gift to the female gender," she mumbled.

Judge Wilson was not inclined to stop her amazing confession. The courtroom stenographer recorded the entire confession word-for-word. The prosecution sat with mouths gaping, their ears burning with embarrassment at such a display of hate from their client.

"Sure...I gave the old man a push down the stairs. It was time for the old fart to meet his maker. I couldn't wait for Marc to give him a shove. It never would have happened. Frozen to the wall, he was. Frightened of his own shadow. I heard the neck crack on the first tumble and knew it was all over by the time his body rolled to the bottom of the stairs."

Liz watched the shock register on William's face, raised her chin and gave a guttural laugh in his direction, as he attempted to rise and was held in place by the two detectives behind him. "You bitch! You murdering bitch!" he screamed, as tears rolled down his cheeks. She laughed in his face.

It was greed that had lured her down this path and she would not give up her sweet taste of revenge. She removed a small revolver from the purse in her lap and hid it from view while making one final statement, as she stared at William. "Don't think any of this was easy, William. It took a lot of hate over many years to reach this point, and it's over now. But you won't put me in prison."

Raising the small pistol to her chest, she quickly pulled the trigger. Her aim did not miss its intended target at such close range. Blood spattered the witness box and the defense Counsel, standing just steps away. The pistol fell to the floor as she slumped in the chair. The courtroom was in chaos.

Reporters and spectators alike lunged for the floor when they heard the shot. Police burst through the back doors of the room, guns drawn to stop anyone from leaving the scene. It was over in minutes, but the smell of death lingered in the air. Members of the jury were stunned and frightened. Reporters were on their cell phones as the police ushered them to the back.

"Wow! Now that's what I call an exit!" exclaimed Grant.

Judge Wilson was banging his gavel on the desk. "Order in the court!" he yelled over the mayhem. An officer approached the witness box. Holding his fingers on the left side of Liz's neck just below the ear, he shook his head. "She's gone," he announced to the judge.

Judge Wilson was still in charge as he spoke to the officers. "You will empty the courtroom in an orderly manner and remove the body." His gavel was heard once again. "This court is now adjourned until tomorrow morning." He glanced at the jurors and added, "The bailiff will see that you receive further instructions."

Dave Barrett clapped Shawn on the shoulder. "Jesus!" I sure didn't see that one comin'," he whispered.

"I don't think any of us did," Shawn muttered.

"Well, one thing's for sure," Grant said. "She was guilty in more ways than one—no doubt about it."

William pointed to Patterson, who was white as a sheet and still seated in shock as his paralegals gathered their reports and other papers. "Gentlemen," the officer said, "I have to ask you to leave the courtroom through the doors at the back so the EMT's can get in to do their job."

"No problem, officer, we're out of here," said Barrett, as the four of them made their way down the center aisle and out the entrance of the courthouse.

~

Standing in front of the court building, William took a deep breath of fresh air as the sun beamed down between the soft clouds now starting to glow with the promise of a beautiful sunset. "So...I'm a free man."

"In essence, yes," said Shawn.

"However, I still need to ask the judge to declare a mistrial, which I'm sure he and the prosecution will agree to."

"And what's going to happen to Marc? Will he still be charged with murder?" William asked.

Shawn thought for a moment. "He might be charged with manslaughter. It wasn't premeditated murder on his part. He was duped into following orders from a serpent of seduction and deception. The judge might also consider the fact that he killed a person accused of murder by the confession of her own daughter. However, he will most likely serve fifteen to twenty years in prison before being granted parole."

"I want you to help him," William said.

"William, what are you talking about? Do you know what you're saying? They killed your mother and father. You can't be serious," Shawn exclaimed.

"No, they didn't. It was Liz who killed my parents and she used Marc to help. He never would have murdered my dad. I know he can't now inherit the $500,000 dollars that Dad wanted him to have, but I can put it in a trust fund in his name. He can use it to pay your attorney fees and the rest can accumulate until he is out of prison. At least it will help him start a new life. He was good to my father. He took care of him like he was his own father. I will honor my dad's last request. Marc wasn't the bad guy. He was led down the wrong path by a true disciple of Satan."

Shawn gave him a bear hug. "William, my friend, you're all heart. Now you know why I said, "You could never murder anyone.'"

Epilog

Judge Wilson declared a mistrial in William's case the following morning. The news of Liz Carson's confession and courtroom suicide was plastered on the front page of every newspaper you could find.

Arrangements were confirmed for Shawn to represent the defense of Marc Garret. William promised to see the family lawyer and arrange setting up the trust fund. Marc could not believe his good fortune. He had truly cared for his patient, Michael Gordon.

Detectives Barrett and Grant had their lunch at the Musso and Frank Grill the following week, and Dave added his ten-dollar winnings from their bet to the waiter's tip.

Carmen buzzed around the mansion like a busy bee, humming with happiness that Mr. William was back at work writing on his next mystery. The stolen jewels were found in a briefcase locked in the trunk of the BMW owned by Liz Carson. They were put in a safety deposit box at the bank.

Shawn and Sandra gave an Irish dinner party to celebrate St.

Patrick's Day the day after the trial had ended, and everyone was surprised to find a four-leaf clover in their salad. "It's the luck of the Irish," Sandra explained as her green eyes sparkled with mischief.

William made his annual trip to the mountains, where he tossed a floral wreath into the abyss of memories where his mother lost her life, and heard her voice call his name one more time.

Accent

READERS' COMMENTS
on ACCENT

This could happen anywhere, but New York was the perfect setting. Typically people don't want to get involved in a crime and when they do, things go from bad to worse. Your mystery and your characters are true to life. Humor and romance added another layer of interest. Thanks for an entertaining read. —*Valerie W.*

Another suspenseful bedtime story. I didn't want it to end, but then I never do. *Mystery Lover—Joy R.*

You've done it again. The mixture of suspense and drama with all the details—combined with stalking, travel, romance and friendships. I look forward to reading each new volume of Mystery Collection. —*Richard K.*

It keeps getting better with each volume. You're on a roll—don't stop now. Thanks for sharing. —*Robert A.*

I knew when you moved to Merida and started writing, I knew it would change your life. Little did I realize it would lead to mystery, suspense, and intrigue, what fun! You do have a creative imagination. Keep up the good work. —*Tracy M.*

Great finish to a well told story—need I say more? —*Sandra B.*

Chapter One

New York City had begun to experience the onset of an early winter. Pedestrians rushed along the sidewalks in front of the Plaza Hotel on West 59th Street, bundled for warmth against the incoming storm. Shock penetrated every bone in her body, as chills crept up her spine. Casandra Collins couldn't believe what she had just overheard and was afraid to move. A man, talking on his cell phone not more than six feet away, was plotting to murder someone. His back was to her as she stared across the traffic to Central Park. Her hands began to shake, making it difficult to balance the to-go cup of coffee she had just purchased from Billy's Bakery in the Plaza complex.

Should she ignore what she had heard? Most people wouldn't want to get involved. Her mom had always told her to keep out of other people's business, and at thirty-six, she had managed most her life to follow that advice, but this was different—someone's life was in danger. She needed time to think.

It was cold and windy on the streets of Manhattan. The sun had set early, as it does in late October, blotting out any residual glow as thick clouds hovered above the city like a foreboding dark angel spreading its wings, rumbling and ready to strike with lighting at any moment.

The trees in Central Park, across West 59th, stood with black skeletal branches, stretching like the gnarled fingers of a ghostly apparition. Their dried, fallen leaves rustled and swirled around massive trunks, scattering down streets and avenues between the high-rise buildings. She stood frozen with fear not far from where the killer had placed his call, before he dashed across the street between traffic that had paused for the red light. He turned and glanced back in her direction, the shadow of his hat covering his face. Then he vanished in the darkness.

What should I do—call the police? What could I tell them when they get here? I heard a man talking on a cell phone about his plan to murder someone. Would they believe me? Would they take me in for questioning, or think I'm just some lonely woman trying to draw attention to myself?

Of course, they'll want to know what he looked like, but I never saw his face. All I noticed was a shadow, dressed in a black overcoat and hat, as he crossed the street and disappeared into Central Park. That wouldn't be much of a description to go on, with every man in Manhattan bundled up in their coats and hats in this nasty weather. I didn't even hear who he's plotting to kill, or when, and how.

Casandra stood glued to the sidewalk, unable to move. Her mind raced as she thought to herself, *I know it's been a long day at work and I have a lot on my mind. I may even be a little stressed, but I know what I heard.* Passers-by were becoming irritated with her as she stood like a statue in their path, causing them to dodge around her. She twisted and turned—*I'm not crazy*, she wanted to say when they gave her annoyed looks. *Really I'm not.*

Casey, as she is called by her close friends and business associates, had worked late, trying to keep ahead of inventory orders for the weeks of Christmas shopping still to come. As manager of the men's accessories department at Bergdorf's for the past seven years, she knew it was going to be a busy holiday season and she needed to be sure there was plenty of stock available. It wouldn't be wise to run short.

Being a professional business person from the old school of fashion-conscious, well-bred, dignified ladies, Casey is an attractive, sensible, intelligent and mature woman in her thirties, but dealing with murder was not on her agenda. She turned and hurried home to her co-op at 41 West 58th; it was time to get in out of the cold.

All the way home she felt she was being followed and kept glancing back as her sensible heels clacked faster and faster on the concrete walk. It was only a block and a half from Billy's Bakery, but it felt like miles with the wind whistling around her as the temperature continued to drop. Glancing behind her again, she gasped. It wasn't her imagination. She could see a man in a black overcoat and dark hat getting closer and closer. Casey feared for her safety.

I knew it, she thought. *He spotted me and knows I heard his conversation.* Panic set in and she picked up her pace. He was about to catch up with her just as she reached her building.

Casey fumbled with her keys to open the door. The glass-enclosed lobby was warm and inviting as she stepped inside. Sam, the doorman, greeted her as the door closed and locked behind her. "Sam!" she exclaimed with relief, "What a surprise."

"It's no surprise to me, Ms. Collins. I'm here at six o'clock every night, come rain or shine." He stepped from behind the desk where he had been reading the New York Times. "It must be getting really cold out there, you're shaking like a leaf. Here, let me help you with that mailbox key. You look like you've seen a ghost. Is everything OK?"

He took the key from her gloved hand and opened the box for her.

"Thank you, Sam. I'm fine now that I'm home," she mumbled, staring through the glass front of the lobby, eyes searching for the man that had followed her—but no one was there. Perhaps it was her imagination after all—or was he lurking out there in the black void just beyond her vision?

Casey was out of breath as she retrieved her mail, locked the box again and stepped through the open elevator door that Sam was holding for her. "Have a good evening, Ms. Collins, and don't fret so much over the holidays. We all get through them a day at a time, same as every year."

The soothing hum of the elevator gliding her to the third floor was a reassuring and safe sound. Once in her unit, she locked the final bolt in place and breathed a sigh of relief. *What was I thinking?* She asked herself. *In this weather, that person behind me could have been any man in Manhattan—and again, maybe there was no one. My mind is playing tricks.*

She dropped the mail on the entry console, hung her coat in the closet, kicked off her shoes and headed to the bedroom to change out of her work clothes. A clap of thunder made her jump—it had begun to rain.

Casey's co-op, consisting of a single bedroom and bath with combined living room, dining room and open kitchen, was decorated in neutral tones and contemporary furnishings, accented with splashes of pastel colors, offering an up-scale, sophisticated-yet-comfortable look.

Book shelves covering one wall were filled with reading material, knick-knacks and framed photographs. Her at-home work station, complete with computer, printer and short file cabinet, featured a sleek Maguire desk of mahogany and bronze, with bamboo legs tied by strips of rawhide. The dining room and kitchen encompassed the remainder of the generous living space and although she no longer played, a small baby-grand piano occupied one corner near, the windows.

Returning from the bedroom, wrapped in her robe and standing barefoot at the kitchen counter, she made herself a cocktail while the Jacuzzi tub in her black-and-white marbled tiled bathroom filled with hot water. Sinking into the warm liquid, she pushed the button. As steam rose from the water's surface and bubbles swirled around her, she set her cocktail on the short table next to the tub. Slowly she relaxed from the day's events and her memory returned to the man outside the bakery and his frightening phone conversation.

She tried her best to remember every detail. His voice had been deep and clear and he spoke in English, but with an accent she couldn't place. It wasn't French or Spanish, but definitely European; perhaps German or Hungarian. Whatever it was, she would recognize it in a minute if she heard it again. She swore she would be able to pick him out in a line-up with the lights off.

Casey closed her eyes and allowed the stress of the day to float away. Time passed quickly. The water began to cool and her cocktail glass was now empty. Stepping from the tub, she wrapped her wet hair in a towel and slipped back into her long-sleeved white terry robe. The bubbling bath waters that had soothed her muscles drained away, taking her stress with them, while the Scotch on the rocks had warmed her inside.

Suddenly, Casey was hungry. It was time to order-in some Chinese for dinner and stay safely indoors for the night. Joe's Shanghai restaurant was close by, and their crab soup dumplings were just what she craved to take the edge off this gloomy weather and thoughts of murder.

Sam buzzed her intercom, announcing the delivery boy's arrival and she greeted him at the door as the aroma from the crab soup met her nostrils, making her mouth water with anticipation. She watched the young Chinese man retreat as he walked down the hall to the elevator and noticed that he had a slight limp. Instantly she recalled—the man with the phone had appeared to limp as he crossed 59th Street. However, he was much taller than the delivery boy. That's another detail she needed to remember to tell the police.

Sitting at the kitchen bar-counter with a glass of white wine while devouring her crab dumplings, Casey grabbed a notepad and allowed her thoughts to retrace the events of the evening after leaving work.

It's strange how little details resurface in your mind several hours and even days after something happens. Casey thought to herself, *perhaps I noticed more than I thought I did.* Although, I wasn't eavesdropping on his conversation, I seem to remember he mentioned something about the Metropolitan Museum and fashion before he said, "He's as good as dead. I'll take care of it." Of course, it was those last two sentences that jarred my attention and the rest was rubbish—but maybe not.

The carton of crab dumpling soup was empty and Casey was full as she turned off the light, stretched, and headed for the bedroom. I'll let it rest tonight and perhaps call the police in the morning. It's my civic duty to report something like this, even if nothing ever comes from it. I always see things clearer in the light of day. But wait—although I never saw his face, I wonder if he could see me from across the street when he turned and looked back. Oh my god—now I'll never get to sleep.

Chapter Two

Casey slept restlessly, with frightening visions of being chased through Central Park in the dark by something evil; something she could never see, but only hear with every crunch of a leaf or crack of a twig. Daylight could not have come too soon. Rays from the morning sun began to slice like knives down the east-west streets, funneling between the tall buildings. The storm had passed and the rain had cleansed Manhattan. The fall morning was crisp and cool, with a crystal-clear sky and no wind.

Casey, sitting at her desk by the window, had been awake since 5 a.m., staring at the traffic on West 58th—watching but not see-ing—listening but not hearing—she was in a trance-like state, deep in thought as she attempted to recall any detail she could about last night's encounter with the man on his phone.

Was it *his* cologne or someone else who passed by? I would recognize the fragrance of Hugo Boss cologne anywhere. It's one of my favorites. She jotted this memory on her notepad, now full of details about the mysterious man. She glanced at the clock on her desk and reached for the phone to call her friend Jill Clark.

"Jill. It's Casey. Sorry to ring so early, but can you join me for breakfast? I need to talk to someone and I trust your judgment."

"Why, honey, is something wrong?"

"I'm not sure." She hesitated. "I need another woman's opinion on an important matter and I value your advice."

"Well, that put a feather in my hat. When and where do you want to meet? I just got out of the shower and need time to dress."

"How about the Great American Health Bar on West 57th? Say about 7:30? I can't be late this morning. I scheduled a department meeting with the sales staff."

"Is this about work?" Jill said.

"No. It's something very serious and you won't believe me when I tell you. You need to help me make a decision."

"Oh my god! You've met a man. Now I can't wait. I'll be there at 7:30 on the dot." There was a click as the phone disconnected.

Casey bit her lip and breathed a sigh...*And I thought she had a head on her shoulders. What was I thinking?*

She stacked the paperwork for her meeting, and placed it in her briefcase, along with a copy of the *New York Times,* which she hadn't had time to read. Selecting an Ann Taylor navy suit and a cream-colored silk blouse, she dressed quickly. Checking her appearance in the full-length mirror, she nodded with satisfaction. If you look professional, people will see you as a professional—that's what I tell my sales team. Time to face the world—but first, Jill. She headed for the elevator.

Sam, dressed in his gray uniform, was standing by the lobby door and tipped his hat.

"Morning, Ms. Collins. You look mighty sharp, as usual."

"Morning, Sam. I wish I felt as sharp as you think I look."

"Well, the day's still young, Ms. Collins, and the sun is shining—the gloom is down the drain, as my wife would say."

She smiled and asked, "How are Martha and the kids? I bet they're anxious for Christmas to get here."

Sam grinned and shook his head, "Always, Ms. Collins, always. You have a good day." Casey tugged on her gloves and was out the door in a flash.

Jill Clark had arrived first at the breakfast bar restaurant and was seated next to the wall. Casey smiled and waved as she entered and joined her at the table. Jill took one look at her face. "You don't look like a woman who's found a new love, honey. So what's up?" The waiter arrived with fresh coffee and they placed their orders. Casey waited before answering Jill's question.

She glanced around to be sure no one else was listening, and in a whisper she asked Jill, "If you overheard a person who is planning to murder someone, but you don't know who, when, or where, and you don't even know what this person looks like because you never saw his face, would you think it necessary to report it to the police?"

"Holy cow, sweetheart! What have you got yourself into?" Jill could tell this was not a joke as she studied Casey's serious face.

"It was all quite by accident," she admitted, filling her in on the details of the previous evening. She sat back in her chair, waiting for Jill's response as the waiter delivered their omelets, topped off their coffees and disappeared.

Jill clutched her pearl necklace in shock. "Jesus, Mary and Joseph! Honey, of course you should report it. I would have been on that phone last night. Why on earth would you hesitate?" As a court stenographer, who works daily with lawyers and judges, Jill's advice would of course follow the rules of law.

"I wasn't sure I wanted to get involved."

"Honey, you're already involved. You overheard a murder being planned. Did this man see you? Does he know where you live? Lord, Casey honey, you could become one of his victims—or at the very least, an accessory to the crime if the police find out you knew and didn't report it. Make that call, meet them during your lunch break today and pray the murder hasn't already taken place." Jill was like a mother hen. "I'll come with you, if you want."

"I don't need anyone to hold my hand, but it would be nice to have a little support. Are you're sure you can get away from court today?" she asked.

"No problem, sweetie, the jury's out for deliberations until Monday. I'm taking the day to organize the documents, like any good court reporter. Buzz me and let me know where to meet you. I'll be there."

"Thanks. You're a dear and I knew you would have the answer," Casey replied as she flagged the waiter for their check.

Jill shook her head. "You're not out of the woods yet, Ms. Riding-hood. Let's hope the wolf's eyesight wasn't any better than yours, and he doesn't know who you are. Perhaps the police will have someone watch you for a few days, just to be sure. Better safe than sorry, my mom used to say. And on that note, you had best get to work or you'll be late." She left a tip on the table. "Thanks for the breakfast and remember to call me."

Jill took off in a different direction while Casey paid the check, then maneuvered through the pedestrian traffic as she headed east to Bergdorf's. As she glanced in shop windows on her right, she felt she was being watched— she continually noticed a reflection of the same person across the street. She waited until the right moment, just as a truck passed by, and quickly ducked into the employee entrance at Bergdorf's, hoping that he didn't see her disappear.

Chapter Three

Overnight, the merchandise display department had worked a miracle, decking the store's many floors with holiday trimmings. Red, white, and silver sparkled on all the display platforms. Christmas trees and garlands were laced with colorful ribbons and glittering ornaments, while the mannequins were dressed in the finest holiday attire. Casey joked at the meeting with her sales staff, "Christmas always comes earlier than Thanksgiving in retail. So put on that holiday smile and let's dazzle the customers and beat last year's figures." The opening buzzer sounded. "It's showtime!" she added.

Stepping off the floor and into her cubical of an office, Casey made the call and set up her appointment with the police, then she called Jill. "We're all set. They'll meet us at Serafina Osteria on East 58th at twelve-thirty. Are you still willing to join me for lunch with the cops and hold my hand?"

"Of course I am. And Osteria is one of my favorite restaurants.

I'll see you there. You're not having second thoughts, are you? You sound worried." Casey's mind was on the stranger who appeared to be following her this morning and she didn't answer. "Cass, are you there?"

"Yes, I'm here. The problem is, I think I was followed this morning when we separated after breakfast, but I can't be sure. I kept seeing a reflection in the shop windows of a man across the street. I'll tell you about it at lunch. Meanwhile I've got some work to do. See you later."

The morning hours flew by with business as usual, but nothing too stressful, as noontime rapidly approached. Casey was on the phone most of the morning, placing orders for additional merchandise from the buyers. Her inventory notes from the night before indicated the hot items she was selling out of. Without any warning, she heard a familiar voice speaking with one of the sales clerks. She froze in the middle of her conversation, leaving the buyer on the phone hanging mid-sentence. "Ms. Collins, are you there? Ms. Collins?"

She hung up the phone and listened but was afraid to move from her desk, as thoughts raced through her brain. *That's him! That's his voice.* She would swear it was the same person. *What's he doing here? He mustn't see me.* She pushed the door to her office almost closed, leaving a small opening so she could still listen, while she hid in silence. Her hands were trembling and her throat was dry. The conversation was over quickly, as the clerk finished with the sale.

"Thanks for shopping at Bergdorf's and have a great day."

Casey closed her eyes and said a little prayer, then peeked around the door only to see the back of the customer leaving the department. "Danny, step into my office quickly," she whispered.

He stared at her frightened face. "Yes, Ms. Collins. Did I do something wrong?"

"No, no. The man you just waited on—what did he purchase?"

"A pair of black leather gloves. Why? Is that important?"

"It might be. Did he pay with a credit card?" she whispered.

Danny shook his head, not sure where this line of questioning was leading. "No ma'am. He paid cash."

"Too bad we didn't get his name or address," she said as she wondered what she should do next.

"Should we call security?" Danny asked.

"No," she said shaking her head. "He hasn't done anything wrong—at least not yet." Danny had a puzzled expression as she waved her hand in dismissal. "It's OK. You can get back to work." Casey looked at her watch. It was 12:10. Time to head for the restaurant. I hope he's not waiting outside for me to leave. She slipped on her coat and gloves, closed the office door and headed for the security office at the employee exit. "Please God—don't let him be waiting outside," she prayed silently. Stepping through the doorway she looked right and then left, but there was no sign of him.

Casey arrived at Serafina Osteria. It was still an early lunch hour for most New Yorkers. She spotted Jill siting alone at a table in the far corner and joined her. "Honey, you look like a mouse who just saw a giant cat. These guys we're meeting are just police officers. They won't bite you head off." Unable to find her voice for the moment, Casey nodded her understanding. "How will they know who we are?" Jill asked as she flagged the waiter to catch his attention.

"I told them what I would be wearing and that I would be with a friend. We better go ahead and order lunch, they might be late." Taking their orders, the waiter disappeared. They watched as two men approached their table.

"Am I correct to presume you are Ms. Collins?" the older one said flashing his badge of identification.

"That's correct," she said. "And you are?"

"Sergeant Willis—NYPD. And this is Detective Brandon. May

we join you?"

"By all means, please, have a seat. This is my friend, Jill Clark."

Sergeant Willis began. "I know you mentioned you don't have much time, but if you could supply more details regarding our phone conversation this morning, perhaps by the time you finish lunch, we'll have a better picture of what we're dealing with."

Casey took out her notepad and began to fill in the blanks as the waiter delivered the food they had ordered. Willis and Brandon ordered coffee. "So," Detective Brandon added when he thought she had finished her story, "you think he may have followed you this morning, but you said you don't know what he looks like."

Casey sat back. "Yes, I did and no I don't. I know it sounds confusing, but that's not all. He was in the store this morning and purchased a pair of leather gloves in my department. Unfortunately, I didn't get to see his face. I was in my office when I heard his voice and was afraid he might see me, so I stayed behind the door. He paid cash for the purchase, so we don't have a name or address to go on."

Jill was beside herself. "Cass, you didn't tell me all this."

"I know and I'm sorry, but I didn't have time before the Sergeant and Mr. Brandon arrived."

"Who was the salesperson that handled the transaction?" Willis asked.

"A part-time employee named Danny Dumont. We've hired several new people for the holidays as we do every year. Why?"

Brandon understood that Casey's mind wasn't running on all cylinders. "If he waited on the customer, most likely he would be able to give us a description of what the man looked like. We could then get a police artist to make a sketch of this person and distribute it around the city," he said.

Casey's hands flew to her cheeks in embarrassment. "Oh my god! That completely slipped my mind. Of course he saw him. I should have asked him myself."

"Don't worry. You're a little stressed right now and that is perfectly understandable. We'll walk you back to the store and perhaps you can arrange for us to question Mr. Dumont," Willis said. "In the meantime, I'll arrange for someone to keep an eye on you, in case this character is a stalker," he added. Lunch and their meeting was finished. Jill took Casey aside while the detectives made some calls. "That detective, Brandon has eyes for you. I could see it in his face."

"Jill, honey, let's not go reading romance into this meeting with the police. I have other things to be concerned with at the moment," Casey said.

"Well, just remember you heard it from me first and don't be surprised. I'll call you tonight and we can have a long chat about romance." She said goodbye and headed back to her office. Casey gave an exasperated sigh as she turned to see the detectives approaching. Willis and Brandon escorted her back to Bergdorf's.

They met with Danny Dumont in a private conference room upstairs. The room had a crystal light fixture hanging above an oval, polished-mahogany table and eight, comfortable, chocolate-colored leather chairs. Brandon, figured it was used for executive meetings. Danny had been thinking about the incident all morning. Brandon explained that he was not in any trouble. "What we need, if you can remember, is a description of the customer you assisted this morning—the one who purchased a pair of gloves. We believe him to be a crime suspect."

Danny was all excited, and his description of the mysterious customer was detailed and clear. "I would say he was about six feet tall. He had broad shoulders, and maybe weighed around 200 pounds. He was wearing a black felt hat, but I think his hair was dark brown because his mustache was dark brown. He may have been bald, but I couldn't tell. His eyes were a deep blue, like the tile around the pool at my gym."

Brandon asked the questions while Willis took notes. "Can you describe his facial features—anything unusual about his appearance? Our police artist needs to know what his face looked like.

"That's easy," Danny said. "He had a square jaw and wore a small gold stud in his left ear. His eyes were squinty and lips were cracked and thin. Oh, and yeah…he must've been in a fight at some time, there was a scar on his nose. Maybe it was broken and he had it fixed. His left hand had been burned. I noticed the scars. My cousin's a fireman. He burned his hands once, so I know what that looks like. Probably why he wanted the gloves. He was really kind of nervous. Just wanted to make his purchase and leave. Didn't ask for a box or bag. Just paid cash for the gloves, put them on, and left."

Willis was still writing this down as Brandon asked, "Is there anything else you want to add to this?"

Danny thought carefully, then added, "Not that I can…" he paused, "come to think of it, he had a limp as he walked away—not much, but a limp. I can't recall anything else." Willis's cell phone rang and he stepped outside the private room to take the call.

Detective Brandon handed Danny a card. "Drop by the Midtown police department when you get off today—address is on the card," he pointed. "We should have an artist's sketch for you to take a look at and make any changes that are needed to go with your description before we post it around town. You've been a big help, thanks for your cooperation. You can get back to work now."

Willis returned as Danny was leaving and grinned at Brandon. "That was Mark Gibson. He's on surveillance detail for Ms. Collins. I told him to wait at the employee security entrance. Store security can introduce them when she leaves today. Nancy Kelly can start on the sketch as soon as we get the description to her. I'll call her right now with the details. How about a late lunch before we check in. My stomach's growling and I'm starved."

"That's funny. You don't look like you miss too many meals to me." Brandon chuckled.

Willis gave him a sarcastic look. "Smart ass. I learned a long time ago on this job—you never know when you'll have time for your next meal. Let's stop downstairs and give Ms. Collins the good news. It ain't much, but it might make her feel a little safer. She's probably already cornered Danny for a description of this guy."

"I still think she's a looker even if she is in her thirties," Brandon said.

Willis grimaced, "Don't go getting involved. The boss won't like it."

"Whose boss? Yours or mine?" Brandon needled.

"Don't ask for trouble kid—it'll find you soon enough without an invitation."

Chapter Four

The Metropolitan Museum of Art bustled with excitement as they prepared for the spring fashion show of Italian designer Gianni Scarlatti, the name on everyone's lips in Rome, Milan, and Paris. This would be his first showing in America since his Sicilian design partner, Gabriella Vescucci, and he had severed their business contract and gone their separate ways.

Rumors connecting the Vescucci family to illegal activities and claims of tax evasion were spreading in the Italian fashion industry. Gianni, at the top of the fashion world and envied by all as the idol they aspired to be, had no desire to be associated with the Vescucci family and the rumors that were circulating, including Sicilian Mafia connections.

By the young age of 35, Scarlatti had trained at several of the major fashion houses in Europe—Dior, Fendi, Gucci, Dolce & Gabbana, Chanel, and Van Cleef & Arpels, where he had learned the ins and outs of couture fashion. Gianni was flying high on his own merits, without Gabriella to add her touch to his designs any longer.

The New York fashion scene was buzzing with anticipation to see the designer's exciting spring collection, hidden in secrecy and touted in Milan Couture News as the "eye-popping extravaganza" of the season. The entire collection had been designed by Gianni from head to toe. Gowns, cocktail dresses, business suits, casual ensembles, shoes, gloves, and handbags—everything from outerwear to underwear, for both women and men, had been created with European flare by the handsome young genius, Scarlatti.

The debut of the season would be held in the Egyptian atrium of the Temple of Dendur at the Metropolitan Museum of Art on Halloween Eve.

Set among monumental stone arches and columns carved with ancient hieroglyphics sparkling in a giant mirror-like reflecting pool and guarded by massive stone Egyptian Pharaohs, the room is an atrium with an entire angled wall of protective glass.

Guests with tickets to the event are encouraged to attend in costume suitable for the festivities and the theme of a "Night on the Nile." The Manhattan garment industry was in a fashion frenzy to out-do their competition with lavish and inventive, custom-designed costumes. The gala event had been in the planning stages for weeks.

As Casey read about the coming fashion event in the newspaper, it suddenly dawned on her that it could be connected to the conversation she overheard concerning a possible murder attempt. She quickly phoned Detective Brandon to warn him of her suspicions. "I know this may sound far-fetched, but I have a strong feeling that something is going to happen at that event."

"I appreciate your desire to help, Ms. Collins. And I can assure you it is already on our radar. There'll be plenty of security at the event, both in and around the Met. Will you be attending?"

"Oh heavens no! I may work in the fashion industry, but I'm not in that elite group of the rich-and-famous, high-fashion society. I'll watch it on the news and be thankful I'm not there," she sighed.

"It's probably for the best. If you were in the crowd and the would-be assassin recognized you, you would not be safe. Right now, you and Danny are the only two people who can identify the suspect. Danny is of no concern to him at the moment, but you are. He believes you not only overheard his phone conversation, but also saw him that evening."

"You really know how to make a person feel comfortable, Detective. However, there hasn't been any further sightings of this person and I'm sure the police officer who's been following me around is beginning to wonder why."

Brandon had to be careful not to offer too much of the information his department had learned from their investigation of the possible suspect. "Your protection is our main concern, Ms. Collins. Your report to us has led us to believe that your life is in danger, and our further investigations have revealed that to be true. I cannot stress how important your safety is and we will do everything in our power to maintain that security." It was not his intention to frighten her, but to let her know he cared.

"Why do I get the feeling there's something you're not telling me?"

"I can only stress your need to stay alert. There is danger involved, but I can't say anymore until we've made certain arrangements, which we are in the process of doing. Would you allow me to take you to dinner this evening? I should have more details to discuss by then."

Casey's heart was racing as she paced the floor of her co-op. Having dinner with Detective Brandon might have a calming effect and perhaps she could learn more about the suspect. "I would be delighted to have dinner with you this evening." Her voice wavered even though she tried to sound confident.

"Great! I'll pick you up at eight. There's a restaurant in the Village I've been wanting to try. It's called The Spotted Pig."

"Sounds intriguing, see you at eight," she said, ending the conversation she would revisit later at dinner. She phoned her friend Jill immediately.

"Hey, there!" Jill sang happily as she answered on the first ring. "I was just about to call you. Did you see the article in the paper about the big fashion show coming up at the Met?"

"Yes, I did—and that's why I called you. I just got off the phone with Detective Brandon and he says my life is in danger. There's more to this story than meets the eye. I'm having dinner with him tonight, so maybe I'll have more information tomorrow."

Jill always looked at things from a different point of view. "Casey, honey...why don't you just try to have a pleasant dinner with the nice, handsome detective, and try to put this stalker thing out of your mind for one evening?"

"Jill...I can't let it go. If this has something to do with international crime, which it very well may, I'm involved and that's hard to shake and makes me nervous." Casey was on her fifth cup of coffee and getting a caffeine high. "I can't sleep at night because I keep hearing his voice in my dreams. I cringe at the thought of going to work for fear he's somewhere out there, waiting to follow me.

"And now that I know what he looks like in that police sketch, I keep seeing his face everywhere. And to make matters worse, you're the only person I can talk to about this. The police have warned me not to speak of it to anyone. I can't even trust our doorman. What the hell have I gotten myself into?"

"Calm down, sweetheart. How many cups of caffeine have you had this morning? Don't answer that. It's obvious the detective is going to fill you in on the details and you need to listen to him and follow his instructions and advice. Now, go take a cold shower and try to get some rest before your date this evening," she advised.

"Jill, dear, this is not a date this evening," Casey said.

"Well you'd better not tell the sweet detective that. I'm sure it would be a great disappointment."

Casey sounded surprised. "Oh good lord, girl... you can't be serious."

"I told you he had eyes for you when we met for lunch. Now go freshen up, get some rest, put on a sexy outfit and try to look like you're having a good time tonight. Call me in the morning and we'll meet for breakfast." She could always count on Jill to throw romance into the scheme of things.

Chapter Five

The day of the big event had arrived. New York traffic was in chaos, not to say it isn't every day, but the police have cordoned off Fifth Avenue for blocks in front of the Metropolitan Museum. Reporters and TV camera crews took up their positions surrounding the entrance to the museum to capture the elegant and outrageous costumes of the social elite as they make their way up the steps on the red carpet, stopping to pose for the cameras before they disappear into the inner sanctum of the museum.

The fashion designers in New York had pulled out all the stops for this event, with lace-and-sequined plunging necklines, backless gowns with flowing ostrich-feather trains, see-through caftans of the thinnest linen stenciled in colorful hieroglyphs, and, of course, Egyptian headdresses and wigs of every shape and design that Cecil B. DeMille could conjure in his wildest dreams for Paramount Pictures. Cleopatra eye make-up was *de rigueur* for both men and women and there were more pharaohs than there were slaves.

As a group of museum officials gathered at the entrance made their way to the top of the stairs on the red carpet, a motorcade approached, accompanied by a motorcycle police escort. The mayor was sparing no expense for this event or perhaps he had been warned of possible dangers.

A single black limousine slowly pulled to the curb and Gianni Scarlatti, along with his male companion, emerged from the auto to an enormous applause of welcome. They began to climb the carpeted stairs but Gianni's foot caught on the carpet and he stumbled forward just as a shot rang out over the cheers of his fans. A bullet ricocheted off the carpeted concrete stairs and a scream echoed from the crowd as the museum's events planner, Andrea Nevo, collapsed in the waiting group at the entrance.

Suddenly the police were swarming through the scattering mass of humanity. They appeared from every angle as if materializing from bushes and shrubs in pots and from behind the massive columns at the top of the stairs. Andrea Nevo was carried into the museum as Gianni and his friend were surrounded by police and escorted through the entrance. A bullet had grazed Andrea's shoulder and she was being treated by theEMT's that she had arranged to handle any guests' emergencies that might happen.

The gala in the Temple of Dendur was in full swing and the guests were unaware of the events outside. Andrea knew it was best not to mention what had taken place as Gianni arrived. She was not going to allow anyone to put a damper on this occasion. As quickly as she was able, with her arm in a sling, she arrived with a smile on her face and a story that she had slipped on the marble floor and sprained her wrist.

Gianni, although a bit shaken, had no idea that the bullet was meant for him. He never even heard the shot, but knew something had taken place when he was rushed by the police and hustled into the building. Andrea stressed that the show must go on as she took to the stage to announce the opening of "A Night on the Nile" and the fashion extravaganza of the season with none other than fashion icon Gianni Scarlatti.

Meanwhile, the security at the museum was in full force and the NYPD scurried like ants on an anthill that had been disturbed by a predator. The shot appeared to have come from the apartment building at 1001 Fifth Avenue, directly across from the main entrance to the museum near the corner of East 82nd Street. Making a door-to-door search, the police located the empty apartment where the assassin had attempted his kill. The smell of gun powder still lingered in the air, but there was no sign of the suspect who had fired the single shot.

The newspaper reporters had their connections and the following morning the artist sketch of the suspect was on the front page of the *New York Times*. Unfortunately, it told the assassin that they knew what he looked like. It also told his boss that he missed the mark and the job would have to wait for another opportunity. But first he needed to silence the woman who had identified him. He didn't appreciate her interference. She had betrayed him and he doesn't take betrayal lightly. He knew where she lived and would be sure she didn't live much longer.

After several interviews and guests appearances on TV, Gianni Scarlotti was on a flight back to Italy, having survived the attempt on his life. He felt he would be safer in Milan.

Detective Brandon picked Casey up at precisely eight o'clock. She had already been glued to the TV watching the news about the attempted murder on the steps of the Met. She was jumpy as a frog in a lily pond, and almost canceled her dinner with the detective. However, her instincts told her she would be safe and she needed to hear what he had to say.

It was a short drive to The Spotted Pig restaurant and Brandon did his best not to mention the shooting on the way over. Casey knew he was having difficulty avoiding the conversation point and tried not to make him uncomfortable. The Spotted Pig is an upscale, neighborhood restaurant in the Village, where they could enjoy quiet dining at a corner table without being on display.

They ordered a bottle of wine and made their dinner selections before the conversation began. "So," Casey said, "tell me about the attempted murder at the Met. I assume you were there."

"Actually, no, I wasn't on the scene." Brandon said with a grin. "The police and added museum security were on the alert, but it was good that you had tipped us off with your segments of overheard conversation.

"I'm a detective and don't usually get involved with police security for major events," he continued. "However, that brings me to another point regarding personal security of valued witnesses, so I'm glad you asked." The waiter returned with their first course and refilled the wine glasses. Brandon began to eat his crispy pig's ear salad with a lemon caper dressing as Casey sat pondering his last statement.

She picked up her fork and began pushing her grape salad with tarragon, pickled shallots and candied hazelnuts, around on her plate. "You mentioned on the phone that I might be in danger, but my police shadow and I haven't seen this mysterious person for several days now. He's already made his murder attempt and failed. So where is the danger? With his picture in the papers and on the news, wouldn't he be trying to disappear before someone recognizes him?"

Brandon knew he shouldn't be mixing business with pleasure, but his need to confirm his plans with Casey gave him the opportunity to express his desire for a more intimate relationship. He finished his salad and cleared his throat with a sip of wine. "Unfortunately, it's not that simple. That's why I didn't want to talk about it over the phone—for that and various other reasons.

"The suspect is a person known to the FBI. He's an international criminal, suspected to be a member of the Sicilian Mafia, which is why we need to take every precaution at our disposal with regards to your safety." He paused as the waiter returned to remove their first course. Speechless, Casey had barely touched her salad.

"Detective Brandon..." she hesitated.

"I wish you would call me Tom. That's my first name," he said sincerely.

"OK. Tom." Casey's voice was wavering as her hand, resting on the table next to her wine glass, started to trembled. "Are you saying that I'm suddenly involved in a case with a mafia hit man?"

He reached across the table and covered her shaking hand with his own. "I know how this may sound, but you must trust me. I have been working all morning to make arrangements for your safety."

"No, no, stop a minute...let's go back a few paces. How is he connected with the Sicilian Mafia and why is he here in New York? I don't understand." He squeezed her hand and it seemed to offer her reassurance. His hand felt warm and comforting, but her mind was not on romance.

The waiter returned to the table with their entrées and poured them both more wine. Tom relished the aroma of the grilled skirt steak with roasted sweet potatoes, Cipollini onions and a béarnaise sauce. His mouth watered. Casey watched as the waiter placed her order of Arctic char with lardons, fresh beets, and pickled red onions, topped with a crème fraiche in front of her. She wished she felt like eating, but her mind was not into food at the moment.

Tom raised and clinked his glass with hers. "I know I shouldn't be drinking while having this conversation, but I am off-duty, so I hope you won't tell." He gave her a sheepish grin.

She gave him a serious look. "I promise not to tell if you will please answer my questions." Casey had sunk her teeth in and was not going to let go. She was frightened but wanted to know the truth. Her hand was now grasping his with a firm hold as she waited for him to speak.

"Casey, I don't have all the answers, but I will tell you what I can. I won't confuse you with a lot of names. Suffice it to say, our suspect has many aliases. It's our understanding that he is a member of the Vescucci family from Sicily. His sister was the partner of Gianni Scarlatti until they recently separated, under not so friendly circumstances involving finances and tax evasion. We believe he's out for revenge and to keep Mr. Sacrlatti, his intended victim, from testifying. Possibly his sister is involved as well." He paused, as she processed this information.

Casey shook her head and wrinkled her brow. "But what does that have to do with me? Why would he be stalking me? I don't have anything to do with the Italian fashion industry, Gianni Scarlatti or this guy's sister—what's her name?"

"Her name's Gabriella Vescucci, and she's currently under house arrest until her trial. It appears that Gianni is the star witness in her case of embezzlement and tax evasion. Our attempted assassin, I'll call him Max, as he is known by the FBI, is under the suspicion that you can identify him because of the artist picture that appeared in the newspapers."

"But I didn't see him! It was Danny who gave you that information."

"I know," said Tom, "but Danny didn't overhear his conversation about the murder plot. He doesn't care about Danny. He was only a customer to Danny, but he believes you could put him behind bars if you testify you overheard him plotting to murder someone. We have to catch him before he can leave the country."

Casey had been holding her breath, and she let out a heavy sigh. "So what am I supposed to do?" she asked, her lips beginning to tremble as she held back the tears in her eyes.

"Have you ever heard of a safe house?"

"Only on the TV show, *Law & Order*," she sniffed. "Isn't that where they put witnesses to protect them from the criminal until they're caught and brought to trial?"

"That's correct." He glanced up to get the waiter's attention and ordered another bottle of wine. The stress had made their wine vanish quickly, and there was still the arrangements he needed to discuss with Casey.

Chapter
Six

Tom and Casey were doing their best to enjoy their meal, but the subject of conversation wasn't helping to make this seem like a date. The food was delicious and the atmosphere lively and inviting, but the tension in the air was like walking on eggs. One wrong statement or misunderstanding could easily cause the shells to crack.

Tom was trying his best to approach the subject he needed to address without causing Casey any more anxiety and fear than she was feeling at the moment. He wanted this to be a date, and even though it appeared like one, Casey's curious mind was running ahead to the next question.

"So...are you suggesting I need to be placed in a witness protection program?" she mumbled in a hardly audible voice.

Tom reached for her hand, and the warmth of his touch made her feel secure. "Casey, I want you to understand that you are a valuable witness in this attempted murder. Your safety is top priority.

We will catch this guy. It's only a matter of time. But until we do, I want to protect you."

Casey held up her other hand to interrupt, "Does that mean I have to be locked up in a safe house somewhere until he's captured?"

Tom could see she was about to cry again. "I can't just up and leave my job. We're going into the Christmas season. I have obligations and a staff that depends on my guidance and that doesn't even take into consideration what Bergdorf's would say. They'd probably fire me."

Tom whipped out his handkerchief and handed it to her. "Hang on a second and let me explain." She nodded, holding the handkerchief to her nose as she breathed in his masculine aroma.

Attempting to regain her composure, she smiled meekly and apologized. "I'm sorry to sound like such a ninny, but it isn't every day that I get involved in a murder plot. You'll have to forgive me."

Tom gave a deep chuckle. "Hell, I'm involved in them all the time, and believe me, it never gets any easier. If you asked me, I would say you're doing better than most people." Her smile turned into a laugh as both felt a bond of friendship.

The waiter removed their entrée plates and suggested something for dessert, but they decided to pass on the sweets and enjoy their wine. Casey reached for his hand. She needed the security it gave her. "Tell me what I need to do," she paused, "and then I'll tell you if it's possible."

"Fair enough," he said. "We can arrange everything with your employer so there will be no loss of employment or earnings while under the security program, so you can get that out of your mind. It will be treated as a leave of absence with pay."

Casey drew in a breath. "It will be the first Christmas vacation I've had since I started working in retail."

Tom was a smooth talker and had her attention. "How would you like to spend that vacation time in a warm climate?"

"You're kidding! You mean I won't be in New York?" She was surprised.

"I've arranged for you to be placed at a safe house in Georgetown, on the coast of South Carolina. It's a small tourist town with lots of museums and other activities to keep you busy. The sheriff there is a friend of mine and is happy to accommodate my request."

"Oh my god. How long will I be there?"

This was the question that he didn't have an answer for. "You'll have to stay hidden away until we catch this guy. It could be several weeks or it could be several months. He's very good at hiding himself, but he's bound to make a mistake eventually—they always do."

"Will I be able to have company? Can my friends come visit me?"

He knew he had reached the hardest part of the instructions and it was important that she understand his next few statements. Taking a sip of wine, he filled their glasses once again, searching for his best approach. Be direct and don't beat around the bush— a motto his dad had taught him.

"Casey, honey," he began. Her defenses melted when he called her honey. "I know this is going to sound harsh, but it's for your own good. You are not allowed to have guests visit. You are not allowed to contact anyone except a single family member once a week. And you must..."

Casey stopped him mid-sentence, protesting, "But I haven't got any family members to contact."

He heaved a sigh. "Then you will be allowed to call a friend— with my permission only—and you must not disclose where you are. I can't stress how important that is. We will keep your cell phone here. You will be supplied with a different phone each week that will not be traceable."

"You mean he's that smart?"

"Max is smarter than you think, and even more deadly. He's

suspected of murder in three countries. He's a professional criminal and a master of disguise, who also speaks five languages; which is why you probably couldn't detect a particular accent when you overheard him on his phone."

Tom had decided not to hold anything back. It was best if she knew the dangers. The more information she had, the more apt she would be at handling a situation if need be. He could tell that Casey was a strong, sensitive and intelligent woman—one who knew how to make rational decisions. Tom had always been a good judge of character.

Casey stared out the window. Is he out there? Is he watching us, hiding in the dark, waiting to pull the trigger? A chill ran through her body raising goosebumps on her arms as Tom watched from across the table. "Casey? Casey, honey...you're not listening."

"Sorry, Tom, what were you saying?" She gazed into his eyes—he'd called her honey again.

"I know it won't be easy, but I'll be your main contact person. There'll be an officer in Georgetown you'll also be able to contact with the push of a button. Both numbers will be programed into the phones we supply for you. Contact should be kept to a minimum. I know you'll be wanting information updates, and I will do what I can to keep you informed. This is not a full-fledged FBI witness program. You won't have to disappear forever. You are under Detective Tom Brandon's personal protection. Any questions?"

"Hundreds! But we don't have all night. How soon does all this have to take place?"

"Is tomorrow evening too soon?" he smiled.

Casey was shocked. "Holy cow! You don't waste any time, do you?"

Tom chuckled, "This is Tuesday. You're off Wednesday and Thursday. We can fly you down on Friday and get you settled in. It's all been arranged."

"And how did you know I would agree?" she said tilting her head as she grinned.

"I didn't," he said, "but I didn't think you would let me down. You see, I'm pretty fond of you. If I had to, I would have hog-tied you and carried you on that plane myself."

She laughed and shook her head. "You sound just like a Texas cowboy."

"No, ma'am—I was born on a ranch in Wyoming."

She touched her glass to his as she gazed into his eyes. "Well, here's to Wyoming, and please, don't call me "ma'am"—I much prefer "Honey."

Tom was grinning from ear to ear. The night was turning out to be a success after all, and the chief would be proud of him. He was looking forward to reading his report about the evening to Sergeant Willis.

Chapter Seven

Friday had arrived and her flight out of LaGuardia airport was due to depart in less than one hour. Tom had made arrangements to fly down with her and make sure she was settled in before returning to New York the next day. With time to kill before boarding, they had been having breakfast together. "I'm going to step into the ladies' room before we head to the gate," Casey said.

"I'll come with you." Tom replied.

"I'm afraid the airport would frown on that," she giggled.

He blushed, "I meant I would come and wait for you outside the entrance." He flagged the server for their check and escorted her to the ladies' room.

When she returned he was not where she had left him. Glancing around, Tom was nowhere in sight—but she heard a familiar voice close by. It frightened her and she quickly stepped back into the restroom. Her heart was racing as she fingered the lucky charm on her necklace. She felt people staring at her as she returned to one of the empty stalls. And locked the door. Where was Tom? What had happened to him? She heard over the speakers that her flight was now boarding. She couldn't stay in this cubicle forever.

Suddenly a woman's voice called her name, "Casey? Casey? Are you in here?" She opened the door and answered.

"I'm here."

"Oh, good," the woman said, "a man named Tom was worried. He's waiting just outside."

"What does he look like?" she asked.

"You mean you don't know him? Is someone stalking you?"

"No, no. I don't have time to explain. Can you just describe this Tom person?"

The woman gave her a strange look, "Well, he's tall, good looking, has nice blue eyes and is wearing a tweed jacket. Does that help?"

She heaved a sigh and gave the woman a quick hug, "You're an angel. Thank you and bless you." Casey hurried out to a pacing Tom and they raced towards their gate, leaving a confused woman standing at the entrance of the ladies' room shaking her head.

"I stepped over to grab a magazine and was worried when you didn't come out. Is anything wrong?" he asked as they cleared the boarding area and made their way down the ramp to the plane.

"I heard his voice," she said glancing behind them.

"Where? In the restroom?" he asked as he looked behind them.

"No. I came out of the restroom but didn't see you. He must have been close by talking on a phone, so I ducked back into the lounge and was hiding in one of the stalls, when the lady came in calling my name. Oh god, Tom. I was so frightened. I don't know if he saw me or not."

"He couldn't know what flight we're on. We're listed under different names, but he could have followed us to the airport. I'll make some calls before we take off. We'll beef up security at the airport in Charleston for any flights coming in from New York, just in case," he reassured her.

"Charleston? I thought we were going to Georgetown."

"We are, but we're stopping in Charleston first. It's a little surprise," Tom said.

~

Tom had a car reserved by the Charleston police. He decided they would stay in town for the night and had booked a couple of rooms at The Planter's Inn in the heart of the market district of downtown Charleston. He managed to reserve a table for dinner at the Peninsula Grill. Tom was determined they were going to have a proper date before he had to return to New York.

Casey was delighted. She had never been to Charleston and was looking forward to an evening with her handsome detective. For appearances, Tom had reserved their rooms on different floors, but on arrival, had changed his room to be next to Casey's so he would be closer, after her experience in the airport.

Casey had packed sensible clothes suitable for beach wear, and casual, about-town outfits—but just in case there was a need, she had thrown in a couple of fancy dresses. She was glad she had made that last-minute decision. Tom tapped on her door at 7 p.m. and stood there, speechless, when she appeared in a Kelly-green, off-the-shoulder, flowing chiffon cocktail dress. Her gold lucky charm, hanging from a chain around her neck, glittered against her flawless smooth skin. The caterpillar, who had been hiding at Bergdorf's in New York, had changed into a fashion butterfly right out of Vogue magazine. Casey had arranged her blonde hair in a French twist, and the dress enhanced her green eyes, accented by a peach blush to her high cheekbones.

Tom stammered as he handed her a small box. "I thought you might like some flowers. I was told the gardenia is a traditional flower of the South."

"Oh, Tom! How beautiful, and I love their fragrance. Shall I wear them on my wrist?"—she placed the corsage on her left arm—or at my waist?" She held them next to her hourglass figure.

"I think they would look great in your hair," he said, mesmerized by the transformation.

"Perfect. Wait here. I'll be right back." She stepped into the bathroom, where she quickly pinned the flowers in her hair. "Are we going far? I brought a light shawl in case it's cool, being near the coast," she called from the bathroom, standing in front of the mirror, making a final adjustment to the gardenias.

"Not far at all—the restaurant is here in the hotel." He turned to see a beautiful woman posing with her raised hand on the doorframe of the bathroom and her other hand resting on her hip. "Wow!" was the only word that came from his lips.

"I take it that's an approval," Casey smiled, "Shall we be off? I'm starved." She reached for her handbag as they left the room.

The dimly lit Peninsula Grill was buzzing with customer conversations and the bar didn't have an empty stool as the maître d' led them past to a romantic corner table. Casey was trying to relax and move her life ahead. After fifteen years without a man in her life, it was time.

They decided to start their meal with oysters on the half shell served with a Champagne mignonette and horseradish cocktail sauce. It had been years since Casey had eaten raw oysters, and it brought back fond memories.

Tom ordered a bottle of Champagne to enjoy with their first two courses. "This restaurant is famous for their she-crab soup, made with lump crabmeat and drizzled with sherry. I was told not to miss it. Shall we give it a try?"

"I'll have to admit, I'm at your mercy. I've never been further south than New York. But I'll also confess, I'm easily spoiled." He could tell that Casey was enjoying the attention.

Tom gazed into her eyes. "It's my pleasure to spoil you and I intend to keep you safe, so I can continue to do so." In the dim light, she couldn't see the blush on his face, but he looked so much younger than he had in New York.

"It's time we got acquainted. I want to learn all there is to know about you," Tom said.

Over the hum of conversations around them, Casey laughed. "Well, that shouldn't take very long. You could put most of my life in a nutshell. Where should I start?"

Tom smiled. "Start at the beginning. Where were you born?"

Casey's head bowed as she stared at the empty oyster shells on her plate. "I was born in Boston. As I said earlier, I've never been further south than New York. My mother was a seamstress and my father owned a small clothing store. I've worked in retail most of my life. I married a school mate, Brad Collins, a guy I had dated since I was in high school. We moved to Cambridge, where his parents had purchased a new home and he attended law school while I worked in a local department store.

"My parents died in an auto accident one winter returning from Cambridge to Boston. I sold the clothing store in Boston. Shortly after that, Brad's mother died of cancer. His father passed away of a heart attack on his yacht a year later, and Brad came into a rather large inheritance."

Tom didn't know she had been married, and she saw the surprised look on his face. "I've been divorced for fifteen years, Tom. I should have told you the night we were at The Spotted Pig, but with the intense conversation we were having about Max and the Brandon protection program, it slipped my mind. I didn't want to spoil the evening. I was enjoying being in your company and that was more important. You made me feel special again and I needed that. Will you forgive me?"

He smiled as he squeezed her hand. "There's nothing to forgive and it doesn't change anything," he said.

Casey breathed a sigh and continued. "I couldn't have children," she confessed, "and Brad wanted a family. It was an amicable separation, with a very generous trust fund that included my co-op on 58th Street in the heart of Manhattan. I don't have to work, but it helps to keep active and I've always loved the challenge of retail and working with the public." She paused as Tom stared at her. "So that's the short story of my life. Not very glamorous, but I have no regrets."

Tom cleared his throat as the waiter brought their soup to the table, topped their Champagne glasses and disappeared. "I suppose you want to know more about me," he said.

"Turnabout's fair play," she said, tasting a spoon of soup. "Oh my god! I've died and gone to heaven. This soup is fantastic!" Tom stopped his conversation to take a sip. "I'm sorry, I didn't mean to interrupt. You were about to say..."

Tom could tell this was going to be a long evening. He was enjoying Casey's company and hoped he didn't scare her off with his unique ambition to be a police detective, plus his desire to solve mysteries. He was glad he had made arrangements for the extra night in Charleston. Tomorrow afternoon, they would have to say goodbye and he didn't know how long they would be apart. He wasn't looking forward to that, as they were just getting acquainted.

"The nutshell of my life isn't much bigger than yours. I was born on the dining room table at a ranch in Wyoming on a snowy winter night."

"Wait a minute. Didn't I read this in a book somewhere?" she asked.

"Not if it was about me—but it probably sounds like one of those mystery stories. Maybe that's why I've always had a curious mind about mysteries. But if you keep interrupting, it might take all night to get this out."

"Sorry, I'll just eat my soup; please continue. I've been forewarned."

"As I was saying..." he began again.

Casey was fascinated with the story of his young life on the Big Creek Ranch, east of the Rocky Mountains, in southern Wyoming. The wind-swept grasslands were home to cattle, elk, deer, and buffalo. The nearest town of any size was Ryan Park, a distance of seventeen miles. Tom had been schooled at home until he moved to Denver, Colorado. He took up residence with his aunt and uncle while attending high school. He joined the army at the age of eighteen and received his military training at Fort Carson, near Colorado Springs.

Three years later, he attended the Denver Police Academy and worked with the Denver Police force for the next five years, before moving to New York, where he had been with the NYPD for the past seven years—the last four of which he's worked as a detective.

"And now that you're totally bored, our dinner is about to arrive." He noticed the waiter heading their way, weaving through all the tables that were now filled.

Light jazz was playing in the background and the volume of the conversations around them had increased. They had decided to share an order of the roasted breast of duck with oyster mushrooms, rainbow carrots and Cipollini onions in a chimichurri sauce, complemented by an order of asparagus with an olive tapenade and a side of goat-cheese smashed potatoes. This called for a full-bodied red Italian wine and like magic, it suddenly appeared. Tom had pre-ordered a Sangiovese wine and Casey was impressed.

"How much time did you spend with the sommelier while I was getting ready for dinner?" she quizzed.

"Oh, once I suggested what we might order for dinner, he was a great help, and I'll have to agree he knows his wines."

Casey was curious. "I thought cowboys from Wyoming would be beer-drinkers."

Tom shook his head. "Not me. I can't afford to get a beer-belly in my line of work. We have to stay in shape."

"Well, you certainly do a good job at that," she said.

Tom blushed at her response. "It's really the job that keeps us on the go. Not a lot of time to sit around. New York City can wear out a lot of shoe leather."

They had managed to eat most of their dinner without even mentioning why they were in South Carolina, but all good things must come to an end.

Casey looked across the dining room. She wanted to remember the smile on his face and not see it change.

"When do we leave for Georgetown?" she asked, staring into the crowded room.

He was quiet as the bubble burst in front of him. His voice took on a sad tone for the words he didn't want to utter. "Tomorrow, after breakfast. It's not a long drive. We should be there before noon. I'll get you settled into the Inn at Prince and Cannon before heading to Myrtle Beach. I fly out of that airport in the afternoon."

They took a long walk around Charleston before turning in for the night.

Chapter Eight

Morning arrived with the first rays of sunlight streaming through the open window of her room. Casey stretched, her eyes still closed to the narrow streak of light piercing the dark room as it sliced through the center of the blackout drapes gently moving with the ocean breeze. There was a gentle knock from the hallway and something was slipped beneath the door. She sat up on the side of the bed and padded to the door in her bare feet. It was a note from Tom—*Rise and shine or you're going to miss breakfast!*

She showered and quickly put on her traveling clothes, but hesitated as she started to open the door. Perhaps I should ring his room first. Dialing his number she waited, but there was no answer. He must be in the dining room downstairs. Cautiously, she opened her door, looked both ways, and stepped into the hallway, moving quickly to the elevator as she noticed the fragrance of Hugo Boss cologne lingering in the narrow passage. It can't be the assassin, she rationalized. There must be hundreds, probably millions, of men who wear that cologne. Just stay calm, she said to herself. Calm.

The elevator door opened and Tom was standing there. "I was just about to come get you. Is something wrong? You look white as a sheet! Was it too much dinner and wine last night?"

"No, it wasn't the food and wine. It was the fragrance in the hallway. She stepped into the elevator cab. I'll be fine with a little fresh air." She couldn't remember if she had ever mentioned smelling the Hugo Boss cologne to Tom, and she wasn't even sure the Mafia man was the one wearing it that night. Fear has a strange way of affecting one's imagination.

Tom interrupted her thoughts as he pushed the lobby button. "I thought we would have breakfast at Toast. It's listed number one on Trip Advisor and is just a few blocks down Meeting Street."

Casey gave him a smile. "Lead the way. I'm getting used to this Southern cooking, but I can't wait to go for a run on the beach."

"There's lots of beaches on Litchfield Island, just a short bike ride from Georgetown," Tom said as they left the hotel.

The restaurant was packed. They finally finished their orders of eggs Benedict with hollandaise sauce, served with southern grits and a side of biscuits and gravy that Tom had requested. Returning to the hotel, they loaded the car and headed north to Georgetown.

The Inn at Prince and Cannon, a two-story, white-clapboard cottage with a brown shingle roof, is in a quiet neighborhood with lots of shade trees and a beautiful garden, complete with colorful flowers and a fountain.

Her cottage, with four-poster bed and private bath, was small but comfortable and had a separate living room with a large TV. The inn offered a complimentary continental breakfast, free WiFi, a washer and dryer for doing laundry and a free bicycle for getting around town. It combined all the conveniences of a hotel with the privacy of a guest house. Casey was pleased.

After saying their goodbyes, Tom was soon on his way to Myrtle

Beach International Airport and his return flight to LaGuardia airport. He had introduced Casey to Officer Frank Short, her police contact in Georgetown, assured her she would be safe, and said he would keep her informed of their progress weekly. He stressed once again the importance of keeping her location top secret and not sharing that information with anyone.

~

Tom was in a rush when he arrived in New York. He wanted to get back to work and solve this case quickly. He never noticed the gray-haired old man with dark glasses and a cane sitting close to the gate as he exited. Max Vescucci had been patiently waiting around the airport for the past two days, hoping to learn where the detective had taken his next victim.

He was aware that Charleston had been their destination when they left New York. His contact in Charleston knew they had headed north out of town, but lost them when they turned off for Georgetown. Max now knew that the detective had returned from Myrtle Beach and Casey would be alone. It was time to disappear and he had worked out his plan to avoid the police and extra security. There wasn't any hurry. Casey wouldn't be going anywhere until he got to Georgetown.

It took him a few days, but he managed to arrange a ride with an ex-con driving an eighteen-wheeler, heading south on Interstate 95. Once they were out of New York, it was smooth sailing. The trucker had several stops to make along the way, dropping off goods and loading new merchandise for Florida deliveries.

After five days on the road, he had reached Myrtle Beach, but Georgetown, his final destination, would be by taxi. He had chosen to stay at Baxter's Brewhouse Inn. Renting a car wouldn't be necessary and he had a plan to learn where his victim was staying. Once he found her, he would watch her habits and wait for the right moment to stage an accident. He knew the police in Georgetown would also have Casey under surveillance, so he will need to be careful, but they aren't expecting him and will eventually become less attentive. He'll strike quickly, like a snake, and disappear in the night.

~

Casey's name had been changed to Connie Collins. Keeping her last name made it easier. When people called her Ms. Collins, at least she wouldn't totally ignore them. She eventually got used to the name Connie, but three weeks later living around strangers was starting to get on her nerves. She didn't go out much and was beginning to get cabin fever. She wasn't used to long vacations and had managed to visit every museum in town twice.

There was nothing new to report whenever she and Tom spoke on the phone supplied by the local police each week. She missed New York and her job. It had been weeks since last she spoke with her friend, Jill. No one knew where she was except the police. In the eyes of her friends, she had vanished overnight without a trace.

Casey decided to get a part-time job. One where they don't ask a lot of questions about your background and prior experience. Strolling along Front Street, she noticed a Now Hiring sign in the window of a men's boutique shop carrying casualwear she was familiar with at Bergdorf's. Patagonia, Costa, Chaco, Loggerhead, and Buff were all brands she had sold before.

The Black Mingo was not a very large shop, but the contemporary interior and outerwear stock was well organized. The owner, Grace Sheffield, was anxious to hire her after a brief interview. "You don't know how difficult it is to find people with retail experience in a small place like Georgetown. With the knowledge you have of the merchandise we carry, I'd be foolish if I didn't start you tomorrow. By the way, can you start tomorrow?"

Casey liked Grace and felt they would get along fine working together. It would be different not to be the boss for a change. "If casual clothing is appropriate, what time should I report for work?" she said.

Grace was delighted. "I get here at nine in the morning, so if nine to five works for you, we can get started checking in new merchandise and restocking the shelves and garment closets before people finish with breakfast and begin to shop. Doors open at ten."

"I'll be here at nine." Casey was about to leave as Grace took her arm and stopped her.

"Listen Connie, I don't ask a lot of questions and I don't mean to pry. I know you said you don't know how long you will be in Georgetown and you didn't have any friends in town. If you're trying to get over a divorce, I know a lot of single men in town who would be happy to be seen with a companion as attractive as you. I would be delighted to introduce you around."

Casey smiled. "The truth is, I miss New York and I will be moving back one day. Georgetown is a charming place to visit, but I'm a big-city girl and it's in my blood. I have someone that I'm attached to, and as soon as things work out, we'll be back together. Meanwhile, I just need to keep busy. But thanks for caring. See you in the morning."

Casey stopped next door at Sweeties chocolate shop before heading back to her bed and breakfast—she suddenly had a craving for chocolate.

Frank Short, her contact police officer dropped by the inn to give her a new phone. She had talked to Tom the night before and decided she would call Jill. They hadn't talked since Casey abruptly left New York. Jill's number rang several times and she was about to hang up when Jill finally answered.

"Hey girl. What's happening?" Casey exclaimed.

"Oh my god! Casey! Is it really you? Where the hell are you? Are you OK, honey?" The barrage of questions caused Casey to laugh.

"Of course I'm OK. It's so good to hear your voice," she cried, wiping the tears from her eyes.

"Oh, sweetie, you don't know how worried I've been. Why haven't you called?"

"I've been whisked off to a witness safe house in South Carolina. I can't tell anyone where I am and I'm not supposed to call anyone except on a cell phone that they provide once a week."

"No wonder I didn't recognize the number. I almost didn't answer cause of all the crank calls people get now days. So tell me more."

Casey needed to hear a friendly voice. "I've enjoyed the vacation, but I'm going crazy not knowing what's going on, and I miss my friends." She opened the box of chocolates and took a piece.

Jill was consoling. "I wish I had something I could tell you, sweetie. I've asked around, but no one can tell me anything. I thought the guy had kidnapped you and they were keeping it hush-hush. Even Tom wouldn't tell me anything. Thank God you're OK."

Casey took another piece of chocolate, "Guess what? I start a new job in the morning." She explained about the men's boutique shop and the lady who owns it. An hour, later sitting on her bed with a half-empty box of chocolates, she finally said goodbye to Jill—making her swear she wouldn't tell Tom, and promising to call her again in a week.

Chapter Nine

Tom contacted Casey once a week, even if he didn't have any news about the suspect in the attempted murder of Gianni. They had had several good leads and hundreds of calls that lead to dead ends. The police were able to locate an apartment where he had been staying on Old Fulton near Front Street in Brooklyn, but he had disappeared, leaving dirty dishes in the sink with finger-prints all over them.

The place was a red brick flophouse for vagrants, with windows so dirty you could write your name in the dust and the window shades had rips in them. The kitchen table was covered with a faded red-and-yellow checkered oilcloth, a single wooden chair lay on the wood floor where it had been knocked over. A single, bare light bulb hung in the middle of the room as roaches scurried to hide from view. The layer of dust on everything told them no one had been there recently.

The place was devoid of any additional furniture except for a worn-out, overstuffed chair with olive-green frayed upholstery. A small closet stood open and empty. The sleeping area in this single-room dump consisted of a thin soiled mattress resting on the floor. The bathroom sink revealed that the suspect had dyed his hair black, and they found several strands of hair in different colors, perhaps from some of the wigs he wears as part of his disguise. The villain was getting careless.

The artist sketch had been reprinted in the newspaper along with a photo from Interpol. The FBI had agreed to join the case late in the game but hadn't been much help. Sightings of the suspect had been reported as far north as Yonkers and as far west as Morristown, New Jersey, but nothing had panned out and there was no further evidence. Tom was sure Max was on the run and desperately looking for Casey.

Casey told him about her job, but he could tell that she was homesick for New York. "I'm glad you found something to do and it's good to be around people during the day. I'm sorry it's taking so long, but at least I know you're safe." She didn't tell him she had called Jill last week. She wasn't supposed to have contact with anyone in New York except him and she didn't want to upset him. However, she was tired of feeling like a prisoner, even if it was in a charming southern town full of friendly people and hordes of tourists escaping the cold clutches of winter further north. It was still two weeks before Christmas, but her spirit wasn't into it.

~

Grace met Casey for dinner the following week at the Alfredo Bistro on Front Street. As soon as they had ordered, Grace asked her if she was surprised. "Surprised about what?" Casey asked.

"Oh, didn't the gentleman drop by and tell you that your mother's house had finally sold?" Casey looked confused. "He had some papers for you to sign and couldn't remember where he had put your forwarding address, but knew you were staying here in

Georgetown. Evidently, he'd been asking all over town and had almost given up hope. Black Mingo was the last shop on his list. When he mentioned your last name and showed me your photo, I told him where to find you."

Casey was upset, "How could you do that, Grace? Did he show you any identification? How do you know he wasn't a stalker or a rapist?" Grace could see terror in her eyes. Upset as Casey appeared, she tried to remain calm as she scanned the tables in the restaurant, hoping she would not encounter his presence.

"Honey, I'm so sorry. He was such a nice man with a foreign accent like a New York realtor and he left his card with me at the store. How was I to know? I was only trying to help."

Casey whispered in a low voice, "My mother died over ten years ago. She didn't own a house. I'm here under a witness protection program to hide from a potential murderer. And now he knows where I'm staying."

"Oh my god! Why didn't you tell me from the beginning? I never..."

Casey cut her off, "I wasn't supposed to tell anyone. If word got out—which it has—I could be in extreme danger. This guy is smart. He has lots of disguises. And somehow he has found out my location in South Carolina, and now my address. He's murdered before. I overheard him plotting a murder in New York and he thinks I saw him and can identify him. The police have been trying to track him down. And that's all I know."

"Good lord, girl!" Grace was shocked. "And I had to open my big mouth. What can I do to make it up to you? How can I help?" Tears were starting to roll down her cheeks.

As frightened as she was, Casey took charge. "First, I'll contact the local police and let them know the situation. Then I need to gather my things at the inn and try to plan an escape. I need to get back to New York as quickly as possible. I can't stay here another night."

Grace was as nervous as a mosquito on a pond full of gold fish, but she wanted to help. "We can call the airport and get you on the next flight out to New York City. I have a car and can drive you to the airport. He might be watching other forms of travel to the airport, but he doesn't know my car. I'll get the car and meet you at the back of the restaurant. Give me fifteen minutes and meet me at the kitchen entrance."

Even if she had screwed up, Casey was glad to have Grace as her friend. Grace paid for their untouched orders and chatted a minute with the restaurant owner before vanishing through the kitchen and out the back door. Fifteen minutes later, the owner escorted Casey through the kitchen to meet Grace in her bright yellow Super Beetle VW and they quickly drove to the Inn at Prince and Cannon for Casey's things.

When they arrived at the inn, there was a white rose on the stoop of her cottage and a note had been slipped under the door. The handwriting was scrawled and hard to read, but there were only two words—You're Next.

Casey packed quickly, while Grace, using her own cell phone and credit card, contacted the airport at Myrtle Beach and booked the only available seat on the very last Delta flight to New York that evening. It would be a rush, but they had to make it.

Casey had called Officer Frank Short at the local police station, but had to leave a message as he was out on another call. She explained what had happened and that she was on her way to New York. Then she called Tom in New York and once again had to leave a message. Where were the police when you needed them? It didn't matter as she raced to the departing gate just in time to find her ticket waiting and be the last person on board. The flight attendant stored her single suitcase and she settled in for the late-night flight. Grace had offered to keep her other two suitcases so she could move quickly.

Max Vescucci had expected her to flee and arrived by taxi

moments after she had boarded her flight. He attempted to have the airlines hold the plane so he could give his daughter a message that her mother had been hurt in an accident, but the plane had already taxied out to the runway. He moved swiftly to the Sprint airlines desk and booked a seat on the next flight to LaGuardia, leaving in fifteen minutes.

Once the flight was airborne, Casey realized she couldn't go back to her apartment. That would be the first place he would look when he realized she had disappeared. She was in limbo, not sure where she should go. Perhaps she should call Jill and stay with her until she talked to Tom. She contacted Jill minutes before the flight landed and begged for asylum. Fortunately, Jill was home at that late hour.

"Are you crazy? Of course you can stay with me. I'll come pick you up."

Casey warned her the plane was about to land and she would take a taxi to mid-town Manhattan on arrival. Even late at night the taxi queue was a long wait. Max watched as she drove off. Yelling "Emergency! Emergency!" He shoved his way to the front of the line and got the next available taxi. "Follow that cab!" he demanded, shoving a hundred dollars through the open glass partition.

Casey sensed she was being followed and told the driver, who nodded his understanding and made some fast maneuvers to lose the taxi tailing him. It appeared she was safe as they arrived at Jill's apartment building. Jill, waiting in the lobby, grabbed Casey in a bear hug before she could set her suitcase down in the marble-tiled entry with its crystal chandelier sparkling on the mirrored walls and polished wood panels. Jill took the luggage out of her hand and guided her to the doorman in his crisp gray uniform, who was holding the elevator door open for them.

"I have some leftovers from dinner tonight at the Chinese restaurant around the corner, but first I'm going to make you a stiff drink, then you can fill me in on the details. And, by the way, you look pretty good for someone who's being chased across country by an assassin." As frightened as she had been, Casey had to laugh. Jill had a way of taking the razor's edge off of a tight situation.

Jill's apartment was full of antiques she had inherited from her aunt. There was a comforting ambiance about the mixture of French Nouveau and American Contemporary, with touches of old-world Italian. Jill was definitely not a decorator, but her personality made up for her lack of design concept. After all, she was a court stenographer.

The desk in a corner, covered with recording equipment, headphones and her computer, was her mini-office. The apartment was not large enough for a separate office space. The cream-colored walls and silk apricot drapes billowing on the oriental carpet gave the living room a rich warmth.

As Jill fixed the drinks, Casey wandered to the window and stared out at the lights of New York. She was home again and it felt good until she glanced down at the street. A man in a black overcoat and hat had just stepped out of a taxi and was standing under a street light as he lit his cigarette. A light fog was rolling in off the East River. Was it the assassin? Either he knew where Jill lived or he had been able to follow her. She quickly backed away from the windo. She had to do something, and she didn't want to put Jill in danger. Her mind was racing as her phone rang and she jumped. She checked the caller ID and recognized the number...it was detective Tom Brandon.

Naturally he was upset that she was back in New York until she explained what had happened in Georgetown and her flight to the safety of the city. "I'm sending a police surveillance team over now to keep an eye on the building. You should be safe for the night. Don't go out and stay away from any windows. I'll make some decisions and pick you up in the morning."

They continued to talk while Casey made a feeble attempt to eat. She had missed her dinner at Georgetown and hadn't eaten since lunch yesterday. It was now three in the morning, but she felt safer just knowing Tom was nearby.

Tom explained they had tracked the killer to Myrtle Beach, but was surprised he had learned of Georgetown. The Georgetown police had picked up her message, and later, questioned personnel at the ticket counters in the Myrtle Beach airport. He had used one of his aliases when he boarded the flight from Myrtle Beach to New York, but was not seen by law enforcement when the passengers deplaned at LaGuardia. The NYPD was waiting for him, but he never entered the airport through the arrival gate, at least not dressed as he was when he boarded the flight. The master of disguise strikes again.

Chapter Ten

Casey realized she couldn't stay with Jill now that the assassin had followed her. It would put Jill's life in danger and she would not do that to her best friend. Tom was right. She would wait until morning and follow his instructions. But with only one suitcase of clothing and precious few other items, she needed to stop by her co-op and gather a few things before reaching her next hiding place.

Jill fixed an early breakfast for the two of them. It was Monday morning and she needed to be in the court room by 8 a.m.; after all, she was still employed. Before leaving, she made sure Casey had keys to the apartment so she could come and go when needed. "Call me the minute you know where you will be staying. Get one of those pre-paid phones so no one can trace your call. If I don't answer, leave me a message. I'm here to support you, so don't shut me out of the picture."

"My god, Jill honey. You are my rock. I don't know how I ever got you involved in this mess, but when it's all over, I promise I will make it up to you," Casey mumbled as they hugged.

Jill patted her on the back. "Lock the door when I leave and don't let anyone in but Tom."

"Yes, mother." Casey forced a smiled as she closed the apartment door. Jill waited in the hallway until she heard the click of the locks.

Casey packed her small suitcase with the few things she had and waited for Tom to call. A knock at the door caused her to jump. Who would be knocking? Wouldn't the doorman call before sending someone up? She stared at the door, like a frightened child, as the knob began to turn and the knocking continued. "Casey! Casey honey! It's me, Tom. Open up."

Her heart beat rapidly. She recognized his voice and quickly opened the door. "I was so worried," she said. "You hadn't called and I thought something had happened to you. Is everything all right?"

Tom nodded. "Everything's fine. I think your phone needs charging or you have it turned off. I did try to call, but couldn't get through." Casey took her phone from her purse. She had forgotten to turn it off after talking with Tom last night, and the battery was dead.

"I called Jill's cell and she told me she left you here behind locked doors. The doorman said you had not gone out, so I knew you had to be here."

Casey chuckled. "Remember the days when people used to have land-line phones? It's amazing how unplugged life is without a cell phone. And doormen are trained not to announce the police."

Tom had to laugh as he gave her a bear hug. "Honey, you're amazing. I can vouch for that."

Casey gave him a serious look. "So, my protective detective, where do we go from here?"

"How does Connecticut sound to you?"

"Why Connecticut?" she asked.

"I have an aunt in New Haven with a rental cottage that just happens to be vacant during the winter. It's not far from New York and I'll be able to see you now and then. You'll have your privacy and the neighborhood is well protected. Her son, my cousin, is the chief of police there. I've made all the arrangements and I will drive you up today."

"Well, I guess that's settled and I dare not refuse. At least it's close to New York," she sighed, slipping into her coat.

Tom grabbed her bag. "You're going to love it and Aunt Hilly will pamper you to death if you let her."

"Please don't mention your aunt and death in the same sentence. Isn't that what we are trying to avoid?" She rolled her eyes and grinned.

Tom checked the street before letting Casey step out of the building. The surveillance team was still on duty and indicated with a wave that all was OK as they pulled away. It was a cool morning but the sun was shining. Christmas was only two weeks away and New York was in the holiday spirit.

"We need to stop by my apartment first," Casey said as she buckled the seatbelt. "I had to leave two suitcases full of clothes with Grace in Georgetown, and my winter things are still here in New York. If I'm going to be in Connecticut, I'll need some warmer clothes."

"No problem," Tom said. He knew better than to argue.

As they merged into the traffic, Casey had a feeling they were being watched. Perhaps it was just the police shadows that had been keeping an eye on the building.

Across the street was a redheaded man wearing dark glasses, standing with one foot on a skateboard and ear plugs on his head listening to music; he swayed and moved to the rhythm. Casey and Tom loaded her suitcase and left Jill's apartment building. He crossed the street and caught a taxi as Tom's car pulled out into the traffic. The taxi was several car lengths behind but followed

Tom easily.

The occupant of the taxi stepped out across the street from 41 West 58th and stood under the canopy of Tower 58 while watching the third-floor windows of Casey's co-op as she opened the blinds to let in some light. Tom's black Ford Explorer was parked in front.

Casey emptied her suitcase and repacked it with warmer clothing. She retrieved a larger piece of luggage from the walk-in closet and filled it with additional items she knew she would need. Her laptop, in its carrying case, was the last item she grabbed before closing the blinds and locking the door.

Pausing at the window, she glanced across the street. She thought she saw someone she had noticed near Jill's apartment, but shook her head at the thought and closed the blinds. Downstairs, the doorman helped them load the car and they were off to Connecticut— number 57 Myron Street in New Haven. Tom and Casey, in heavy conversation and with eyes for each other, were oblivious to the taxi following them.

Aunt Hilly met them at the cottage door with fresh-baked cookies and invited Casey to dine with her family that evening. "I just live across the street," she pointed. "It's the house with the red door, just like the one on this place. You can't miss it."

Hilly's name was actually Hillary Mackenzie. She lived with her husband, Sam, a now-retired, fifteen-year veteran of the New Haven Police Department.

Hilly glanced at a New York City taxi as it slowly drove down the street. The New York City taxi was out of place in that neck of the woods. She would need to remember to tell Sam about it. "Well, best get in here and get settled before we heat the whole darn neighborhood." Hilly's robust figure was easy to understand once Casey had tasted the cookies. She knew dinner would not be a disappointment and accepted the invitation.

Hilly gave Tom a hug. "Hope you don't mind bunkin' in the

guestroom tonight. Andy's here for a couple of weeks to spend the holidays and I already put him in your room. You know how he is about his privacy."

"Who's Andy?" Casey asked.

"My nephew," Tom answered. "He's studying law at Cardozo in New York. He's kind of a geek, but harmless, except when it comes to law. I'm not sure if he wants to be a prosecutor or a defense attorney, but he'd be good at either."

"Wow!" Casey was impressed. "You certainly have the law on your side. Now I see why you like your line of work. It must be something you inherited."

"Mom's side of the family," Aunt Hilly said. Did he tell you that his mother, my sister, was the Sherriff of Carbon County in Wyoming?"

Casey looked at Tom and gave her head a shake. "No...he didn't," she said with a chuckle, "but I'm sure we'll have a long talk about that."

Hilly laughed. "Stick with me honey and I tell you all his secrets." Tom blushed.

"I think we need to let Casey get settled in." He kissed her on the cheek. "I'll pick you up for dinner at seven this evening. We can walk across the street together," he smiled.

"You two make a cute couple," Hilly said as she followed Tom out. "Now don't spoil your dinner eating too many of those cookies. They're for later when you curl up with a good mystery in bed," she added.

"I don't need to start a new mystery. I'm already in one. And as for curling up...I look forward to that when this is all over." She closed the door.

"Know what, Tom? That's a classy lady."

"I know, Hilly. I know."

Chapter Eleven

Dinner at the Mackenzie's was enjoyable. Casey felt like she was part of the family. Sam, a retired New Haven police captain, was full of stories to tell and she, never having heard any of them before, was his captive audience. A six-foot-tall muscular man in his sixties, with salt-and-pepper hair, rosy cheeks, and a full handlebar moustache, Sam didn't look a day over forty.

Andy was a lanky, handsome kid with curly red hair, a la Senator Joe Kennedy III. His black-framed glasses gave him a studious appearance, and his smile, with teeth as white as snow, was rather seductive. It was apparent he was good listener as well as an intelligent speaker on a wide range of subjects. Casey had to agree he would make a great lawyer.

Center stage in Hilly's dining room was a large, oval Early American table complete with twelve chairs. Enough to hold an extensive family gathering.

But tonight there were only five, so they gathered at one end of the monster. Coffee and dessert were served in the main room near the tall Christmas tree with a multitude of gifts tucked beneath. It appeared the Mackenzies were expecting more relatives for the holidays. For the first time since her parents' auto accident, Casey remembered what it was like to have a family.

"Looks like you are expecting more company for the holidays," Casey remarked, with a nod to the presents under the tree.

Hilly smiled. "It'll be a circus as always, come Christmas. Sam and I used to live in Colorado, but don't travel far now days, so the family comes to us. Sissy and Joe, that's Tom's mom and dad, should be here in two weeks, if the weather allows it. Not much to do on the ranch in the winter but feed the cattle." She poured another cup of coffee and passed the pot.

Casey sounded surprised. "That's wonderful. I hope I have an opportunity to meet them."

Hilly chuckled and patted Casey's knee. "Oh, honey, don't fret about that. I'm sure you'll get to meet them." Her eyes caught Tom as he smiled.

It was late when Tom walked Casey across the street to the cottage. She invited him in, but he said he needed to chat with Sam about some things. He showed her how to set the alarm and gave instructions to lock the door before giving her a good-night kiss that she would not forget. She locked the door and set the alarm.

During the night, Casey thought she heard a strange noise. Her nerves were still on edge and being in a strange house didn't help. She lay awake, listening to the sound of the wind as a tree branch scratched against the side of the bedroom wall. A half-moon cast strange shadows on the wall of the upstairs room and lightening flashed to the east. A squall off the Long Island Sound was threating to move inland, but was still in the distance. Car lights hit the garage of the house next door. The neighbors had returned home and the scratching noise disappeared. It must have been her imagination.

The following morning was cool and windy, as dried leaves tumbled down Myron Street. The smell of fresh coffee brewing lured Casey out of bed. So far, the rain had fizzled out. She grabbed a robe and padded downstairs in her bare feet. There was a knock at the front door and the doorbell sounded. She quickly peered out the peephole to see Tom standing there with his hands full. But if he was outside, who was in the kitchen?

A man's voice sounded behind her. "Well, don't just stand there. Open it up and let him in." It was Sam, standing with a fork in his hand and wearing an apron. "Hilly's sleeping in this morning and I'm cooking breakfast over here. Now let the man in." He spun around and returned to the kitchen.

Casey pulled her robe tighter against the cool wind and opened the door. Tom grinned as he entered, "Hey, sleepyhead, how about some pancakes and bacon?" He moved through to the kitchen door and turned to look at her.

"Oh, my god! Don't look at me. I must be a mess." She scurried to the staircase and started up the stairs.

"You look great," he said, "but clothes would help, unless you want breakfast in your robe."

"Cute," she smiled, "Now go warm the syrup while I get dressed," she tilted her head, "and stop looking at me like that, it's dangerous; and besides that, Sam's in the kitchen." Tom cracked up and almost dropped a few things. Casey continued up the stairs.

During breakfast, Casey told Tom and Sam about the scratching noise she heard during the night, and how it stopped when the neighbors got home. Tom looked at Sam. "There aren't any trees or bushes close to the walls on that side, but I'll take a look after breakfast. Maybe something blew in with the wind last night and then blew away." Casey felt safe as she enjoyed having breakfast with two cops. She could get used to this kind of pampering.

Tom heaved a sigh, "I need to take some reports into to New

York this morning, but I'll be back tonight. Hilly and Sam are here if you need anything. We had a sprinkle during the night and everything smells fresh. You might get out for a walk along the dunes, but be sure and take Andy with you. I don't want you out alone. Hilly's working the church bazaar today and Sam needs to make a delivery to Hartford."

"I'll be fine, but I will check with Andy if I take a stroll. However, I'm sure he's not jumping at the chance to be my watchdog for the day."

Tom shook his head. "You can be stubborn when you want to."

She held her chin up and answered. "There's nothing stubborn about being logical. Why would a young man like Andy want to be in the company of an older woman?"

"I can think of several reasons, but we won't go there," he chuckled.

"Tom Brandon! Wipe that silly grin off you face. You know what I mean. Now be off and hurry back! I have dishes to do and the kitchen is calling."

Sam had left out the back door to check the side of the cottage where Casey had heard the noise. It didn't take him long to assess the situation. A side window screen had been cut and there were foot prints in the damp flower garden below the window. He quickly caught up with Tom and let him know. He didn't want to frighten Casey, but he said he would cancel his delivery and keep an eye on the neighborhood until Tom returned.

Hilly was awake and heading off to the church. She invited Casey to drop in at the bazaar if she was out for a walk and they would have a coffee break together. She drew a little map for her to follow. Casey was suddenly aware that Connecticut was not like Georgetown. They were both quaint, old-fashioned towns near the water, but here she not only had friends who felt like a family, but she was also just a short train ride to New York City.

Around eleven o'clock, Casey felt the need to stretch her legs. Dressed in her jogging clothes, she crossed the street and asked Andy if he would like to go for a run by the dunes. "I'm just about finished with some papers for our mock trial. Give me thirty minutes and I'll meet you on the corner of Myron and Townsend, it's just a couple of blocks that way." He pointed down the street.

"Great. I'll meet you there." Casey started down the street. A cloud moved across the sun and cast a dark shadow. A chill ran up her spine as she turned quickly. Someone had just ducked behind the corner of her cottage, but she caught a glimpse of red hair. It couldn't be the same person who was on the street at Jill's and across from her co-op. How would he know where she was staying? Had he somehow followed them?

Lots of people have red hair—even Andy, for heaven's sake. It was probably just the neighbor. Will I ever get rid of this paranoid feeling? I have to put it out of my mind. She picked up speed and without thinking, she was soon running. *I know running isn't going to make it go away, but it gets my blood pumping and I can think clearer when my brain is stimulated.* The fear would still be there, but her strength against it would be stronger.

Reaching the corner, she paused to catch her breath and stretch. The dunes were straight ahead and a salt water mist was in the air as gulls glided on the currents above, voicing their mournful cries. The feeling of being watched hit her like a hammer. He was here somewhere. What was he waiting for? Why was he playing a cat-and-mouse game? Did he intend to rape her before killing her? These were questions that circled in her brain stirred by fear.

Casey continued her slow jog up Townsend Street. The dunes could wait for another time. She headed for the church bazaar at St. Boniface. She needed to be around people. She hadn't charged her cell phone before leaving New York and forgot to bring her charger with her. There was no way to call the police or 911. Her stalker must be getting close, but she was afraid to look back.

"Hey there! Slow down." The voice didn't register. Someone tapped her on the shoulder and her head twisted as a redheaded man jogged alongside."

"What's the hurry? I thought you wanted to visit the dunes."

"Oh my god, Andy. It's you."

"Yeah, it's me. Were you expecting someone else?"

Casey breathed in and out slowly, trying to calm herself as she stretched her muscles. "I thought someone was following me and so I decided to head for the church."

"You mean the stalker Tom and Sam were talking about last night?"

Casey was surprised. "You know about the stalker?" she asked.

"Well, Sam and Tom don't do a lot of whispering, and I have sensitive hearing. I overheard them talking last night and got the general picture, though not all the details. Are you really a special witness to a murder plot?"

Casey scanned the area to see if they were being watched. "Sensitive hearing can get you into a lot of trouble, buster. And believe me, I know firsthand. I'm blessed with sensitive hearing myself, or perhaps I should say cursed." Her eyes kept searching the area, checking for any movement. "Let's jog to the church. I don't like standing here making myself and you an easy target. I'm not supposed to talk about it to anyone, but since you're part of the family, and seem to know all about it, I guess that's OK."

Casey had filled Andy in on the details by the time they reached St. Boniface Church. "Wow! This is cool. A real mystery right here in sleepy old New Haven." His eyes, behind the spectacles, were as big as saucers.

"This is definitely not cool Andy. You have to promise me you won't say anything to anyone about what I just told you, especially your uncle. And you need to understand that I may have put your life in danger just by association. You're studying law. I don't know how I can make it any clearer."

Andy stared at her and smiled, "You just helped me make a decision. I'm switching to criminal law. Civil law is so boring."

Casey heaved an exasperated sigh. "Oh my lord! I hope I didn't give you any ideas like that."

Aunt Hilly suddenly appeared. "Hey guys! You're just in time for a coffee break. Follow me to the rec-room. I need to sit down. My feet are killing me."

Casey took another look around at the crowd but didn't see anyone who looked suspicious. "Don't worry," Hilly said, "you can shop after I have a rest. Come on, they have pastries and donuts to give us energy. It's been a busy morning." *You don't know how right you are,* Casey thought.

Chapter Twelve

M eanwhile, Sam had been busy at home. He contacted the local
police and met them at the cottage where they made a cast
of the footprints in the garden and checked the screen and window
sill for fingerprints. A striped awning over the window had kept the
area dry from the rain that blew in from the northeast. He waited
until Casey and Andy were both out for the morning. Sam didn't
want to frighten her or get Andy involved. He also arranged with his
son for extra security patrol in the neighborhood and a surveillance
officer to keep an eye on the place.

He phoned Tom to let him know his findings and when he could
expect a report from the New Haven police that would be sent
directly to his office. Tom had planned to leave early but said he
would wait for the report. Perhaps it was just a prowler thinking the
cottage was empty. He knew that the attempted assassin, Max, was
clever, but it was a long shot that he would be anywhere near New
Haven. Fingerprints, if there were any, would be the best identifica-

tion. In the meantime, he couldn't reach Casey—her phone was still dead; but he knew Sam was on top of things in Connecticut.

Sam arrived at the church bazaar and surprised everyone. Hilly was the only one who suspected something was up. Sam doesn't go to church bazaars. "Just in time for donuts, old man. How's your morning been?"

"Oh, don't your worry. I've been pretty busy." He winked at Hilly and she got the hint not to pry any further. They had their own secret signals after so many years of marriage.

"I hope you brought the car, I don't feel like walking back home," Hilly said.

"I guess you read my mind, sweetheart. Your chariot is waiting if you are done here."

"If they can't handle this event without me by now, then they need to get a new chairperson. I need to get home and start fixing lunch," she said.

Andy laughed. "How can you even think about lunch after that pastry you just finished?"

Hilly squinted her eyes and gave him a stern look. "We may not all be beanpoles, but we're all a healthy family. Are you comin' or not?"

"Lead the way. I won't argue this case," he said.

"Cause you know you'd lose," Sam grinned.

Casey joined in. "I'll help in the kitchen. Just tell me what to do." She didn't want to be alone at the cottage.

"Now there's a volunteer I'm happy to have. I'm sure I have an apron that will fit you just fine," Hilly beamed.

~

Tom arrived a few minutes before dinner and joined Sam in the family room while the women cooked in the kitchen. "Any news from the labs?" Sam asked.

Tom nodded. "The lab results were positive. The fingerprints were a match. He's getting careless, and that spells dangerous."

"We both know he's under pressure and it's making him forget-ful. How long before he makes his next move?"

Tom hesitated, as he considered the situation. "He's clever like a fox, with the instincts of a bloodhound. He ducks and hides, waits and follows. He can smell a trail and doesn't give up. I don't know how he did it, but he followed Casey to Georgetown. Fortunately, she spoiled his plans and fled back to New York when she learned he was in town. We've been leading him on a chase, and so far, have managed to keep a step ahead, but he's bound to strike soon."

Sam spoke in a whispered tone. "I hate to say this, Tom, but he might want more than just to kill."

"I know. That thought crossed my mind too, but I won't put Casey in that danger. I have a plan to keep her out of it and..."

"Keep me out of what?" Casey asked as she stood in the kitchen doorway, drying her hands on a dish towel. Sam and Tom were silent.

"You look great in that apron. How's dinner coming?" Tom said.

"Thank you for the compliment, but you didn't answer my ques-tion."

Sam cleared his throat. "Tom and I were just making some plans. It's nothing important."

"I appreciate you trying to help, Sam, but if it includes me, I think it's important. At least it is to me." Casey crossed her arms and waited.

Tom crossed the room and took her in his arms. "I can't let you get involved. It's too dangerous."

"Sorry, detective. But aren't you forgetting something? I got involved the day I reported overhearing a stupid conversation about a plot to murder someone. I didn't ask to be involved, but there you are—I am. So if there are plans to end this game of cat and mouse, the mouse wants to be included."

Tom smiled and shook his head. "Damn, you're a stubborn woman."

Casey smiled back. "So was my mother. Now, what are your plans?"

"Let's discuss that after dinner." Hilly chimed from the dining room, "I don't want this food to get cold. And if we're making plans, you better include me, too."

"Now you know why I married her. She's not only a great cook, but she's got a head on her shoulders and can organize just about anything."

"Oh, Sam, you say the sweetest things. Now get in here and eat. There's plenty of time for talk later." The boss had spoken and they followed her orders.

They sat around the dining table with coffee and apple pie, speaking in low voices so that anyone with a listening device would have difficulties hearing them. They decided to set a trap for the stalker. Tom took the lead. "It's going to take a day to set the trap up. Casey, you'll stay here tonight. You can have the guestroom and I'll sleep in the attic. I don't want you alone in the cottage."

He explained about the footprints, the cut screen and the fingerprints on the window frame. "We confirmed he's here in New Haven, and he knows where you are staying."

"So, I did hear someone. It wasn't just my imagination."

"Don't worry." Sam said, "We're going to set a trap tomorrow night and I'm confident we'll catch the rat."

Tom continued. "Sam's arranged for additional security and help from the police tomorrow. I'll stay in the house, so it looks like you are there." He touched Casey's hand. "Criminals are creatures of habit and usually repeat their actions. He tried to enter the house by way of the window on the first level but was chased off by the arrival of the neighbors. Most likely, he had cased the cottage and felt that was the least visible spot, avoiding the front and back entries. We believe he'll try the same entry. Sam also discovered the security alarm wires had been cut. He left the scene as he found it, so it doesn't look like we discovered his plans."

Everyone listened intently as Hilly filled their coffee cups around the table and returned to her chair. The dishes would have to wait. She didn't want to miss anything. Even Andy was taking notes for future reference, to be analyzed later. Casey had been quiet while putting the pieces of the puzzle together in her mind. She was good at catching any flaws that others might overlook.

Sam took up the conversation. "I'll be stationed in the garage keeping an eye on the back door while we wait. I have a feeling he's getting tired of the chase and is ready to spring. He doesn't just want to kill, he's looking for pleasures first and that's why Casey can't be involved."

Casey spoke quickly and without hesitation. "Sam, haven't you been listening? I'm already involved. I've been questioned, sequestered in hiding, cut off from my friends, removed from my job, and chased from New York to South Carolina, back to New York and now to New Haven. I've drawn all of you into this nightmare and I refuse to be excluded and shut away."

"I know how you must feel, Casey, but you are a valuable witness and have to be protected." Tom added.

"No," she swallowed a sip of hot coffee, "no. You can't know how I feel. I'm tired of running and hiding, living in fear and paranoid of running into a man I don't even know—a person with numerous disguises who speaks five languages and has a built-in radar system to find his prey."

Not a voice was uttered. Not a sound was made. She had the attention of everyone at the table as she glanced at each person. Hilly taped her fingers on the table. Andy was rapidly writing in his tablet. Sam was deep in thought, trying to figure out her next move. And Tom's puppy-dog face had an apologetic look as his head bobbed in agreement.

Casey continued with calm and concise statements. "It's me

he's after. I'm the one he believes can identify him. You can't pull the wool over his eyes. He'll know I'm not there. He's not stupid. He won't go near the place unless he's sure to get what he wants. You have to put the cheese in the trap if you want to catch the mouse." She waited for a response.

Tom shook his head. "Casey, I can't let you do that. You'd be putting your life in danger, and I can't take that chance."

"My life is already in danger, Tom, and you can't control that. I'm finished with running away. I want this resolved so we can get on with our lives, which I hope will be together. But I've come to the end of the rope and I won't let go without a tug. Maybe I'm stubborn like my mom, but she taught me to always have hope. I'm not ready to give up living, so I hope we can find a better plan, and that's that."

Hilly and Andy gave her a quiet round of supportive applause, while Sam and Tom glance at each other. Perhaps they could make some revisions to their scheme. They still had the night to think it over. Hilly and Casey cleared the table and did the dishes while Andy retreated upstairs to his computer. Sam and Tom put their heads together and worked on a new approach to the plan.

Casey said she needed to get some things from the cottage if she was going to spend the night. "No need for that," Hilly answered, "We're like a hotel around here. I have everything you need, toothpaste, toothbrush, fresh towels and we even changed the bed linens this afternoon."

"But I didn't bring anything to sleep in."

"Oh no need to fret about that. Tom has a fresh pair of pajamas in the drawer. They might be a little big on you, but you're not going to be in a fashion show anyway."

The words "fashion show" made Casey laugh. "Well, you could say, that's how all of this got stated, but we won't go there. I'll tell you the story someday if I live through all this."

"It's a deal. And I'm sure it will be interesting," she chuckled.

Chapter Thirteen

Next morning, Hilly was busy fixing breakfast in the kitchen when Casey finally made it down the kitchen stairs. "That was the first good night's sleep I've had in months. I can't believe I overslept. Where is everybody?"

"Andy's in the dining room. Sam and Tom headed into town to meet with the local police and the sheriff. Sounds like they've worked out the kinks, want to coordinate with law enforcement to get the go-ahead. I'm glad they're leaving the FBI out of it. Too many cooks spoil the broth."

"Hey, Casey," Andy hollered from the dining room. Got a minute? I need to go over some of these quotes you made last night."

"Oh lord. Am I to be immortalized in literature?" Hilly smiled as she handed Casey a plate with pancakes, sausage, and scrambled eggs.

"Syrup's on the table and coffee's in the pot. Humor the boy. He's finally found his calling and we shouldn't discourage him."

"Oh Hilly, have I opened a can of worms or what? Your family's going to end up hating me."

"I doubt that, honey. Our family is like a chain. Some of the links are strong and some are weak. Not all of us have been law abiding citizens. There are a few black sheep in the flock, but we keep their secrets hidden. If you ask me, I think you're a strong link and I'm sure Tom feels the same. Now go eat before those pancakes won't melt the butter. And stop fretting. It's all going to be fine."

"Are you coming or not?" Andy whined.

"OK, OK, I'm here, but you better not misquote me. I get pissed when people misquote me."

"Can I put that in the story?"

"Not if you use the word pissed." They could hear Hilly's laughter coming from the kitchen.

~

Tom and Sam returned around 10 a.m. Once again they were all gathered around the big table. "We have to go over everything. I think we've covered every angle and replayed the scene a dozen times. Each of us knows our position and our part. And I'm pretty sure Max is anxious to play his part." Sam explained.

"So what's my part and what's the plot?" Casey asked.

"At your request, you're the cheese in the trap." He used her precise words.

"And what does the cheese do?" she continued.

"Nothing," he said. But as she started to protest, he held up his hand to stop her. "Well, not exactly nothing. I'll let Tom explain your role." Everyone turned to face Tom.

"What he means is, you were right. Max won't come around unless you're there. But we've worked out a way that makes it appear that you are in the house alone."

"I don't think I understand the magic in this show. How do I appear to be alone and yet not alone? Is there a genie in the bottle or a rabbit in the hat that suddenly appears?"

Hilly tapped on the table like a judge in court. "Hang in there, honey. Give Tom a minute to explain."

"As I was saying...I'll walk you over to the cottage after dinner tonight. He's bound to be watching the place. We say goodnight and you step inside. I'll head back to Hilly's. A police officer will already be in the cottage. Before dinner, Sam will drive around the block and sneak into the garage the back way. If Max is watching this house because you're in it, he won't be watching the cottage."

Casey was starting to get the picture. "So what do I do once I'm in the house?"

"You lock the door, go upstairs, turn the bedroom light on, and wait. And don't come down until we call you. Agreed?"

"Agreed, but what if he smells a trap and doesn't come?"

"Trust me. He'll come." Tom mumbled.

~

Andy wasn't at dinner that evening. He was meeting with a friend to do some research work and grabbing a pizza later, so it was just Hilly, Tom, and Casey. The pork roast with potatoes and gravy was enough to feed a family of ten, but Hilly knew it would be good left over. The quiet meal was punctuated with chimes from the grandfather clock as the hours passed in slow motion. Tension hung in the air as thick as the fog rolling in from the Sound. Another squall was brewing in the distance. Sam had driven Casey and Hilly into town earlier, hoping to draw Max away from the neighborhood so things could be organized. He made sure they were followed without putting anyone in jeopardy. The trap was set.

At the stroke of ten, Tom walked Casey to the cottage, kissed her goodnight and she closed the door. He listened for the lock to click and turned to cross the street. Suddenly there was a scream from the cottage. Drawing his revolver, he kicked the door in and stood to the side. No shots were fired, so he entered. Casey was staring at a body lying on the floor; bleeding, bound, and gagged. It was the police officer.

A voice came from the staircase. "Drop the gun detective, or your girlfriend gets it first." Max's gun with a silencer attached was aimed at Casey. Tom followed his instructions. "Bad planning, detective. You should have known I'd be expecting an inside guard." The front door, hanging on its hinges, was still open. "Close the door behind you. We wouldn't want to draw the neighbor's attention, would we?"

Tom realized he needed to keep Max talking to give Sam time to sneak in from the kitchen. "You're speaking pretty good English, Max. What happened to the accent?"

"I speak five languages fluently and not always with an accent." Casey was sure it was the same voice, even without the accent. And his face was the same as Danny had described, down to the scar on his cheek from his mouth to his ear. His eyes were like orbs of black onyx surrounded by white foam, and she detected the aroma of Hugo Boss cologne, as she stood speechless and helpless.

"So, Max, what are the plans now?" There was a groan from the officer on the floor. He was still alive. A bullet had grazed his head, but he hadn't been killed.

"It's the age-old story: love, unfaithfulness, and revenge."

Tom could see a shadow movement through the kitchen door. Sam was now in the cottage moving cautiously like a cat, waiting to pounce. He was out of view from Max and on his left. Max was left-handed. *I have to keep him talking*, Tom thought. "I don't quite follow. Perhaps you could explain."

"It's simple. I shoot you. Then, with your gun, I shoot the man on the floor. I have a little fun with your girlfriend upstairs and then I kill her with your gun. Love triangle and tragedy. It happens all the time."

Sam was now in position. His aim would be true if only something could distract Max's attention from Casey.

There was a sneeze from the coat closet at the base of the stairs. Max turned slightly. A shot rang out and the gun in his hand fired, dropping to the floor. Tom retrieved the pistol at his feet and fired a shot at Max's leg as he rushed past to the doorway. The door opened and two officers caught him as he fell forward.

Casey's knees gave way and she collapsed on the sofa. Tom rushed to her side. Sam came out of the kitchen and faced Max. "A bullet in the hand and one in the leg. Looks like you won't be doing much walking or writing in prison, Max. Take him in, boys, and keep a good eye on him. He's slippery as a snake."

"Yes, sir. We know how to handle snakes." They walked him out to the waiting paramedics.

Sam untied the officer on the floor. The bullet had grazed his head on the right side. The paramedics helped him out the door. "Max must be losing his touch," said Sam.

The closet door opened and out came Andy, white as a sheet. He looked at the bullet hole in the door frame of the closet and felt it with his hand. "Sorry about the sneeze. I couldn't hold it in any longer."

"That's alright, son." Sam patted him on the shoulder. "You played your part and we didn't even know you were there. What the hell were you thinking, putting your life in danger?"

"Well, to be honest, I didn't want to miss out on the action. I came over early today to interview the officer for my story, but he wasn't here yet. Then I heard someone coming in through the back door and thought it might be the killer, so I hid in the closet—no one ever looks inside closets. I must've waited a long time, then all the action started. I heard a scream and a bang, then voices. I tried to stay quiet, but couldn't hold the sneeze any longer. Then there were gun shots and I crouched in the corner of the closet until I realized it was all over."

"Andy, my man, we might make a detective out of you yet," Tom called from the sofa.

"Thanks, but I think I'll stick to law. It's less dangerous."

Chapter Fourteen

It was three days before Christmas and the Mackenzie and Brandon kin were about to descend for the holiday gathering. The table in the dining room was laden with food to snack on, as their arrivals were never all at the same time and everyone was always hungry when they got there. Hillary and Casey had been in the kitchen all morning fixing snacks and baking cookies, while Sam and Tom were busy repairing damages at the cottage.

Casey had moved her things into the guest room with Tom. After all, they were adults. Casey's friend Jill was driving up from New York. She had no family to spend Christmas with and Tom had invited her to surprise Casey. He had arranged for her to stay in a neighbor's guest house three doors down the street.

The wave of arrivals came early, as kids of all ages ran through the house. A light snow had begun to fall, but no storms were in the forecast.

"Let's take a stroll in the snowfall and get out of this madhouse for a moment." Tom suggested.

"Let me get my coat upstairs and I'll meet you on the stoop. Hilly has everything and everyone under control. I don't think we'll be missed."

Snowflakes swirled around them as they walked hand-in-hand. Casey could tell that Tom was pensive and she waited for him to speak first. "I've been doing some thinking these past few weeks. So much has happened in such a short period of time."

Casey laughed. "You can say that again."

Tom smiled. "The thing is, I don't want to lose you. I know we haven't known each other very long, but I felt something the first day we met. I was wondering if you might ever consider marrying again."

Casey stopped walking, tilted her head, and smiled at him, "That would depend on the person asking to marry me."

"Would you be willing to consider a detective, whose line of work is dangerous, unpredictable, and has demanding hours both day and night? Someone who loves you very much and will take care of you?"

"Well," she said, "I guess I'll have to think about this, but can you answer one question?"

"Sure, shoot."

"Was that a proposal?"

He laughed. "Guess I'm not too good at this, am I? But to answer your question: Yes, it was a proposal."

Casey crossed her arms like a mother scolding her child, "Well then, the answer is yes, but please don't use that word 'shoot' when you get down on your knee and ask me properly."

By the time they returned to the house, everyone had arrived. Casey was delighted to find Jill mingling with the family. She had introduced herself to everyone and was already helping Hilly refill the bowls and platters on the dining table. As they gathered around the table for dinner that evening, Tom announced their engagement.

Jill was beside herself with happiness. "See there? I was right all along. I told you he had eyes for you that first day at lunch."

Casey patted her hand, "Jill, honey...you're such a romantic."

Andy was entertaining the kids with his story about how his sneeze helped to capture the criminal. Sissy and Joe, Tom's parents, were eager to hear all about the prior evening and the arrest of a wanted criminal.

Tom explained how the assassin-stalker would be processed through the New York Police Department and handed over to the FBI for federal prosecution. The FBI wasn't pleased that they had been out-smarted by the NYPD, but they were happy to finally have the murderer behind bars. Some feathers were ruffled and a few harsh comments made, but the end results were legal in the eyes of the law.

The house was full of laughter and conversation mixed with the aroma and flavors of a banquet. Presents circled the tree as lights twinkled and the fireplace roared. A blanket of snow now covered the ground outside, glittering in the light of a full moon as clouds gave way to a clear sky. All was well in New Haven.

Merry Christmas, one and all.

Vortex

READERS' COMMENTS
on VORTEX

I finished *Vortex* yesterday—and liked it! I like science fiction, so the combination of that element plus mystery was a good one. I thought that the sudden, bizarre twist introduced by the Bob Cat enigma was well-developed as the story progressed—and got even more bizarre. —*Edward B.*

An amazing story! I was hooked when the suspense began in Death Valley and couldn't put it down. Reminded me of *The Twilight Zone* TV show. —*Evelyn K.*

Another winner—Felt I was on the road trip with Patrick and Nick. What a surprise twist—Hope there's more to come. —*Carolyn L.*

A most ingenious plot. Enjoyable Si-fi/Mystery with twists and turns that surprised us from Death Valley to Sedona. —*D. Garner*

You've done it again! I look forward to reading more mystery stories when *D.G. Heath Mystery Collection—Volume Three* is published. —*G. Lebow*

I just finished *Vortex*—I was really into it. I admire your imagination and how you fit things together. This cries for a sequel! Have you started one? —*Maryretta A.*

Chapter One

I was having that recurring dream once again. I was hiking in a desert searching for a lost treasure in the Valley of the Dead. I didn't have a treasure map and had no idea what the treasure was. Suddenly a large black raven was sitting on my shoulder squawking at me... "Wake up dude—wake up! It's 5 a.m.—time to hit the road." I was being pushed and shoved—then suddenly I was blinded by a bright light. Nick had turned on the bedside lamp and was staring at me with a wide grin.

This was the first day of our planned road trip and Nick had already packed the car and made the coffee. He was an early riser and always full of energy, even when he stayed out all night partying in college. I groaned and stretched. "Do we really have to leave so early? It's not even daylight outside."

"Stop whining wuss. Get dressed, brush your teeth, and comb your hair. I'll be waiting in the car with fresh coffee. We need to beat the rush-hour traffic." I hurried around as quickly as I could at that ungodly hour. Grabbing my backpack, I locked the door and met Nick at the curb.

"Are you sure you've got everything?" I said quietly so as not to wake the neighbors. It was o-dark-thirty and I hate getting up that early, but Nick wanted to be ahead of the morning traffic. People think that getting out of Las Cruces is easy. You just hook on to I-10 and head east or west. The concept may be true but hitting the highway truck traffic at any time of the day is a challenge. People who say that New York never sleeps should try living in Las Cruces where highway I-10 traffic never stops.

Nick and I had been roommates since our college days at the University of Texas. Twenty-eight-year-old Nickolas Se with his jet-black hair and deep onyx eyes, had come to America from Tibet to study astronomical science. However, he didn't really need to study much. Nick knew more about the planets, the stars, and the universe than most of his professors. He was an honor student by day and a "frat-rat" by night when it came to his social life. Nick currently works at the Apache Point Observatory in Cloudcroft, a short 45-minute commute from Las Cruces. We'd known each other for the past seven years.

My name is Patrick O'Donnell. I'm a redheaded Irish dude of twenty-seven, with emerald green eyes, freckles, and a "Luck of the Irish" attitude. I was raised in Sedona, Arizona, before being shipped off to boarding school in Connecticut, while my parents got a divorce. Dad moved to Texas and mom decided to stay in Mexico where she had met a handsome plastic surgeon with his own medical facility in the city and a huge country estate where he raised racing horses.

My major at UT was archaeology, with a minor in anthropology. I spent my school months in Austin and summers in the Yucatan, working side-by-side with experts at Mayan villages and temple excavations in southern Mexico, feeding my passion for exploring archaeological sites and learning more about ancient civilizations.

Nick was getting impatient. "I've got everything that will fit in this car except for you, so hop in and we can be off on our adventure." We had no way of knowing the adventures we would soon encounter. This was our first road trip together, and I had spent weeks planning this tour through several of America's national parks. We were loaded with camping gear to be on the safe side, even though I had managed to secure reservations at hotels and motels for the whole trip. Nick's motto—"Always be prepared"—reminded me of my younger days as a Boy Scout.

I've always enjoyed traveling through the southwest. The desert landscape, although at times only a barren waste, is pockmarked here and there with a variety of strange cacti, colorful rock outcroppings and giant pieces of petrified wood from ancient forest that once covered this now desolate part of southern North America.

I can picture in my mind imaginary bands of native Indians on horseback, standing guard on the flat low mesas as the heat rises in waves from the hot sands of the desert floor, and vultures slowly circle overhead searching for their next meal. An occasional coyote or javelina scampers across the road, and small herds of desert antelope scatter and disappear into the landscape as we pass.

Nick stayed off of the interstate highway as much as possible, taking scenic back roads whenever available—we weren't in any hurry and wanted to enjoy the scenery. Without the use of a GPS, he seemed to know which roads to take as if he had memorized them before we left Las Cruces.

The morning sunlight was just beginning to glow a soft apricot in the sky above the Chihuahua Desert when we pulled into the Flying J truck stop at Lordsburg for a hearty breakfast. Driving was easy in Nick's bright red four-wheel drive Explorer, which he had packed to the gills. We made a few stops to stretch our travel legs, allowing our blood a chance to circulate.

The parking area, surrounding the buildings and gas pumps at the Flying J, was filled with about twenty eighteen-wheelers and dozens of smaller trucks, campers, and autos. Inside, the place was jumpin' with truckers and travelers of all shapes and sizes.

Truck stops are like a big-box general store offering everything from shower and laundry facilities, to beverages of every kind, candy, snacks, energy bars, clothing, caps, motor oil, windshield wipers, books, magazines, and toys. Or, as my mom always said, "Everything under the sun."

Truck-stop restaurants put local diners to shame. You can't miss the aroma of bacon frying on the grill or the sound of hash-brown potatoes sizzling in a skillet. Combine that with the smell of fresh baked biscuits and black pepper sausage-cream gravy wafting from the kitchen. That's enough to cure anything that ails you. No wonder truck drivers are rarely sick. They may put on a few pounds, but they're hardly ever ill.

We slid into an empty booth by the window and suddenly menus appeared out of nowhere. "OK boys...what'll ya have?" asked the gum chewing waitress with pink spiked hair, a silver ring through her nose and tattooed muscular arms. Quite possibly she was a reject from some punk-rock band working a day job to make ends meet. The bags under her fashionable smoky-eye makeup were packed for a long voyage. She filled our coffee cups to the rim with precision—never once needing to glance at the mugs.

I placed my order for chicken fried steak and giant biscuits smothered in cream gravy, served with hash-browns and a side of scrambled eggs. Nick selected the fruit bowl with granola and honey yogurt.

"That'll be out in a jiff. Name's Madge," the waitress offered, setting the carafe of coffee on the table. "Just holler when ya need a refill on the java." Madge swung her hips as she sashayed off with our orders.

"What a hoot!" I whispered to Nick making him chuckle.

Stuffed to the gills, I didn't have room after breakfast for apple pie or even a cinnamon roll for dessert, but on our way out of the place we purchased a couple of energy bars and a bag of potato chips for road nourishment. Nick slipped into the driver's seat without even asking—he knew I would be asleep in five minutes after eating so much food, so he volunteered to continue driving. Far be it for me to refuse his offer as I drifted into a state of comfortable oblivion.

The morning had brightened quickly while we enjoyed our dining experience. Leaving the truck stop, we stayed on Interstate 10. Dirt roads in the open desert can be difficult to follow and often are washed out by sudden rains that flow like rivers on the flat surface. Time passed quickly as we zoomed through Tucson and Phoenix with only one pit stop to relieve our bladders, of the never-empty coffee mugs, thanks to Madge, our morning *fashionista* in Lordsburg.

Just before crossing the Colorado River at the border of Arizona and California, I had pinpointed another Flying J Truck Stop. It was time for lunch and a gourmet dining experience with giant burgers, crispy French fries and chocolate shakes. Good thing I was driving or Nick would never have taken the right exit. You can probably tell by now that I travel on my stomach.

Back on the road, Nick headed northwest through Joshua Tree National Park where he proceeded to get us lost. It was late in the afternoon when we finally located the junction of state road 62 and Highway 247 to Barstow. It was pitch black by the time we reached Highway 15 to Baker and turned north into Death Valley National Park and our waiting reservation at the Furnace Creek Inn, arriving at midnight and too late for dinner.

The lodge or, inn and ranch resort as it is called, is a sprawling complex of lodging facilities with two restaurants, an Olympic-size swimming pool, multiple tennis courts, an 18-hole golf course, an Old-West style village, and the Borax Museum.

Surrounded by low mountain ranges with several tall peaks, Death Valley is sunken 134 feet below sea level. Borax made the valley famous in the TV show *Death Valley Days* with Ronald Regan and the 20 Mule Team wagons pulling tons of borax mined from the local quarries in the valley. Giant boulders scattered in the flat landscape offer shaded refuge from the heat of the sun and sand during the day.

The scruffy looking man at the check-in desk appeared unable to find our reservation but I showed him a copy of the printed confirmation from the parks department reservation services.

Getting lost and no dinner had pissed Nick off. "Well what the fuck are we supposed to do—sleep in our car in this 100-degree weather?" he huffed at the old geezer.

"Now just a dang minute there sonny-boy." The old guy said shaking his finger at Nick with an angry stare. "You ain't due here until tomorrow night if you look at that-there reservation, so don't go gettin' all huffy with me."

Standing at the counter, I took the form and checked the date on the confirmation. He was right. "I apologize for my grumpy friend here, and I'm sorry we're a full day early, but we really need to find lodgings for the night, if you're sure we have a room here tomorrow. We planned to stay two nights here in the park."

"Well—that's a lot better," he said smiling at me with milky hazel eyes and nodding towards Nick. "Your friend there needs to let off some steam and I know just the place," he grinned through coffee stained teeth with large gaps. "I got a buddy over yonder at the Bob Cat B&B. I'll give him a jingle and see if he's got a vacant room."

"It's not far is it?" I asked. "We've been driving most of the day and really need to rest."

The man shook his head and mumbled as he reached for the landline phone, "People—always in a hurry now days." I pulled my cell out of my pocket and checked—no signal. This really is *Dead-zone Valley*, I thought. No need to tell Nick, it would just piss him off even more, as he huffed once again from the bench.

The stop in Death Valley was my suggestion. It was part of a dream I had about finding a hidden treasure. I hadn't mentioned the dream to Nick because I knew he would think I was crazy.

"You'd better ask if it has air conditioning before you make any decisions." Nick offered quietly with a look of disgust on his face and sweat beading on his forehead, as he sat on the wooden bench against the wall, arms folded across his chest.

"Believe me—we'll be fine if it has windows and a ceiling fan. The desert cools down at night remember?" Nick's eyes appeared to be on fire and I could almost see smoke coming out his ears. I shrugged and turned back to face the counter.

Mr. No-name hung up the phone. "Yep...Bud's got a vacant room. That'll be one hundred bucks—you can pay me right here. He'll hold the room fer ya. I'll draw directions on this here map," he said, reaching under the desk.

Nick looked up from the bench where he waited, "Isn't a hundred bucks a little steep for a B&B in the middle of nowhere?"

The man chuckled, "May be Sonny Boy—but beggars can't be choosers now, can they?"

I thanked Mr. No-name, paid the hundred dollars in cash and with the map in hand, quickly ushered Nick out the door before he could explode. I could tell Sonny Boy wasn't happy with the answer.

Chapter
Two

Using the directions on the map, we found our way to the Bob
Cat B&B after passing their small road sign three times which
is easy to do in the pitch-black darkness of the desert. Fortunately,
Bud was waiting on the front porch along with five rather rough
looking characters whose Harleys were parked in front. He grinned,
"Wondered how many times you were gonna pass that sign before
you slowed down enough to read it," he said. "Come on in and sign
the register. I'll show you to your room."

The Bob Cat B&B was a cluster of double-wide trailers joined
together and placed at right angles to form a U-shape. Inside, the
main trailer was air conditioned.

"Are the gentlemen outside your other guests or neighbors?" I
asked following him inside to a small counter.

"They just be passin' through. Not many neighbors around these
parts."

I took the pen and with a shaky hand printed both our names

in the book. "Nick and Patrick—now ain't those cute names?" Bud mumbled, as we followed him across the compound. "Stinky said you boys got here a day early."

"Excuse me," I said, a bit confused, "Who's Stinky?"

"He's the man you paid the fifty dollars to for your room here at the Bob Cat."

Well...if the shoe fits, so did the name. Nick was about to say something but I put my hand over his mouth and shook my head in warning. Bud was obviously not aware that his friend was charging double for the lodging and I wasn't prepared to start a feud—at least not while we were still around.

Our room had no air conditioning but a single open window allowed the cool night air of the desert to drift in from outside and offer some comfort. Nick gave the room a quick once-over inspection. "Holy shit! There's only one bed in here," he griped.

"Don't worry...I don't have rabies and I won't bite," I smiled. "It's only for one night. You'll get over it and I promise not to tell." I ducked into the bathroom before he could throw a pillow at me. Once in bed, the clacking sound of the old ceiling fan finally lulled me into oblivion. It had been a long day.

~

I slept like a log and felt like one the next morning. I stood in the narrow shower allowing the tepid water to sooth my sore muscles and wash the salty night-sweat from my body. No desert views could be seen from the sealed frosted-glass window near the sink. I toweled dry and stepped out into our tiny room.

"What the hell is this mattress made of?" Nick grumped as he sat on the side of the bed. "I feel like I just spent the night on a waffle iron."

"No wonder." I said, lifting the fitted bottom sheet. "We slept on box springs only—no mattress."

"No mattress!" Nick rolled his eyes. "No wonder I feel like shit.

Too bad we didn't bring our sleeping bags in for a little fifty-dollar cushion."

I grimaced and leaning my head towards the bathroom. "Get in there and take a shower. You'll feel better and I can smell breakfast cooking. We don't want to be late."

As we entered the dining trailer across the yard, we discovered we were the only people there. Bud heard us talking and stuck his head around the kitchen door. "Have a squat—breakfast should be ready in a jiff."

"Where are your other guests?" I asked.

"Oh hell—they took off around 5 a.m.—wanted to miss the morning heat ridin' on them bikes. Headed north to Salt Lake for a big rally. Coffee's on the side cabinet. Help yourself."

Grabbing a mug of strong black coffee made hours earlier, we took our place at the table. Minutes later, Bud appeared holding our plates full of scrambled eggs with green peppers, sausage, country fried potatoes with onions and a stack of white toast.

"Chow down guys. You'll need some strength if you're plannin' to hike around today." I was starving and couldn't wait to try the delicious smelling sausage.

"Do you have any fruit or yogurt?" Nick asked.

"Too late. Cacti done flowered in the spring. Fruit's all gone by now—but I got some pickled okra," Bob replied with a smile.

Nick rolled his eyes. "No thanks—I'll pass."

"Wow! This sausage is great. I've never tasted anything like it." I spoke with my mouth full. I hadn't eaten since lunch the day before.

"Made it myself," Bud noted with pride. "Ground prairie dog and javelina meat, chopped desert onions, lard, and some Mexican spices.

"That sounds gross," said Nick shoving it to the side of his plate.

"Hey bud...this ain't the Marriott Hotel. You're in Death Valley at 134 feet below sea-level with temperatures up to 130 degrees. You take what nature has to offer and make the best of it. No one's gonna force you to eat it." Bud turned and stomped out of the trailer and across the yard to the office.

"Nice going, Yogurt-man. I'll eat your sausage if you don't want it."

Nick stared at me in disbelief. "You've got to be kidding."

"No, dude," I smirked, "I'm hungry. If you remember, we missed dinner last night because you made that wrong turn."

"There's something weird happening to you. You're not the same sane person I've been rooming with for the past seven years. What have you done with my roommate and who are you?" Nick demanded.

"I don't know what the hell you're talking about."

Nick sat in his chair and gazed at me deep in thought. "You're the one who wanted to do this road trip," he said. I nodded. "It was you who selected the parks you wanted to see." I continued to nod. "You're the one who made all the reservations."

I held up my hand and he stopped. "Yes," I said, "But you're the one who got the dates screwed up and got us here a day early. So, don't blame me if you're feeling miserable."

"OK...I admit that might have been my fault and I don't know how that even happened. But this trip had better start getting better or I'm heading to Vegas." He paused. "You're welcome to join me."

"Right, dude...now let's go exploring."

Bud met us in the yard. "Be sure and take plenty of water with you. Lots of people have died out there from heat stroke. Desert creatures strip the meat off their bodies and leave the bones to bleach in the sun before the sheriff ever sees the vultures circling for what's left of them." He was shaking his head as he headed to the kitchen to clean the dishes.

"Thanks for the cheery advice," Nick said, "But I think we know how to take care of ourselves. And by the way...that room doesn't have a mattress on the so-called bed. I don't know how you can legally call this place a bed and breakfast—more like "springs and garbage."

Bud wasn't smiling and I was totally embarrassed as I headed for the car and didn't look back.

"Stinky's going to hear about those remarks—you can be damn sure about that," I blurted as he got in the car.

"Look, let's just forget Bud and Stinky and go hunt for your treasure."

"Wait a minute. How do you know about the treasure?"

Nick wiggled his eyebrows and smiled. "You talk in your sleep."

Chapter Three

We decided to spend the morning hiking around Death Valley, visiting all the tourist attractions since we couldn't check in at the lodge until later in the day. It was after one o'clock when we stopped for a rest. Sitting under one of the few large trees in the park, drinking water, and taking a break from the scalding heat, I noticed a shiny object partially hidden at the base of a large boulder.

I started to say something, but Nick was leaning against the tree with his eyes closed snoring like a buzz saw. He was exhausted from lack of sleep the night before on the firm box-springs we had shared as a bed. I knew from college experience not to wake him—it would only serve to stir his foul mood.

Quietly I stood and moved towards the metal object catching the sunlight. Making sure there were no scorpions or snakes nearby, I crawled under the overhanging rock and picked it up. The metal surface was smooth and cool to the touch as I held it in my hands.

The object was lightweight and measured about ten inches. On closer inspection, the strange tube appeared to have an iridescent metallic glow. I had studied metallurgy in college but couldn't place the type of metal used. I wondered where it had come from. Perhaps someone hid it for safe keeping or dropped it by mistake and it rolled under the bolder.

As I turned the tube-like object in my hands, my eyes were quick to notice what appeared to be three circles or recessed buttons in a straight line. There were symbols, like hieroglyphic markings beside each button that resembled Egyptian or Mayan writings, but I couldn't be sure. Although I had worked in the Mayan ruins, I never got the hang of the symbols they used for written words.

I glanced over at the tree where I had left Nick, he had studied Egyptian writings in his astronomy classes, but he wasn't there. "Nick! Where the hell are you?" I hollered standing there feeling deserted and alone in the rugged landscape surrounded by sizzling hot rock formations.

"Nick!" I yelled louder in a panicked voice.

"Hey, dude, knock it off. Can't a guy have a little privacy to take a piss?" he said from behind one of the boulders.

I dropped the strange object into my backpack and hung it on my shoulder as he rounded the large cluster of rocks.

"Sorry I frightened you. You had your back to me and I didn't think I needed your permission to take a leak," Nick said. "How about we head back to the lodge, have some lunch, and take a swim. I think this heat has affected your brain." He shouldered his back-pack and we trudged our way for a quarter mile back to where we had left the car sitting in the sun.

"Ouch. Damn this seat's hotter than hell," I yelped.

Nick laughed and tossed me a beach towel from the back of the trunk. "Use this to cover the seat. It should help until the A/C cools it down inside."

"How can you sit on that hot seat? Your ass must be made of

asbestos," I said. He shook his head and smiled ignoring my comment.

"I'm done with hiking for the day. Ready to hit the pool and cool off—maybe even take a siesta. Hope you reserved a room with two beds. Otherwise you'll be sleeping on the floor in your bed roll tonight," Nick smiled.

"All the reservations I made were for two beds. Last night was just a screw-up and it wasn't my fault...so get over it."

Nick was pissed with my attitude so I decided not to mention the metal object until I had more time to study it.

When we arrived at the lodge, he waited in the car while I went to check us in. I was greeted by a stocky woman with blazing red hair pulled back in a ponytail. A narrow leather cord hanging around her neck held a large turquoise pendant almost hidden in the suntanned cleavage of her ample bosom. "Welcome to Furnace Creek Inn and Resort. How can I help you?" she asked.

"We need to check in and I hope we're still in time for lunch." I handed her the reservation confirmation.

"Mr. O'Donnell." She smiled as she checked the registration book. "Looks like you're a day late, but I still have your room available. Unfortunately, I have to charge you for the two night's lodging."

"Excuse me?" I questioned, "The gentleman on duty last night said we were a day early and he didn't have an empty room until today."

"Well I'm sorry to disagree, sweetheart, but it shows here on your confirmation," pointing as she handed it back to me, "that you were supposed to be here yesterday." I studied the confirmation carefully and she was correct. Was I too tired to notice it last night?

"My name's Lucy Balls and I own this here inn along with my husband Harry who was on duty last night. "Harry," she hollered out... "Leave that damned TV for five minutes and come help us out."

"What's up sugar?" he replied standing in the doorway to the back office.

"This here is Mr. O'Donnell who was supposed to check in last night. He says that a man here told him he was a day early and we didn't have his room available."

Harry extended his hand, "Harry Balls the name," It took all the control I could manage, to keep from laughing out loud, as he noticed the expression on my face. "That's all right sonny, I get that look all the time—I'm used to it. Grew up with it and busted a few heads over it. I had the evening shift last night as I usually do," he said, glancing at Lucy, "but I never saw you. Who was this man you spoke to?"

"I didn't get his name, but his friend Bud from the Bob Cat B&B called him Stinky. He called from that phone on your desk to see if he had an empty room for one night."

"What did he look like?" Lucy questioned.

"Sort of an old geezer—bout six feet tall with dirty gray hair, and a few missing coffee-stained teeth and dirty fingernails. That's about all I can remember."

Lucy and Harry looked at each other and shook their heads. "No one around here by that name or that description either and the Bob Cat's been closed over two years, ever since old Bud wandered off in the desert during the night and was never seen again. Had Alzheimer's bad. Sheriff never even found his bones."

"But I'm telling you, we spent the night there last night and had breakfast this morning," I stated firmly with a confused look on my face and my head tilted at a slight angle—as if to ask—*What are you not understanding?*

"That's impossible," they said in unison.

"That place burned to the ground two years ago sweetie," Lucy added.

"Got struck by a small meteor what set the propane tanks ablaze. It was all the buzz here in the valley for weeks—made headlines in the Valley News. Nothin's left now but the foundations," she sighed staring at me with a skeptical eye.

I couldn't believe what I was hearing. My stomach started to churn. Something pretty strange was happening and I needed time to chat with Nick about it. I know I'm not going crazy—but a little reassurance couldn't hurt.

Lucy patted my hand on the counter and with great concern on her face said in a quiet voice, "Sweetheart, let me show you to your room and you and your friend can get a bite to eat in the restaurant. Its three o'clock now, but they serve lunch until four then get ready for the dinner crowd at eight. I think you've been out in this heat too much."

Harry agreed with her. "Yes sir...the desert heat can play some mighty strange tricks on people. I've known some who said they saw space ships landin' and takin' off, and others who said they were abducted by aliens and returned to earth. Must'a been rejects," he chuckled. "There's always someone with a crazy tale to tell around the campfire at night."

Patrick followed Lucy out of the office and tapped on the car window to wake Nick, who had dozed off while he kept the engine running and the car cool in case they needed to drive to Baker for lunch. He rolled the window down.

"Follow us over to the room. We'll turn the A/C on and go have lunch in the restaurant."

I motioned to Nick.

"Is something wrong?" Nick asked. "You sound really strange like you're off in never-never land."

I could see flames in his shining black eyes as he stared at me with a questioning expression on his face. I shook my head—must have been my imagination. "I'll fill you in on the details over lunch, but you're not going to believe it. Do we still have that map to the Bob Cat B&B?"

"I think it's in the glove compartment," he reached to open it. "Don't tell me we have to go back there again," Nick winced as he rummaged in the compartment. "Did you leave something in the room?"

"Don't look for it now. I'll explain later," I continued to whisper so Lucy couldn't hear.

The room had two beds and Nick was happy. Leaving the luggage in the room we took our backpacks with us and moseyed over to the restaurant. There weren't many people eating at that hour, so we found a table in the corner. Nick attempted to eat his Caesar salad while I related the strange mystery about our reservations to him. I pushed my order of barbecue ribs around on my plate, having lost my appetite.

"So—you want to go back and find the B&B?" he said between bites.

"Of course I do. Aren't you even curious to know if it's there?"

"Dude, I know it's there. I still have the marks on my butt from those damn box springs to prove it."

I gave him a pleading glance. "It won't take long and maybe we will find some answers to what is going on."

Chapter Four

I searched the glove compartment in the car but there was no sign of the map that Stinky had given us. My memory is pretty good and I was sure I could find the right roads. I gave instructions to Nick: "Two miles down the main road and make a left, then three miles and make right." Driving slowly, Nick followed directions. "It should be just past that pile of rocks, close to that big tree on the left."

Nick slowed the car to a crawl as we stopped at the small, barely readable weathered sign nailed to a leaning termite rotted four-by-four, and we viewed what remained of the Bob Cat B&B. Our jaws dropped as we read each other's expressions of disbelief. We pulled onto the dirt drive and stopped. Stepping out of the car we stared in denial, shaking our heads at the faded black charred remains scattered on the old foundations.

"This can't be the place," Nick finally exclaimed while I was busy scouring the ground under the large tree. "What the hell are you looking for?" Nick growled with impatience.

"Tire tracks," I uttered in return. "Remember the motor cycles that were parked here last night?" Nick nodded and stared in silence. Unfortunately, the sand and small rocks were undisturbed—no tire tracks could be found. It appeared untouched—not even a foot print. The smooth grains of sand were void of any recent signs of life. I was speechless—and for me, that is rare.

Wrapping my head around what had taken place with the mysterious Mr. Stinky, the date changes on our confirmation letter, the place where we stayed the night—now only charred remains of a B&B destroyed two years ago, made it sounded like a Rod Serling story out of the *Twilight Zone*.

And then there was Bud—the man with Alzheimer's who went missing two years ago and the five bikers that we never heard leave early that morning. There were numerous questions without any answers.

"Let's go back to the lodge for a swim. This heat is draining all my energy," Nick grumbled as he headed for the car and cranked up the air conditioning.

We drove back to the room without speaking, both lost in thought. A note was pinned to our room door when we returned. Lucy had a message for me at the office. "You go ahead to the pool and I'll see what this is about."

Harry Balls saw me coming before Lucy did. "You didn't believe us did you?" he mocked with shifty eyes and a head that bobbed like it was on a spring. "Had to go check it out for yourself."

"Leave the poor man alone Harry," came Lucy's voice from the back office. Can't you tell he's mixed up? Don't pay him no mind sweetie. He thinks he's in control of the universe, but he keeps me warm on cold nights so I let him think what he wants. I'm the one with the brains in this outfit."

I wasn't sure where this conversation was leading but thought I would change the direction quickly, "You left a note on our door about some message for me."

"Oh...that's right, you had a visitor while you were out—said his name was Kaleb. At least I think that's what he said—a tall man, about six-two, with a bald head, and dark skin like your friend. He had piercing hazel eyes and spoke in a strange accent that sounded hollow like one of those recordings on an answering machine. Kind of gave me the willies if you want to know the truth."

"Sorry but I don't know anyone by that name or description," I muttered, as my mind floated in a haze.

"Well, he certainly sounded like he knew you. Said you have something that belongs to him and he would meet you later to pick it up. He also said I should warn you not to try and use it—whatever it is. I offered him a pen and some paper but he didn't want to take his gloves off to write the message down—just made me promise to tell you."

"I'm sure the man's mistaken me for someone else," I uttered, searching my memory for any recognition of the name or description.

"Well I'm not the kind of person to say 'I told you so,' but just remember who gave you the message," she admonished.

"Thanks for the warning. I think I'll join Nick at the pool and cool off."

"Good idea, sweetie. Be sure and put some sunscreen on—with that fair skin of yours, you'll burn to a crisp in no time." I nodded in agreement and hurried off to change into a swimsuit and find Nick. Sipping margaritas while submerged in the crystal-clear refreshing water of the pool should have been relaxing. However, the unexplained, inconceivable, freakish events over the past twenty-four hours had me twisted in knots.

I waited until dinner that evening to tell Nick about the message. No point in spoiling his margarita magic-moments while in the comfort of the cool waters. Nick appeared intrigued and concerned about the mysterious person who had left the message. "What do you have that belongs to him?" he queried, "and how did he know where to find you?"

"Got me, dude," I shrugged. "I don't even know who the guy is or where he comes from. I was trying to think all afternoon around the pool but couldn't come up with any answers."

Nick got a faraway look in his eyes staring into the space between us—not really seeing me on the opposite side of the table. His next questions surprised me. "Did Lucy say what he looked like?"

I explained Lucy's description of the guy and watched as Nick's brow furrowed and a dark frown crossed his face. "How did he spell his name?"

"How the hell should I know, man? He didn't write it down. Lucy said he wouldn't take his gloves off to write the message. Why? What difference does the way he spells his name make?"

Nick was shaking his head. "It's a long story and I'm not sure I can talk about it. I thought...but I guess it doesn't matter what I thought."

I placed my hand on Nick's shoulder, "Hey man. It's OK. You don't have to solve this mystery—but answer just one question. Do you think you know who this guy is?"

He nodded in response. "And believe me—we need to be on guard. He may appear to be friendly but he's not. He can be dangerous. I'll fill you in on the details in the morning. Meanwhile, I need to contact some people and see what I can learn."

"Good luck with that," I offered. "We're in a cell phone *dead zone*. But maybe Lucy or Harry will let you use the phone at the office."

"Don't worry. I just have to drive a short distance to make contact. Hang out with the other guests at the campfire tonight until I get back."

"Are you saying that I shouldn't be alone?" I mumbled, wrinkling my forehead as a foreboding chill engulfed my body.

"That's exactly what I'm saying—at least until I can find out what's going on. I'll explain what I can later. Be sure to keep your backpack with you. Don't leave anything in the room, and settle the bill tonight. We'll leave before dawn tomorrow."

I nodded in agreement. What else was I supposed to do? My National Parks vacation adventure was rapidly turning into a reality mystery with quirky, phantom individuals and now a sinister and possibly threatening character.

Nick scooted around the booth and placed his arm across my shoulders. "Trust me, dude."

Chapter Five

Sitting around the campfire as the desert cooled off for the night, several guests and a few neighbors were more than eager to share their travel experiences. My mind was elsewhere, wandering through the strange happenings since our arrival in Death Valley.

Lucy strolled around the pool to the fire pit, took a seat beside me and began to chat in a whisper so as not to disturb the guest telling his story. "I went to your room but you weren't there." She surveyed the guests. "Where's your friend?"

"Oh... he took a short drive to see if he could get a cell phone signal—needed to check in with his family."

Lucy scooted closer. "Well I thought you might want to know what I discovered at our ladies' poker club today. I'm not sure everything those old biddies gossip about can be taken for the honest to gosh truth, but you never know."

I was staring into space. "I'm sorry Lucy—I have a thousand things tumbling around in my head right now. What were you saying about poker?"

She glanced at me and smiled. "Not about poker honey—it's about the man you say you saw in our office last night and I thought I should share it with you."

"So, there was a man and it wasn't our imagination."

Lucy grimaced and shook her head. "Well not exactly."

I crossed my arms, "So—what does 'not exactly' mean?" I said with a smirk.

"Well—I don't know how you're gonna take this but here goes. I was tellin' the ladies your story about the man you said was here the night when you tried to check in. They was sittin' on the edge of their seats with cards laid flat on the table, ears perked up like little Chihuahuas. Then Pip...that's short for Priscilla." She said...

"That sounds like the old miner. Remember that scruffy old codger who used to come around now and then, pullin' his mule behind him?"

"Wait a minute. You mean there really is an old man and I didn't just make it up?" I said.

"No, no," she patted my knee. "Just listen to me for a minute. There used to be an old prospector who wandered through the valley searching for gold. Bud over at the Bob Cat and he became friends. Bud would feed him and let him rest up when he was around. They used to sit on the porch at the BC and jabber away till the wee hours of the morning. But after Bud wandered off, we never saw the old man again. Some said he was in the Bob Cat the night it got hit by the meteor, but the sheriff never found any remains. They both just up and disappeared."

I gave her a questioning glance. "So—Stinky and Bud both vanished without any trace."

Lucy nodded with a sigh and stood up. "Sure looks that way, sweetie. We never knew the prospector's name, but Pip used to put out some of her husband's old clothes for him and saw him once or twice up close when he'd leave her a tiny nugget of gold in their place."

This sad bit of news only added to my confusion as Lucy headed back to the office. I glanced around the group of remaining guests that now numbered only three couples and two single women traveling together. Car lights flashed casting eerie shadows of the local cacti on the buildings as someone arrived—it was Nick.

I breathed a sigh of relief. It was time to turn in for the night. I would tell him about the prospector tomorrow at breakfast. Sleep tonight would be needed for the journey tomorrow as we headed to Utah and Zion National Park. For now, the metal object I found in Death Valley would remain my secret—at least until I had time to study it closer.

~

Pitch black is the only way to describe the desert at five in the morning during the month of September. Fall was in the air over San Bernardino County, California, but its stretching tendrils had yet to reach the pockmark on the face of the earth known as Death Valley. As silently as possible, we departed from The Furnace Creek Inn heading to the small town of Baker and an early breakfast.

At night, the desert-scape takes on a desolate foreboding shroud of the deepest dark black velvet. Driving on single-lane roads, one encounters little or no traffic. On cloudless evenings, the multitude of stars twinkle in the distant atmosphere. Car lights shine in the staring eyes of small desert dwelling creatures hiding off to the side of the road. An occasional coyote or mouse will scurry across the pavement in the headlights, but the bleakness of the desert night can play tricks on a person's vision while enveloping them in a sense of loneliness and abandonment.

I insisted that Nick stop at the world's tallest thermometer on Baker Boulevard and take my picture so I could send it to my mom. The thermometer at 41 meters tall is an electric sign built in 1991 at a cost of $700,000. It commemorates the record-breaking temperature of 134 degrees Fahrenheit in Death Valley on July 10, 1913. I hadn't been able to send mom a text without any signal in the valley and I knew the photo would put a smile on her face.

Pausing to fill the gas tank at a Shell station, we spied a fast-food place a short distance up the road and pulled in for breakfast. Denny's is open 24 hours a day but at that hour of the morning only a few die-hard truck drivers were filling up on green chili stew, breakfast steaks, mashed potatoes, biscuits, and anything containing carbs before hitting the road for the long haul to their next stop. Our personal destination was at a distance of over 350 miles. With stops for lunch and to stretch our legs and do some sightseeing, I estimated it would take us about eight or nine hours to reach Zion.

As I drove northeast, the morning sun slowly began to change the color of the sky to a soft apricot, brushed with wisps of golden clouds, adding a stark contrast to the grayness of the desert still hidden in muted shadows and rock formations etched with black crevasses.

The vast desert plain consists of sand, rocks, and cactus, with only four nondescript pitstops, sporting motels and casinos, that can be missed in the blink of an eye. There is little to draw one's attention between Baker, California and Las Vegas, Nevada. The highway cuts through the city on the west side of the Las Vegas Strip.

Multiple tall hotels and casinos line the famous South Las Vegas Boulevard as monuments to the world of greed and indulgence. I hardly cast an eye in that direction as the traffic had become crowded, requiring my attention to maneuver the highway in our route to Zion National Park.

We squeaked through Las Vegas on Interstate Highway 15 without stopping to gamble a dime and I waved goodbye to the poor gamblers who were sucked into the one-arm bandits, roulette wheels, and games of chance. I was driving after breakfast so Nick could get some sleep. He had been up most of the night working on the new laptop his folks had dropped off on their last visit with us. It was a brand I had never heard of and had more bells and whistles than even Bill Gates could imagine.

Once Nick was awake I filled him in on some of the strange fireside stories from last night and the tale about the old prospector that Lucy had heard from Pip, her lady poker friend. He didn't show much interest so I let it pass. Something was bugging him but I knew better than to pressure him for information about his contacts last night. He would tell me when he was ready. Four years as roommates in college and three years living together in New Mexico, most people would think we knew all there was to know about each other, but to be honest, we really didn't.

Nick's large family, of six brothers and four sisters, was from Tibet. He was raised in the remote mountain village of Ngari, also known as *the roof of the world* located at 4,500 meters above sea level. Ngari is surrounded by lakes, rivers, glaciers, vast grasslands, and views of spectacular snow-covered mountains. I never thought he looked at all like someone from Tibet.

Nick didn't have an Asian profile. He reminded me of an Egyptian priest—tall and muscular—with shiny cocoa-colored skin, black hair, and large hands. His father had the same strong features, while his mother, though tall and slender, was blessed with strands of silver hair that glistened like tiny jewels when she moved her head.

One night, during midterm, while sitting at a local bar in Austin, drinking far too many shots of tequila, I asked Nick what his father did for a living. Not that I wanted to pry, but I was curious. He gave me a look as if to say, *it's none of your business*—then smiled.

"I suppose you could say he's a diplomat. But I can't really discuss his work because of diplomatic regulations. I'm sure you understand," he said in a serious tone. And of course, being the intelligent, although inebriated student I was at the time, I decided to drop the subject. Questions not asked are rarely answered. A profound statement if I do say so myself.

Chapter Six

As I drove into St. George, Utah, Nick stirred in his seat, stretching and yawning. "Where are we man?" he murmured, rubbing the sleep from his eyes.

"St. George, Utah. How was your little nap?" I needled sarcastically. "You missed your chance to gamble in Vegas, dude."

Yawning once again he smiled and vigorously rubbed his wavy hair. "Life's a gamble, my friend, and those hours of nap as you call them made up for the ones I missed last night."

"Oh God—is it going to be one of those days of profound intellectual statements?" Before he could answer, I asked, "Are you ready to stop for lunch and switch places?"

His eyes opened wide. "Wow that's one big building up ahead."

"That's the St. George Mormon Temple," I said. "But you didn't answer my question. Are you hungry?"

"Sure. Let's find a place to eat and then come back and see if they offer a tour of the temple. That building reminds me of..." he stopped midsentence.

My curiosity bell ran with anticipation. "Of what?" I asked.

"Oh—nothing. It was just a childhood dream," he said as his voice faded in thought.

I finally found George's Corner Restaurant on North 100 Street. A friend in Las Cruces had said it was a cool place for lunch, so it was added to my list of things to do in St. George. The place was a busy hangout, full of college students from Dixie State University with typical pub grub, burgers, and beers accompanied by promising young entertainers strumming their guitars.

After lunch we had a chat with the musicians and I paid our check while Nick stepped into the restroom. Rather than wait inside, I went to start the car and get the air conditioning going. Studying the map while the car cooled, I glance up to see a tall, bald-headed man standing in front of the car staring straight at me through the windshield. He resembled the description of Kaleb, the guy that Lucy said had left a message for me in Death Valley and he was wearing a pair of black leather gloves.

I reached for my cell phone in the side compartment on the door to take a photo of him but when I looked up he was gone. The driver's door opened and I jumped—it was Nick. "Sorry man—didn't mean to scare you." He slipped behind the wheel, "Thanks for putting the air on. Where to next?" he asked backing up and heading for the parking lot exit.

In my head, I was still trying to figure out what happened to the man in front of the car—how did he vanish in the blink of an eye just as Nick appeared? "I'm not sure," I mumbled.

"Not sure where we are going or not sure which street to get us back to the Temple. You promised we would see if it was open for a tour, remember?"

"Oh shit—I'm sorry—yes, we're on North 100—make a left out the exit and go to 500 South and make a right. That should get us close enough that we can see the temple and figure it out from there."

"Are you OK, dude? You sound like you're miles away wandering through the canyons in your mind."

"Yeah—right—someone should write a song about it."

"They did, dude—so out with it. What's bugging you? All that crazy stuff back at Death Valley? If you asked me, those people do that stuff to promote the 'Woo-woo factor' to sell the tired hikers and unsuspecting tourists on attending their campfire ghost stories."

"Are you saying that those strange things never happened in Death Valley? We never slept on those damned box springs and ate javelina sausage? You're telling me that Stinky and Bud weren't real people?" I asked with astonishment.

"Not in those exact words, but think about it. Strange weird things happen all over the world all the time. People see flying saucers and little green men with big eyes from outer space. They follow moving specks of illumination across the dark sky only to see them suddenly vanish in a flash. These things are not paranormal—they're normal reactions. People want attention and some will do anything to get it. Who's to say what's normal anymore?

"I'm not saying it's right and I'm not saying it's wrong—and I can't honestly say none of it is true. Everything in the universe happens for a reason. We don't always know what the reason is, but nothing happens at random," he stated with conviction.

"There's the temple. Make a left here. Sorry—I didn't mean to interrupt your lecture." I rolled my eyes. He smiled back and chuckled raising one eyebrow.

"Too much?" he asked.

"Yeah... but I got the message. Thanks."

"Professor Niki Yangkey Se will give you a test after we tour the temple and have absorbed the knowledge of the Second Great

Awakening."

"Well, since we weren't around for the first I'm not sure it will do much good, but I'm willing to give it a try," I smirked.

"And how do you know I wasn't around for the first?" he said in his deepest secretive voice.

My eyes lit up and a smile crossed my lips, "Yeah, right. I can't wait to hear this story, dude."

Chapter
Seven

We toured the temple in silence listening through earphones to the recording as it described in detail the beautiful interior spaces. However, I was having some difficulty with Nick's last remark. He was joking of course, but his profound knowledge about the universe and the people of the human race was obviously true. There are a lot of crazy insecure people all over the world. Many of whom believe the happenings that their minds have allowed them to create.

I remember reading somewhere that *there is a thin line between genius and madness.* My mother would swear I was a genius, but my father believed I had crossed over that line.

Being a lawyer, he made politics his career of choice. Mom refused to be a politician's wife and filed for a divorce. She was tickled that I was not a chip off the old "block-head." Of course, that's a family joke, but only Mom and I still laugh about it.

I like the career I've selected. I enjoy studying old bones, ancient artifacts and civilizations, vanished cultures, and historical happenings. Putting together pieces of a puzzle that tell a story of life long ago takes time, patience and an immense amount of research.

Leaving the temple feeling newly awakened, we made our way back to State Road 9 and headed east to Zion National Park. I didn't have a specific agenda other than just to enjoy the monumental rock formations of amber, gold, and red that created the scenic views.

Flannigan's Inn in Zion had our rooms ready. A very cute young girl with a great smile and a pleasant voice processed our information. I was mesmerized by her sparkling brown eyes with flecks of gold that seemed to dance as she spoke, and her golden hair pulled back in a ponytail that bounced when she turned her head. Her voice made a sound like tiny bells or a distant wind chime. It was a relaxing sound.

Standing at the registration desk, waiting for our room keys, I glanced at the mirror on the wall behind the desk and froze. I saw a reflection of the bald-headed man who had stared at me outside the restaurant in St. George. I nudged Nick, who was in conversation with the young lady.

"What's up, dude?"

Not saying a word, I twisted my head and tilted it towards the mirror. Nick followed my lead and looked up.

"What?"

"It's him," I whispered as if I thought he might hear me.

"Him who?" Nick asked, whispering back with a blank look on his face.

I glanced back at the mirror. He was gone. I turned and searched the small lobby but he was nowhere in sight.

"I saw him—plain as day. He was standing right there by the door. It was Kaleb—or at least, the man we think is Kaleb."

"You wait here and get the room keys. I'll check outside." Nick hurried out the entrance door.

The young lady retrieved our keys and returned to the desk. "Here are your keys, Mr. O'Donnell. I put two in the envelope and there was a message waiting for Nick in the key box." She handed the envelopes to me. "This is a map of the Inn and your room is located in building C, past the pool to the back of the complex. It's a nice quiet space with a private terrace and some great views."

Nick had not returned, so I listened to the girl's instructions explaining, on the map, where everything was located. "Please enjoy your stay with us and if there is anything you need just ask— my name's Cheryl," she smiled seductively.

"Oh brother, that's all I need right now—two people pursuing me," I mumbled to myself.

"Did you say something?" Cheryl queried.

"Uh no, thank you Cheryl, we'll be just fine I'm sure." Nick walked into the lobby turning his head side-to-side searching for our mysterious stalker. I met him halfway across the lobby.

"Follow me out of here. I'll show you where our room is...and watch out for the cute young tiger at the check-in desk. I think she's on the prowl—'*if there's anything you need just ask,*' " I mimicked and gave him a wink.

Nick chuckled, "I thought she had an eye for you, you handsome fox."

"Don't give me any of that shit, dude. You were the one who struck up the conversation in the first place."

"*We've been on the road so long—you sure are a sight for sore eyes.*"

"Where did you come up with a line like that? Sounds like something Bob Hope would have said to Dorothy Lamour in the old *Road to Rio* movie."

"Hey, don't knock my old movies—they're classics, dude."

"Speaking of classics, did you find the invisible man or did he vanish into thin air?" I asked.

The banter and jokes had been our way of escaping the reality of the pendulum swinging over our heads. Nick thinks he knows who the man may be. However, he hasn't revealed this secret and it is starting to set my nerves on edge, but I promised I would wait until he was sure of his identification.

It was getting near dark as Nick took his turn in the shower. I was dressing in the room when the phone rang. Who would be calling us on the room phone? We both have our cells with us and no one knows where we are. I walked slowly to the desk reaching for the phone but hesitated to pick up the receiver. I feel like Grace Kelly in *Dial M for Murder*—what the hell am I afraid of? And why are all these old movies popping into my head?

On the eighth ring, I picked up the receiver as I looked behind me, searching to see if someone was hiding behind the drapes at the French doors. "Hello?"

Silence filled the room. There was a click and the line went dead. I hung up then picked it up again and punched the button for the front desk. "Did someone just try to put a call through to this room?"

"Not to my knowledge, Mr. O'Donnell. Hold on and I'll check with the operator."

Nick stepped out of the bathroom. "Who just called? I heard the phone ringing." I put my finger to my lips to silence him.

The clerk's voice came back on. "Sorry to make you wait, but it was an outside call and it appears the caller disconnected the call before the line was answered."

"Do you know the number of the person who placed the call?"

"I'm sorry, sir, but we don't have a record of that. We only keep records of internal calls."

"Thank you." I said, hanging up the receiver as I stared at Nick with a questioning look.

"What?" he exclaimed.

"How did you hear the phone ringing all the way in the shower with the bathroom door closed?"

"So, what am I guilty of? Can I help it if I have sensitive hearing?" he shrugged.

"Sorry, I'm just on edge tonight. Whoever it was hung up. Get dressed and let's go eat."

Chapter Eight

We finished an early breakfast the next morning, and as we crossed the lobby to join the hiking group, we ran into Cheryl, the cute girl behind the counter when we registered.

Putting on her sexy smile she hurried to catch us. "Hi guys! Going hiking today?"

"Yep, we're taking the tour that starts at eight o'clock. Want'a come along?" Nick asked.

"Sorry," she frowned, looking at me instead of Nick. "I've got to work. But I tried to call you last night to see if you wanted to join us at the local saloon down the road. You must have been out because no one answered." Her beautiful eyes danced with those flecks of gold as she looked directly at me.

I must have turned three shades of red as Nick gave me a suspicious sideways glance. "Yeah, too bad, we were probably having dinner," he said, giving her a wink as I rolled my eyes in disbelief.

"I've got some night courses at Dixie U this evening but I hope

I'll see you tomorrow before you leave." She couldn't stop staring at me with a smile on her face as if she knew something that I didn't.

"Sure," Nick replied as she headed for the registration desk with a backward glance over her shoulder and a flip of her golden hair.

"See you tomorrow," she called, as tinkling bells sounded in the distance.

"Not a word. Not one word," I commented as we joined the hiking group for the tour.

"Did I say anything?" Nick asked with a look of amusement.

"No, but I know what you were thinking," I smirked.

"You're kidding!" he said looking astonished.

The hiking trail began at the end of the parking lot. There must have been about thirty people of all ages, shapes, and sizes. Everyone had their backpacks stocked with plenty of water, sunscreen, and the forever useful sweat towel.

Sunglasses and hats or caps were recommended. Cameras and iPhones were hung around necks and stuck in pockets. Two ladies carried umbrellas to protect their delicate skin. It was a multilingual group with people from various parts of the world. Several people were equipped with mini-recorders and ear phones with a version of the tour in various languages. The park ranger issued trail maps with information written in four different languages.

Nick and I hung out at the rear of the hikers as they moved like a school of fish from one point to another while the ranger offered his monologue. The canyon had been carved by a rushing stream, creating rugged rocky cliffs and stone outcroppings in colors of ochre, orange, pink, and red, the perfect invitation for an artist's paint brush, and there were several artists standing at their easels along the stream's edge, capturing their personal vision on canvas in the clear morning light.

I paused in the middle of the path. "Now what's wrong?" Nick asked.

"Have you ever had the feeling you're being watched, but you can't see who's watching you?" I whispered.

"I know the feeling you mean. I can sense his presence too," Nick agreed.

"What does he want? I'm not rich. I doubt my father would pay a ransom if I were kidnapped. I don't carry any valuables and I don't have any drugs. What else could he be looking for?"

"If it's who I think it is, he won't give up until he gets what he's after. You must have something he wants or he wouldn't be hanging around."

We now stood some fifty yards from the last hiker in our group. As I started to protest my words fell like a short safety line to a drowning man. "But I haven't got..."

And then as if struck by lightning I remembered the object I found in Death Valley, still hidden away in my backpack. "No, that's impossible. At least I think it is. How would he know?"

"Dude, you're not making any sense—you're talking in circles. What are you trying to say?"

"I can't show you here," I stammered. "I found something when we were hiking in Death Valley and was going to show you once we checked in to our room, but when all the strange things started happening it didn't seem important."

Extremely agitated with my confession, Nick's brow furrowed in deep concentration. "What did you find?"

"I don't really know what it is, but I'll show you when we get back to the room."

For the next hour of the hike we hardly spoke to each other. Nick was trying to read my mind and I was doing my best to think of more archeological things. The guide pointed out Indian signs that were etched into the stone walls bordering the trail and pointed to caves on the opposite side of the stream that served as dwellings centuries in the past.

Both of us kept our eyes open searching for any sign of the disappearing stalker. Someone in our group pointed to a ridge high above us and clicked a photo with his camera as he asked the ranger, "How'd that guy get up there. Is that where this trail takes us?"

The hikers all gazed up the steep rocky side of the hill but no one was there. "Shouldn't be anyone up there," said the guide. "That trail's been closed since last year's rains washed most of it down the side of this cliff. It's too dangerous for any hikers until we can get it repaired."

"But I'm sure I saw someone up there," the man insisted.

"Impossible," the guide said. "You probably saw the movement of an animal, maybe one of the mountain goats that live around here. Anyone up there would have to have wings or hooves to scale that path."

The tour was finished and we had turned around to head back to the inn. Nick caught up with the man who said he saw someone on the closed trail. "Did you get a shot of whatever you saw on the ledge back there?"

The guy shrugged and reached for the camera hanging around his neck. "I think so. Let's take a look."

"There he is, standing on the edge," the man remarked, showing Nick the photo. Nick peered at me over the top of his dark sunglasses, his face hidden in the shadow of his red baseball cap, and gave an imperceptible nod as I read his thoughts.

He patted the guy on the shoulder. "Thanks bud," he said as the man rushed to catch up with the ranger and show him the photo.

We lagged behind as the group moved on ahead. The ranger needed to make a report about the person on the closed trail. "Looks to me like the vulture is circling. Our stalker knows every move we make. It's time to fess-up, dude. I can't help if you keep me in the dark," Nick implored.

I folded my arms across my chest and huffed, "As I said before, I was going to show you earlier but with the mixed-up reservations, people disappearing, a B&B that vanished overnight and a strange man delivering weird messages, my little discovery paled in comparison."

Nick was getting insistent. "Well, we're in the labyrinth now and it's time we opened Pandora's Box to see if we can find our way out of this maze."

I decided it was my turn to flip the page on Nick. "Remember when you left me to join the guests around the campfire at the lodge while you drove off to find a phone signal? You said you needed to contact someone about this man but you never said who. Not once have you said who you think this man is and how you might know him. You haven't been yourself on this trip and you appear to be hiding something from me as well. I think it's time we both came clean."

Nick shook his head. "It's not as easy as that. I've wanted to tell you for a long time now, but I need permission from the Council. I've spent seven years getting to know you, learning all about you and all that time you've never pried into my background. You know very little about me and yet we've become close friends."

I wasn't sure where this conversation was going as I tried to wrap my head around what he had just said. I thought I knew Nick, but realized what he said was true. Perhaps I only knew what he wanted me to know. Who is this person I have lived with for the past seven years? Why has he spent this time getting to know all about me? And who or what is this Council he speaks of.

As if reading my thoughts, Nick continued, "I'm waiting to hear from my father. He's speaking to the Council on our behalf. I contacted him again last night and he's aware of the man who follows us and of the dangers he represents to our mission and to humanity. I can't say any more right now and may already have said too much, but I know I can trust you and that goes both ways."

Chapter Nine

Back in or room, I placed my backpack on my bed as we sat facing each other. Opening the top zipper, I reached in and pulled out the metal cylinder I had wrapped in a sweat towel for protection and handed it to Nick. His onyx eyes glistened with surprise. He opened his mouth but words escaped him. He turned it around in his hands feeling the smoothness of its surface as he inspected every inch.

He stared directly at me and without moving his lips, he spoke with his thoughts, and his voice filled the room. "*Where did you get this?*"

Astounded that I could hear his thoughts as clear as if he had spoken them, I answered, "*That's what I found in the desert while you were asleep under that big tree.*" I was stunned—I can't believe I just said that without opening my mouth. We were conversing in a form of telepathy. A chill ran up my spine. Was Nick actually able to read my thoughts? How long has he been able to do this?

"Since I was four years old," he said with a smile on his closed lips.

"You bastard," I said—words pouring freely from my mouth. "If you can read my thoughts, then you knew all along that I had found that...that thing," I said pointing my finger at the object in his hands.

He nodded—and speaking in a clear voice, his lips moved. "I knew you had found a treasure. I didn't know what it was but your thoughts told me you considered it a treasure and I knew you would share this find with me when you got the time. However, I'm sure this object is what the man is seeking, but there are two questions the Council will want answered. How it came to be in his possession and how he came to lose it?

"Since you found it, it belongs to you. Remember what I said about destiny? Nothing happens that isn't meant to happen and everything happens for a reason. That being said, I must tell you not to use this tool until you have been given instructions and permission to do so from the Council," he warned.

"Several times today you have mentioned the Council. I'm curious to know—who or what is the Council—and what is this object?" I thought, without speaking aloud, getting the hang of this ESP communication. Nick read these thoughts as he handed my treasure back to me, stood, and crossed the room. Standing by the glass doors to the terrace he answered with his back to me.

"Because you have been chosen, you will know in due time about the Council. All will be revealed and your lessons will commence very soon. The object you hold in your hands is not a toy but a sophisticated scientific instrument that someone with your skills and knowledge of ancient civilizations and cultures will find useful once you know how it works."

He turned with a gleam in his eye. "But right now I'm hungry. Put that tool in your pack and bring it with us. You should never let it be far from you. I'll show you how it fits on your belt later."

In total awe and confusion, I followed his instructions and rolled my treasure in the towel, placing it back in the pack. A sense of excitement swelled within me. I was on the edge of discovery and my journey was about to begin.

The restaurant was busy, but the hostess found us a quiet table in the corner. Our server appeared out of nowhere. "Hi! My name's Jill. I'll be taking care of your table tonight," she spoke in sing-song fashion as she placed the menus on our table. "Can I get you something from the bar?" Jill, with her blonde ponytail and bangs, was a character right out of *Beach Blanket Bingo*. I almost expected Annette Funicello to pop up behind her doing a little tap dance.

"I'll have a Negro Modelo Dark." Nick said.

"Have you got any Bohemia Dark?" I asked.

"No," she said, "We have…"

"Never mind," I interrupted with a wave of my hand, "Make it two Modelos Dark, and bring me the wine list, I feel like celebrating." She smiled with enthusiasm and sashayed off in her white tennies, her ponytail moving from side-to-side with the sway of her hips.

I glanced at Nick, "You will share some wine with me won't you?" I coaxed.

"Sure, but what are we suddenly celebrating?" he asked.

"Your birthday, stupid. Don't you even remember what day it is?"

"Hell…It's been so long ago I completely forgot."

"Come on man—you're not that old—are you?"

"Remember—I've seen both the First and Second Great Awakenings. I may as well start your education with the simple facts first," he chuckled.

"Holy shit!" I said with surprise.

"I certainly hope not," he countered seriously. There was a pause as we stared at each other and together we burst with laughter.

Dinner was great and conversation never stopped. It had been another long day. We were both tired and the altitude and wine had gone to my head. I lay in bed staring at the ceiling as thoughts raced through my head.

"Will you go to sleep so I can get some rest? All those questions will be answered in due time."

"Sorry, dude. I forgot my thoughts would keep you awake. What other unusual talents do you have that we haven't discussed?"

Nick chuckled. "I'm saving those surprises for later. It wouldn't be wise to reveal everything at once. Now go to sleep."

Chapter Ten

The following morning after breakfast we loaded the car. "Shouldn't we check the car over to be sure the stalker hasn't rigged it to blow up?" I hinted.

Nick studied me with exasperation written all over his face. "Dude, the guy doesn't want to blow you up as long as you have something he wants with you. This isn't a James Bond movie. He knows by now we are being watched by others and he won't make a move until he's sure he can retrieve the device you have in your possession. Stick with me and we will get this figured out—remember, we're not alone."

I gave him an inquisitive look. "Well, it sure as hell feels like we're alone. I haven't noticed anyone else trying to help."

"That's because your sensory perception hasn't been fully developed yet. But we're going to work on that starting today. You get to drive first."

Cheryl was at the desk as we checked out. "Hey guys, sorry you have to rush off, a friend of mine is having a party tonight and I wanted to invite you."

"Maybe next time," I said, "but it was nice meeting you and tell Jill thanks for the great service last night."

"Service? Who's Jill and what kind of service did she give you?" she huffed.

"In the restaurant," I said in defense.

"Oh! Of course—I'll tell her," she said with embarrassment as she blushed. Nick winked at her and waved goodbye.

"You're terrible—you know that?" he chuckled, once we were outside and out of hearing range from the reception desk.

"My reputation precedes me," I said, running my fingers through my wavy copper-blond hair as I slid into the driver's seat.

"Bryce Canyon awaits. What mysteries will it reveal?" I wondered. Nick leaned back with his hands behind his head and his eyes closed. As I exited the parking lot our stalker was standing by the exit. I glanced in the rearview mirror to see if he got in a car to follow, but he had vanished in the wink of an eye.

No need to say anything to Nick. With a quick glance he turned and stared through the rear window. I could tell he had already read my mind.

Our driving time was shorter than I had thought, perhaps aided by the lack of early morning traffic. We arrived in Bryce Canyon and checked into the Bryce Canyon Lodge shortly after two o'clock. The lodge reminded me of a cross between a Swiss chalet and a Western-style ranch with an abundance of massive stone fireplaces and a log-cabin atmosphere. There were lodgings in the main building and several individual cabins grouped in a large cluster.

Three clean-cut college students were working at the registration desk. The young man who greeted us was eager to assist. "Good afternoon gentlemen, I'm Marc, how can I assist you?"

"We just need to check in if it's not too early," I said, handing him the printed confirmation.

"Mr. O'Donnell," he mumbled as he typed on his computer keyboard. "Looks like you are good to go. Your requested cabin is ready. I just need some identification and Rob here will show you the way."

"I don't believe I booked a cabin. We were supposed to be in the main lodge in a room with twin beds." I corrected.

"Your request for the up-grade to a cabin was processed yesterday and paid in advance. All our rooms in the main building are filled. I'm sure you'll find the cabin has more privacy as noted in your request and a great view of the canyon."

Glancing at Nick, I was confused. "Did you change our reservations?"

"Dad must have made the change. He's planning to meet us here sometime in the next three days. I'm sure he insisted on privacy away from the main lodge and prying ears."

"You didn't mention your dad was going to pay us a visit. Is this the results of your phone call last night?"

Nick nodded. "He was going to meet with the Council and get back to me, but he wasn't clear on the timing."

Marc appeared with the keys to the cabin and handed them to Rob. "Number 47 near the Rim Trail. Just follow Rob. Enjoy your stay with us. All the information you need about the park is in the cabin."

We thanked Marc and followed Rob. The accommodations were most generous. The main area with large rustic furnishings and a massive stone fireplace had a view of the canyon. At the back were two bedrooms each with a private bath and two full-size beds per room.

"I assume with the two bedrooms your dad will be staying overnight," I said.

"He might be around for a couple of days. At least until we have formulated a plan to take care of Kaleb, but we'll still be able to explore the park and even take in one of the astronomy nights at the canyon observatory. Mom might join us for one night. There is strength in numbers and she's also a Council member."

"This is starting to sound like espionage in a spy mystery. Is it really that serious?"

Nick stared out the window at the canyon formations, his ESP sending me the answer, *"It's an enormous responsibility to prevent what could lead to catastrophic events that must be avoided at any cost, but decisions have been discussed and solutions resolved. That's all I can reveal for now."*

He turned and smiled. "Meanwhile, a walk along the Rim Trail in the late afternoon is in order. It's one of the best times of the day to catch the sun's reflections on the hoodoos. Don't forget your backpack." He headed out the door as I raced to keep up.

Bryce Canyon is a sprawling nature reserve in the southern part of Utah, known for its crimson-colored hoodoos, which are weathered and eroded spire-shaped rock formations standing like needles reaching towards the sky. Lying below the Rim Trail is Bryce Amphitheater, a hoodoo-filled depression discovered by the Mormon pioneers in the 1850s.

The park covers over 35,000 acres and was proclaimed a national monument by President Warren Harding in 1923. It was named after Ebenezer Bryce who homesteaded the area in 1874. Canyon elevations can reach up to 9,000 feet. The canyon is full of evergreen Douglas firs stretching to reach the sunlight among the tall spires. This is the perfect spot to enjoy the splendor of the stars and planets in the night sky, far from the ambient light pollution of civilization.

As we walked back to the room in the twilight of the evening, Nick pointed out several of the star formations as they began to appear, even naming some distant planets that were beyond my eyesight. I had always been amazed at his knowledge of the universe. Nick's visions were always of the future, while mine were hidden and buried in past civilizations.

The large dining room at the lodge with its raised ceiling supported by numerous timber trusses was filled with tourists. Large round tables for eight to ten people quickly filled with the bus loads of people arriving for the nightly stargazing tours. I could sense that Nick wanted to tell me something as our conversation seemed to meander from one topic to another without cohesive subject matter or direction.

Back in the cabin he announced, "It's time I began your training. I think you're ready to know about Corvid, the Council, and our people. Dad will tell you about our family and Kaleb when he arrives.

"We shall begin without speaking in words. Our minds will be linked." He waved his hand in a circle. "The barrier is sealed. No one else can read our thoughts or hear the words we speak."

Chapter Eleven

He hesitated, gathering his trust and his thoughts, as my mind swirled in a vortex filled with images of places and faces unfamiliar to me. I closed my eyes to secure my equilibrium and keep my dinner settled in my stomach. *"Sorry,"* Nick apologized, *"I forgot we've just eaten. Has everything stopped spinning?"*

"I think I'm OK, but that was the strangest feeling."

"It's easier to get use to when your stomach isn't so full," he smiled.

"What is Corvid?" This was the first thought that appeared in my head.

"Corvid is my home, the planet I come from. It's located in a small galaxy, light years away from Earth."

I just stared at Nick and nodded my head.

"Reading your thoughts just now, I can sense you're not surprised with what I just announced," Nick said looking confused.

I couldn't keep my mouth shut. "Actually, I was wondering how long you would wait to tell me, dude." I was smiling at Nick as I watched his reaction. "After all, I'm not the only one who talks in his sleep, and bunking together in a college dorm for four years gave me the opportunity to get to know you in a more—shall we say, scientific relationship. Surprised? No. Curious? Yes. And as my mom used to say, everything comes to those with the patience to wait."

Now it was Nick's turn to be surprised. *"You're better at this than I thought you would be."*

"Thank you, sir. I was wondering when you would notice. But there are still many questions that require some answers. You've spent years studying the universe and researching plans for the future of the world, while I've spent my time digging in the past to discover how civilizations began. I've long believed that the past had to be influenced by people from the future. But obviously I still have much to learn."

Nick was deep in thought. Where should he begin? "I know you've studied Greek and Roman mythology, so I'll just say...not all of it was a myth. People will believe what they want to believe and that's how myths and rumors get started. Good and evil exist in every galaxy, of which there are many. Werewolves, vampires, gods, goddesses, fairies, witches, and wizards all appear through-out history. Some of them were and are real and some are figments of imagination." His voice was that of a professor.

"I'm sure you must have read Homer's *Odyssey* where Circe transformed Odysseus' men into pigs. And remember how Medusa was turned into a monster with snakes for hair just for having sex with Poseidon in Athena's temple—and Zeus frequently trans-formed himself as a human to approach mortals as a means of gaining access.

"Folklore, ballads, and tales about dragons, demons, beasts, and angels have been recorded in some form in every country on earth. Shapeshifters move in various forms. The Valkyrie maidens appeared as swans. Our people from Corvid transform themselves into birds, but we can take other shapes depending on the circumstance. There are, and have always been, skin-walkers and shapeshifters—humans who can change into animals and animals that shift their bodies into human form. This is nothing new or unusual.

"Even Walt Disney was made aware of fairies, witches, and wizards. Just look at Peter Pan and Tinker Bell, the wicked queen in Snow White, and Cinderella's fairy godmother...where do you think those ideas came from? Not to mention *The Wizard of Oz*, *Beauty and the Beast*—munchkins, and unicorns. There's a thin line between myth and reality."

"OK—OK—you've made your point. I'm convinced. Lesson learned—things are not always what they appear to be. So...where is this leading? What is the scientific purpose for your being here on earth?" My head was spinning as I tried my best to understand, but my curiosity continued to build.

Nick answered with his thoughts. *There are thousands of our people here on your planet, living in peaceful harmony. How many birds do you think there are on this planet? A great deal of them are from Corvid. In many ways, we are very much like you, only with a few more advanced technical abilities. Among those traits, we have mastered the art of time travel and mental telepathy—in which I will have the pleasure to instruct you.*

"Whoa...can we take this a bit slower? I have some questions to ask, if that's possible."

"By all means...feel free to ask your questions. If I am permitted by the Council, I will answer them."

I attempted to put my thoughts in order of priority. *Who are the Council?*

Nick didn't hesitate to answer. *There are 500 members on the Council. My father and mother are both members. On Corvid, Dad is known as a facilitator, or in this world he would be called a diplomat. They are responsible for governing the planet, its people, and the gal-*

axy where I was born. There are no individual leaders, kings, queens, dictators, or presidents. The Council makes all the laws and decisions for our planet, and its people.

So...in a sense, they act much like our United Nations Council.

In a way, yes. However, they do not represent different countries. Their goal is to maintain peace and harmony through rules that apply equally to everyone on the planet. All the people are workers, even the council members, and the elders are cared for without question. We received our wisdom from the ancient ones, who first appeared to the Incas as condors and were revered as messengers from the gods. The population on Corvid is governed and provided for with compassion, understanding, and sharing. We have not experienced a war for thousands of years. Our planet developed long before the earth existed.

Nick was amazed at my ability to continue conversing with extrasensory perception. However, it can cause headaches and be a difficult strain for someone not used to it. *We are here to help—to plant the answers and ideas where needed to advance the human race into the future. We have been doing this since the age of the pharaohs and before. However, it is not a quick process because of the Universal Orders in agreement with our Council.*

"Explain," I said speaking in voice, as my head started to ache like it used to do when I studied late in college.

Nick was trying to think of how best to explain. "Einstein's Theory of Relativity was credited to Einstein—right?"

"Right," I agreed.

"But...where do you think the solution came from?" Nick smiled.

"From Einstein, of course."

"Wrong. The solution was passed on to Einstein through a strict system of thought processing by one of our scientists."

"Oh...so when Newton discovered gravity, one of your people dropped the apple?"

"Actually no...because of gravity apples had been falling from the trees long before Newton claimed his discovery. All he really needed was a little help from someone to put the answer in his head." Nick said with excitement. "Have you got the picture?"

"I think so, but I have a terrible headache. Can we continue with all this information tomorrow morning? I'm sure I'll have more questions," I said with a yawn.

"Not a problem. We both need some rest before Mom and Dad arrive tomorrow. I'm sure they will help fill in a lot of the blanks." Nick put the palm of his hand to my forehead and everything went dark.

Chapter
Twelve

I awoke the next morning and quickly showered while Nick, who was already dressed, stood out on the terrace talking on his cell phone. I don't recall changing out of my clothes or falling asleep, but I was feeling energized when I finally joined him in the fresh fall morning air, as the sun peeked over the mountain ridge casting a golden glow across the hoodoos and rugged narrow fins of solid rock, shaped like a coral reef.

The language he was speaking was unfamiliar. Perhaps it was a form of Tibetan. After all, he had grown up in a small mountain village—or had he? I would remind myself to ask that question later.

Nick ended his phone conversation. "We'd better eat something before we head out. The morning sunrise hike departed an hour ago, they're probably at Sunrise Point by now, but we can do that one tomorrow," he added.

I didn't realize I had slept in so late. "Why don't we do the Rim Trail all the way to Vista Point and back?" I suggested as we headed to the restaurant. Who were you talking to just now?"

"That was my sister. She said Mom and Dad will be here around lunch time. They want to have a meeting after lunch so we'd better hurry if we're going to have breakfast and get some exercise."

"Doesn't your sister know how to use ESP?" I asked.

"Oh, sure she does, but we don't use it all of the time. Only when we feel the need. Her sensory development will continue to improve the older she gets." he said.

"How old is she?" I asked.

"Twenty years by your standard of time measurement. She's the youngest."

"What's her name?" I asked.

"Sherill," Nick smiled.

Why did that name sound familiar?

~

We ate breakfast quickly and headed out for a fast hike.

The morning views of the canyon were spectacular. Two of the most photographed monuments in the park were a stone's throw from the trail's edge. Thor's Hammer is a monolithic weathered hoodoo with a massive square boulder balanced on top. In the morning light, the spire-like stone handle had turned a vibrant orange with vanes of sulfur running like a yellow waterfall to the canyon floor. Further along, we stopped to admire two balanced rocks shaped like the flame on the torch held by the Statue of Liberty.

A group of tourists with their guide was departing Vista Point just as we arrived, leaving it almost empty of people. I stood at the railing, gazing out over the vast expanse of hoodoos and ragged fins that appeared to wave and ripple in the late-morning heat—a mirage of undulating stone and fir trees as far as the eyes could see. I wondered if there was anything so amazing on the planet Corvid.

"What's it like living on Corvid?" I asked, wondering what it looked like, and if I would need to live there in the future.

"Corvid has an atmosphere similar to Earth, perhaps a little more oxygen, making the air thinner but fresher to breath and there is no industrial pollution due to our highly advanced methods in energy, manufacturing, and travel. Corvid is covered in water much like this planet and there are many large islands—not as big as the continents on earth, but with numerous colonies where people can choose to reside. We've developed a single language on the planet, although most of us can speak many languages when necessary."

Nick answered my thoughts, "One day you will see Corvid and visit the island of hanging gardens that are suspended in air like green growing clouds with hanging vines a mile long and flowers of every color and fragrance you can imagine. The island clouds produce their own water and the birds that roost among the island clouds add the nutrients that fertilize their gardens."

A thick cloud, drifting on the winds above, suddenly cast a dark shadow over the colorful vista causing us to do a sweeping visual search of the area on the point. We were alone, yet both had experienced an overwhelming sense of evil and even someone's thoughts of death. But we could see no one.

"Better head back," Nick said. "We should be there when Mom and Dad arrive. I'm sure they will have much to discuss before dinner this evening. I'll have the restaurant send something in for lunch at the cabin."

On our return, Nick called room service and ordered some lunch. He handed me my backpack. "Here, open it and take out the treasure you found."

"Are you sure it's safe?" I asked with a questioning glance.

Nick paused, his eyes closed for a moment as his brow furrowed deep in thought, then his eyes reopened. "I don't sense any hostile presence so it should be safe, and lunch won't be here for at least a half hour."

I pulled the metal object from the pack and held it in my hand.

"Press the bottom of the flat base with your thumb, and hold it there for a moment," he urged. "That will activate the mechanisms sealed inside." I followed his instructions.

The smooth iridescent surface began to change color from silver-gray to blue-green and I felt a slight vibration. "This device is your handy-dandy time-travel magic wand," he announced with a chuckle. "You'll note the three recessed buttons along the length. Do not try to use them without further instructions—they are sensitive to the touch when pressed. This instrument has multiple uses, but I'll explain those later."

I thought to myself, I was glad I had not tried to press them when I found it, but with my training in archeology I had learned that patience is more rewarding that speedy curiosity. "You were smart not to be that curious," Nick said, as he read my thoughts.

"Oh...I was as curious as any archeologist would be, finding an unusual artifact, but I remembered what an old Egyptology professor once said to me: Haste makes waste and can destroy historical discoveries."

"Wise man," Nick replied in thought with a quick nod.

~

Nick's Mom and Dad appeared on the terrace. I slipped my treasure back into the pack as Nick opened the sliding door. "Wow! Time travel is really fast," I said as they entered the room.

"Actually, we were not that far away. We stopped by to say hello to Nick's sister at the university in Utah," said Josh. My ears perked up at that response.

Leizal and Josh looked even younger than they had the last time we had met in Las Cruces. "Patrick, you are more handsome than I remember. Your work must agree with you," Leizal said giving me a big hug.

"You had best watch out Patrick—I'm sure she is going to want something when she talks like that," chuckled Josh with a firm handshake.

"I only want what's best for the boys, Josh and you know it."

"Yes dear, and that's why we're here," he said softly, giving her a one-arm hug.

"Wait a minute—don't I get a hug too?" Nick whined.

"Of course you do dear," she smiled, wrapping her arms around him then standing back, her sparkling amber eyes moving from his head to his feet. "But I think you're putting on too much weight," she giggled with the sound of bells in her voice.

Nick turned to Patrick, "Now you know where I get my wit." His dark eyes danced as he hugged his mom again.

Was I seeing them for the first time? And the tinkling bells...where had I heard them before?

Josh put his hand on my shoulder and answered my thoughts. "You are seeing with eyes that are much clearer and the knowledge you now have of our people will help you to see even more." There was a knock at the door as Rob arrived with our lunch.

Chapter Thirteen

Once lunch was over, the family gathered in front of the stone fireplace. Leizal was the first to speak.

"I know you must have many questions, Patrick. And the Council has given me permission to answer them as I see the need to do so. Nick has already opened doors, which will lead to much important discussion and I'm here to make sure you understand. Josh will also be able to fill in some of the blanks when called on."

She gazed at Josh with her twinkling eyes. "I sealed the room after the server left. We can speak freely without a sound or thought escaping."

Josh cleared his throat and spoke in his deep melodic voice as he watched Patrick. "I was informed that you have discovered a lost object of great importance."

Patrick wasn't sure how to respond as he cast a questioning look at Nick for guidance, wondering how much he had already told his parents.

Josh and Leizal nodded to each other.

"Nick has explained what the found object is. You were chosen to find it and it is yours to keep. However, it's time you learned who the person is that wants it back." Leizal spoke in a calm and steady voice as she began to tell the tale.

"Many years ago, the man committed a terrible crime on Corvid. He was tried, convicted, and sentenced to exile on a distant penal colony in our galaxy. Unfortunately, he killed a guard and escaped with the guard's time-travel device.

"I don't have to tell you how difficult it is to try and find a criminal who is able to travel anywhere in the past or future. However, it was only a matter of time before he would make a mistake, and time is endless."

"What was his crime?" I asked.

"Josh," Leizal said, "perhaps you should answer that question."

"He was guilty of murder and was apprehended before he could escape. However, he murdered a second victim, to make his escape from the penal colony and is now a rogue time traveler and extremely dangerous." Josh paused to let his statement register with me.

"Do you think he would murder again?" I asked.

Josh and Leizal looked to Nick, who had remained quiet waiting for his turn to speak.

"Our main concern is to capture Kaleb again before he can cause greater damage, creating a catastrophic change for the future. And yes, he is capable of many crimes, which we must prevent from taking place. However, capturing him will require your help, and it could be dangerous."

I wasn't sure what help I could be, but I began to realize the only reason Kaleb was hanging around was because I had something he needed.

Leizal knew what I was thinking and calmly explained why they needed my assistance. "You control his only means of escape from this planet. He can no longer travel into the past or the future. He is Earth-bound and will remain close to the time travel device now in your possession."

"So that places me in danger." The thought raced through my brain.

"Patrick my son," said Leizal, "You are not in danger as long as we are with you. Even though you may not see us, we will be close by and we will do everything in our power to prevent any harm to you."

"Won't he know that you are near?" I asked.

"We are capable of disguising our presence and our thoughts by creating a "vision." It acts as a screen that we can see and hear through but he cannot. His ability to see through any vision was removed when he was first apprehended. You needn't worry about us. You are his choice of concentration and he must not lose that connection so it limits his ability to sense other things in his surroundings," Josh assured me.

I gazed into Leizal's twinkling amber eyes seeing a face that I knew I had seen recently. She smiled and nodded, "You will meet her again, but for now, we must set the plans in motion to capture Kaleb."

Nick grinned and cleared his throat. "Kaleb will not show while the three of us are here. There is too much energy in our space. Mom and Dad will stay with us until we leave day after tomorrow. We are waiting for the Council to approve our plans to capture Kaleb. I will not be able to discuss our plans with you because you have not yet learned how to block your thoughts which Kaleb would be able to read. We cannot force you to help us—that must be your choice alone."

Leizal took my hand. "You will have time to think this through tomorrow and I know you will make the right decision, but for now I will clear your mind of this discussion and we will have a pleasant evening enjoying your company." She pressed her hand to my forehead. My eyes closed as I drifted in a warm fog.

~

"That was a beautiful sunset," said Nick, "but I'm starved. Mind if I shower first?"

"Where are your mom and dad?" I asked rising from my chair by the fireplace.

"They said they would meet us in the restaurant. Mom was still enjoying the views from the Rim Trail. With her photographic memory she will be painting a picture of Bryce Canyon when they get back home. You should see her paintings of Tibet."

He was undressed and already heading to the shower while I stood there trying to figure out what had happened to the afternoon. Where had the time gone? Our lunch dishes were still on the table and it was almost twilight.

Nick was out of the shower, dressed and on his phone while I stood under the cascading hot water to relax my tense muscles and sooth the stiffness at the back of my neck. I can't explain why, but suddenly I had a vision of Cheryl, the young girl at the lodge in Zion. She smiled and waved, then blew me a kiss and vanished. I was trying to recapture the vision when Nick knocked on the bathroom door.

"Have you drowned in there? Hurry up, Mom and Dad just headed for the restaurant and my stomach is growling."

I turned off the water and stood there for a second. Now I know where I saw that face before.

"You go ahead—I'll meet you in a few minutes." I called out.

"Are you crazy man? I don't dare leave your side, so get your ass out here and let's go."

I stood in the doorway to the bathroom half dressed. "Since when did you become my keeper, boss man?"

"Since Kaleb popped up on the scene, Romeo...so don't give me any trouble or I'll have to call in the reserves."

I scurried around to finish getting dressed. "Don't forget the backpack." He reminded me as we headed out the door.

"Romeo?—Where did that come from if I may be so bold to ask?"

"You forget...I can read your mind, dude."

"Well—if she's part of your reserves, I'd be happy to see her again."

"You're quick to remember. When did you realize?"

"When I looked into your mother's eyes." I said.

"Ah—well you can't pull any wool over mother's eyes, that's for sure."

I smiled. "And then there were those bells."

"Oh no...hold on, man...you heard the bells?"

"Yeah...what does it mean?"

"It means, you're hooked. Mom will explain later and I'm hungry."

Chapter
Fourteen

Josh and Leizal were waiting for us in the restaurant. I was intrigued to learn more about Nick and his family and they were eager to fill me in. Josh was the first to increase my knowledge as we sat in a quiet corner booth.

"I believe Nick has given you a quick overview of Corvid, but he has barely touched on why you have been selected to join us. The final choice, of course, will be yours to make.

"As he has stated, there are many Corvidians already living on Earth. Our mission here is to create a healthy planet—to end wars and provide the path to peace, harmony, and understanding. Our goal is to offer the intelligence needed to accomplish this mission."

Perhaps this announcement had startled me as I was attempting to grasp his meaning. "So, if I understand correctly, you're here to help our society, but you need our cooperation to make this happen."

"Exactly," replied Leizal. "And to facilitate these changes, we are selecting people here on earth in various scientific fields who want to increase their knowledge and work with us to make this planet a better place to live."

"But my fields and knowledge are of past civilizations and ancient cultures. Why would I be selected for a mission that wants to change the future?" I queried without thinking clearly.

"Precisely!" she exclaimed with the soft sound of bells in her voice.

"If the Council members present will allow me," Nick said, "I think I can draw a clearer picture for you."

Nick's voice was miles away. The thoughts in my head were in the clouds as I heard the bells in Liezal's voice and saw a vision of Cheryl's face.

Leizal smiled, "I'll address that thought later, Patrick." She turned to Nick. "Excuse my interruption son, please continue."

Nick wiped the grin off his face. "The earth is on a path of destruction. It is only with your knowledge of past civilizations and cultures, combined with our knowledge of the future, that we can reverse the direction. Wars, chaos, devastation, famine, and dictatorships will destroy civilization as you know it today if we are not successful in our mission. This is why we must find and stop Kaleb and his followers. If he is able to influence or change events in the past, that could alter how things are in the present and the future."

I was beginning to grasp their intentions and to understand why I had been selected. *But where does Cheryl fit in and why my sudden attraction to her at the inn in Zion?* These thoughts were running through my head too fast to comprehend.

Leizal patted my arm. "You want a simple answer to a simple question, but it isn't that simple. She pronounces her name Cheryl here on Earth, but she is Sherill on Corvid and will be part of your future, but for now, you must concentrate on the present."

I sat in a half daze, surrounded by a cloud, *'Sherill—even her name sounded like bells in my head.'*

"Meanwhile," Nick chimed in with enthusiasm, "it's almost time for 'Nature's Light Show' and we don't want to miss that."

Josh shook his head, "You can take the boy out of the stars, but you can't take the stars out of the boy. Your mother and I are turning in early. Tomorrow will be a busy day. You boys enjoy the galaxy on display. We'll see you in the morning."

Everyone stood to leave the conversation area as Nick pulled at my arm. "Come on Robin, Batman wants a front row seat."

~

A large crowd had gathered for the spectacular event in a moonless night sky. Rangers were using flashlights to guide people to the viewing area where seats had been arranged near the observatory.

The splendor of the night sky, far from the light pollution of civilization, created a sanctuary of natural darkness. Here, in a vast twinkling silver rainbow above, the Milky Way extended from one horizon to the other. On most evenings you can see over 7,500 stars. The planets of Venus and Jupiter are often so bright that they cast shadows from the trees and hoodoos.

Now, I better understood Nick's fascination with the stars and why he cherished visiting this grand sanctuary of natural darkness. We were fortunate to have such a clear moonless night. Satellites could be seen floating overhead as drifting pen-spots of light in space.

I strained my eyes, searching deep into space for a twinkle from Corvid. Nick chuckled with laughter. "What?" I said.

"The day will come when you will visit Corvid, but you will never see it from Earth except by satellite in the future."

I looked at Nick in the darkness. His onyx eyes glowed with a low flame. He had a regal bearing just like his father and yet his facial features were like his mother, smooth and without a flaw. Under the starry sky above, my thoughts were drawn to Cheryl at the lodge in Zion.

As we hiked back to our room, Nick had been hiding his thoughts from me, "OK. I know I won't get any sleep tonight until I answer your questions and I'm sure Mom will agree for my sake."

"Yes...there is a family resemblance—Sherill, or Cheryl as she is call here on Earth, is my youngest sister. I knew she would be at Zion, and she has been wanting to meet you. I honestly had no idea you would hear the bells, but that is something that Mom will have to explain later. Now—will you let me get some sleep tonight?"

"I never said a word. Did I?"

"No—but that's the problem. Your thoughts are flying around my head like drones or large mosquitos deciding where to attack," Nick huffed as he mimicked the sound of a mosquito buzzing around my ear with his hand.

"Why can't you just surround yourself with a barrier to block out my thoughts?" I blurted out.

"Can't do that, dude. It's my duty to maintain mental contact with you until we have captured Kaleb and put him where he belongs." I nodded in understanding.

"So—what are the plans for tomorrow?" I asked, changing the subject.

"I thought you would never ask. While you napped today, we made a small change in our trip schedule. Have you ever been to the Hopi Indian reservation?"

"I've always had that area on my bucket list but never got around to making a visit. Why do you ask?"

Nick seemed a little nervous. "We're heading there tomorrow. I want to tell you everything, but I can't. The less you know, the harder it will be for Kaleb to read your thoughts and that will make it easier to lure him into our trap."

"So," I said, "I'm to be the cheese in the trap to catch the rat. Sounds exciting to say the least."

We had arrived back at the cabin and were now whispering as we stood at the front door. Nick put his hands on both my shoulders and turned me to face him. "I know it's a lot to ask, dude, but we need your help. As Mom said, we can't force you to do anything... the choice has to be yours."

He was surprised when I pulled him towards me in a hug. "I'm on your side, dude—just tell me what to do."

"First...I'm going to be sure you get some sleep tonight. Your mind will be refreshed in the morning and so will mine. I promise... you won't feel a thing," he said.

"I will welcome your handy assistance on two conditions... one, that you make sure I see your sister again soon and two...that you teach me how to do that hand-to-the-forehead go-to-sleep trick."

Nicked laughed. "Patience my friend. I'm sure you will have more than one instructor in the future."

Chapter Fifteen

The following day, we arrived at the Hopi Cultural Center on Second Mesa in northern Arizona where they were having a yearly event. The small hotel and surrounding grounds were full of people who had come to sell their wares, take part in the native rituals and watch the tribal dances.

The place was buzzing with music, beating drums, rattles—the sound of bells jingling from the dancer's ankles and their colorful costumes, as red dust stirred beneath their feet and the ancient ones chanted in their native language.

The people in attendance must have numbered in the thousands. There were tents set up for the artists to sell their jewelry, carved Kachina dolls, weavings, and paintings while the aromas of Indian fry-bread, pozole, and pots of local red beans with chili filled the air.

"Liezal and Josh were already in their room. Leizal had a concerned look on her face, "Perhaps we picked the wrong time to be here with all this going on."

"Nonsense." Josh spoke over the sounds around us. "This is perfect. Most of the people in the area will be drawn to this event and to the evening festivities. That should make our plan work even better."

I wish I knew what their plan was, but as Nick had said, it was better if I didn't know. I had already agreed to play my part and be the bait in the trap, but it didn't make it any easier. At least it sounded better than becoming just another murder victim for Kaleb. The suspense was driving me crazy, but I wasn't going to let it show.

Once we checked into our adjoining room, I wanted to get out in the open and take part in the festivities. "Let's go watch the dancers. This is a culture I have always wanted to know more about. Did you know that the Hopi believe their reservation to be the center of the universe? The legend, according to the Book of Hopi, says that they were brought to live above ground by the ant people.

"They were considered the chosen people, according to their beliefs. It was their destiny to roam the earth until they found the perfect place to live—rather like the tribes of Israel. They traveled south to the jungles of South America, where members of the parrot clan decided to live and make their homes, but the others were not convinced and moved to the northern hemisphere where another clan decided to make roots and stay.

"A study made by a scientist some time ago took the DNA from an Eskimo in northern Alaska and matched it to one of the ancient families here on the reservation in Old Oraibi on Third Mesa." I must have been making conversation just to calm my nerves.

I looked at Nick as we walked through the maze of people heading toward the sounds of the music and the lure of Indian tacos and fry-bread doused with powdered sugar—he was smiling and I could tell he was amused. "Listen to me," I babbled, "spouting off like a history professor. You probably knew all of that information. Right?"

"Not all of it, but you made it sound so interesting, I didn't want to stop you. Actually, the Inca, the Hopi, the Mayan, and the Egyptians were among the first to arrive from other galaxies." My jaw dropped.

"I know—it's shocking. But you'll have lots of time to learn all about that once you can travel back in time. Meanwhile, I'm ready for an Indian taco on fry-bread…care to join me?"

~

Josh and Leisal joined us for dinner at the hotel's small restaurant that evening. It was not a social gathering and I could feel the tension in the air as Josh began to speak in a serious tone. "Nick said that you have consented to help us capture Kaleb. I must repeat—it can be dangerous, but we will do our best to keep you safe from any harm."

My voice trembled as I spoke with quiet conviction. "I've accepted the fact that my destiny lies with your people and your family personally. I've learned that nothing happens by chance— there is a reason and a purpose for everything that takes place in the universe." I glanced at Nick. "I've had a very good instructor— although sometimes I thought he was a pain in the neck—he has always been there to offer his support. I'm close to you in more ways than I could ever have imagined."

Leizal smiled and leaned into Josh. "I believe he's referring to Sherill."

"Of course he is, my dear, but let the young man finish. Please continue, Patrick."

"What I want to say is, that I have agreed to help in whatever small way I can. My future is in your hands and I've already had a glimpse of what awaits after this is all over and done."

"Then we will set the wheels in motion. What have you boys got planned this evening?"

Nick spoke quickly. "I thought we would take an evening drive over to Third Mesa to Old Oraibi. The stars are really bright tonight and I think it's time I gave Patrick a few lessons in mind control away from this crowd."

Josh nodded. "That sounds perfect. Your mom and I wanted to see a couple of firelight dances and turn in early."

Leizal chimed in. "I think I'll send a message to Sherill and see if she can meet us at the Grand Canyon for a day or two. I'm sure Patrick wouldn't complain."

"You must be reading my thoughts," I said to Leizal with surprise as Nick rolled his yes.

"Come on, dude—it's time for your lessons—and where better to start than 'the Center of the Universe' on the Hopi Reservation."

A strange foreboding came over me as I stood dead still next to the car in the parking lot and I began to shiver as an icy chill surrounded me.

"Are you OK, dude?"

I heard Nick, but wasn't able to answer him as my mind was filled with a sense of fear and a blurred vision of something evil. I slipped into the passenger seat and closed the car door. "I'll be OK—just a weird sensation that's all—let's get out of here."

We headed out across the mesa top in the dark of night. There were few vehicles on the road going east and the further we went from the Cultural Center the more stars we could see. Nick placed his hand on my neck and rubbed gently to relieve the tension in my shoulders. I felt a pinch on the side of my neck and suddenly the lights went out and I drifted in darkness.

Nick shifted into four-wheel drive and turned off the main road driving north on a deserted dirt road, away from any signs of humanity—deeper and deeper into the lonely darkness of the high desert.

Chapter Sixteen

My eyes fluttered as they slowly began to open. I felt my neck and rubbed a sore muscle. The car was not moving and the lights were off. Nick was nowhere to be seen and the keys for the car were missing. Perhaps I had fallen asleep and Nick had stepped away from the car to relieve himself—but why would he take the keys? Something wasn't right.

Stepping out of the car, I called Nick's name but there was no answer. I called again, but there wasn't a sound. The silence was deafening as if the desert absorbed all sound like a dry sponge. The only sound I could hear was my own heartbeat. *Where was he? What had happened to Nick?* I wasn't sure I should leave the car—and if I did, where would I go?

Glancing at the sky, I tried to get a sense of direction—but the stars had vanished. A thick ground fog began to roll across the desert floor, but it wasn't a normal desert fog. This fog was an iridescent green in color and swirled like the fog created by dry-ice at a rock concert.

Lights appeared in the distance heading up the road towards me. I slipped on my backpack and waited for the vehicle to arrive—but the car stopped a distance away, with its lights on bright. I heard the doors open and close but was blinded by the lights as I called out, "Nick? Is that you?"

There was a low growl that sounded like a dog as someone stepped in front of the vehicle, the lights formed a glow behind them, causing the person to appear in silhouette. I froze, realizing in that moment that my stalker was approaching, and on each side of his massive frame was a black wolf with piercing yellow eyes that glowed as if shining from within the beasts. "So...we finally meet alone. Your friend Nick isn't here," he roared with a voice like thunder. The wolves growled again in a threating low rumble.

"What have you done with Nick?" I demanded.

Kaleb gave a sinister laugh, "Nick has abandoned you. You're no longer under his protection."

"That isn't true. He wouldn't do that."

"You waste my time. I've come for my possession."

"I don't have it here. It's back at the hotel."

"You're lying!" he yelled, "It's in your backpack." The wolves lurched forward, but were stopped by the chains around their necks. He held them in check with the leashes secured in his left hand. I had to keep him talking. I didn't dare let him read my thoughts about Nick, Josh, and Leizal. I blocked them out of my head.

"What you want, was never yours in the first place. You stole it from a guard and killed him to get it. It's mine now because I found it."

"You're wrong, boy," he paused, slowly raising the pistol I had failed to notice in his right hand. "It's mine and the game is over."

The gun was pointed straight at me and out of the darkness came a blinding flash of light, the sound of the gun echoed in my ears. I felt a sharp sting and something warm flowed out of my body.

Darkness filled the void as my eyes closed and all was dead quiet.

~

The world spun around me. Everything was in a haze. I could hear voices but the language was not familiar. I glimpse people dressed in sheer white linen. Several bare chested young men with shaved heads glistening in the torchlight scurried about while others chanted in the background. I could smell incense burning as several unfamiliar faces appeared above looking down at me.

There was a strange odor of something antiseptic mixed with herbs and a sweet floral fragrance. I stared up at the high ceiling supported by brightly decorated columns with hieroglyphic markings as a handsome face with large almond-shaped eyes lined with black kohl hovered above. "The object passed through the body and exited the back of the shoulder." He spoke in broken English with a Middle Eastern accent. "He is lucky it passed through muscle and didn't affect any major arteries. The transfusion will help him to heal much quicker."

My head turned to the side and I could see Nick, lying on a table next to me with Leizal and Josh standing beside him. I couldn't move, but felt something being injected into my arm. My left shoulder burned as if it was being scorched with a branding iron then quickly cooled like ice as I plunged into darkness once again.

A warmth filled my body with searing heat as I felt energy pulsing through my veins. Even with my eyes closed I could see giant floating clouds with hanging vines and colorful flowers—I felt I had been here before. Then I remembered Nick had told me about the island clouds on Corvid and I wondered if I was on another planet.

In this hypnotic state, I drifted into a deep sleep, and from the swirling darkness visions of Kaleb and his two wolves appeared in shadow. I wanted to run but my feet were like lead and I couldn't move. His giant six-foot-seven frame with shaved head and broad shoulders stood with legs spread. His massive bare chest covered with multiple tattoos and runes heaved as his two black wolves, standing guard on each side, glared with yellow eyes, their teeth glowing white in the black ink of their twisting heads.

He was speaking but there was no sound. I watched as he raised his right hand in slow motion. There was a flash and I fell backwards, hit by an unseen force. I expected to feel pain, but there was none. The flash of light had blinded me and I felt a stinging sensation in my shoulder as I sank further into an abyss of darkness.

~

The sound of soft bells echoed in the back of my head. "Shouldn't we try and wake him? He's been out for three days now. He must need some nourishment." I recognized Sherill's voice.

"We don't want to rush his recovery. These things take time as you well know, and the nourishment he needs he is getting from the transfusion of Nick's blood into his body. But for now, rest is required," said Leizal. You're hovering around him like a guardian angel. Give him time and space to return on his own." Sherill heaved a sigh.

I tried to open my eyes but they felt as if they had been sealed with glue. It took great effort, as narrow slits began allowing light to pierce the veil of my copper-colored eyelashes. My eyelids fluttered. "He's awake—he's awake," she sang as bells began to chime.

I saw her smiling face as she sat on the bed next to me and took my hand in hers. "Where am I? What happened?" I asked.

"Answers will come in due time," said a voice from the other side of the bed. That voice was also familiar. Nick patted my right shoulder. "How's goes it, dude?"

"I'm fine," I said, as I tried to sit up. "Ooooo!... Man that smarts. How did I hurt myself?" Sherill was busy tucking some pillows behind me.

Leizal spoke but didn't answer my question. "Josh should be here any time now and we'll know all the details. Meanwhile, is there anything you need?"

As I looked at myself, I realized I was only half dressed. My chest was bare and under the bed clothes I was wearing a cotton loincloth. *Where did that come from I wondered.* "Maybe some clothes would be appropriate." I said. "Oh my god...my backpack!"

Nick pointed to the chair in the corner of the room, "No problem, dude. It's safe. The rest of your clothes are in the closet. We'll leave you to change. If you need any help—just holler. Come on sis, the man needs some privacy."

Sherill leaned over and kissed me on the forehead. "I'm glad you're feeling better." She said in her melodic voice as they stepped out of the room behind Nick and closed the door.

I stood, but feeling slightly dizzy, I sat back on the side of the bed for a minute and gazed out the window. *"Holy cow...that looks like the Grand Canyon!"* I thought, as I moved slowly to the window.

Nick must have been standing on the other side of the door, as I heard him reply, *"That's right, dude. We're on the north rim. Dad just arrived so get changed...there's lots to hear."* He must have read my thoughts. His ESP was coming through much clearer than before.

I stepped into the bathroom to get dressed. Looking in the mirror I noticed a red mark about the size of a half-dollar on my left shoulder. I couldn't imagine what had caused it. Fingering the circle, with my right hand, I discovered the skin wasn't broken and there were no scars.

I washed my face and hands and as I pulled a T-shirt over my head, I noticed the mark had turned a light pink—almost disappearing. Some of my memory was starting to return as I combed my hair.

"We're waiting for your grand appearance, Mr. Hollywood; this isn't an audition, so get your butt out here." I'll have to admit, Nick had a way with words. I opened the door and he handed me something green to drink. "Bottoms up," he said, waiting for me to follow orders.

The beverage was cool and sweet as it coated my dry throat. "More," I pleaded sounding like Oliver Twist, "Can I have more please?" The group chuckled in unison.

"You can be a real pain at times," Nick grinned as he handed my glass to Sherill for a refill.

"I'm sorry," I said in a waifish little boy's voice, "Have I caused you pain, sir?"

He stiffened like a schoolmaster. "Only a little, sonny-boy—only a little, but I'm over it now." he smiled handing the refilled glass back to me.

I looked him in the eyes and could tell he wasn't joking. What had I done?

Chapter Seventeen

Josh called as he stood by the fireplace mantle, "Come, have a seat boys, I have some great news and we need to bring Patrick up to date. He's missed out on the past four exciting days." We joined him around the large burled-wood coffee table near the fireplace. Leizal and Josh sat across from us, each in a comfortable log chair with cushions covered in geometric Navajo weavings of red, deep blue, yellow and gray colors.

Sherill and Nick sat on either side of me on the chocolate brown leather sofa. Josh was excited to begin. "Kaleb is once again in exile—only this time he's on Soltar."

He explained quickly, "Soltar is a small penal colony planet with many tiny islands surrounded by water full of flesh eating fish. No one has ever escaped from Soltar. Supplies for prisoners are delivered by drones. Most of the islands are not much larger than a mile square. Each island has only one occupant and facilities are minimal—his days are numbered. In his truth induced confession, he admitted to killing the two men in Death Valley, whose spirits you encountered, as well as several others. He will no longer bother anyone."

So, they had once been real people, I thought. I had so many questions to ask. Josh nodded to me, "Yes Patrick, they were real people. Feel free to ask your questions anytime."

I nodded, "I have difficulty putting the sequence of events in order. Perhaps if someone could explain what took place four nights ago on the mesa it would help to relieve the confusion that's been spinning in my head?"

Leizal spoke next. "I believe I should begin the tale and pass the speaker's staff to the next person, as is our custom in Council.

"Four nights ago, we set in motion plans, approved by the Council, to capture Kaleb before he could cause chaos and destruction here on earth, as he had planned. As you know, he was without his time travel device. A device, Patrick, which you will learn more about with the proper training and instructions." She looked at Nick. "Perhaps you should speak about the events that followed."

Nick cleared his throat. "Because you have yet to learn how to block your thoughts so others are not able to read them, I couldn't tell you when, where or what was about to happen. It was necessary to keep you in the dark and I'm sorry about that, dude."

"No need to apologize man. I understood that was part of the plan. Please continue." Patrick sat back to listen.

"While we were driving out on the mesa, I put you under with a pinch to the neck. I didn't want you to know where we were headed. I took off on a deserted dirt road and stopped in the middle of nowhere. We knew that Kaleb would be able to zero in on your location as long as the object of his attention was left in the car with you.

"Taking the keys to the car so you could not leave the spot, I joined mom and dad as we kept watch from a distance, concealed by a vision. We weren't sure how strong Kaleb's senses still were after so many years. You were protected but we could not place you in a shield. It was important that he find you alone with the time travel device."

"So...You set the trap and I was the bait. That I knew was going to happen and fully agreed to be the cheese to entice the rat. I'm glad I didn't know ahead of time. I do remember when Kaleb arrived, with the car lights reflecting behind him and the two wolves that were with him. He demanded his time-travel device and I think I refused. But what happened next?"

Josh, in his commanding voice took the speaker's staff from Nick. "We were prepared to move as Kaleb spoke, but we were not prepared for his quick action with the hidden pistol in his right hand. Kaleb is left handed and we counted on any weapon he might have, to be in his left hand. Our reaction was swift, but not quick enough and you were injured. But we are grateful he was not a good shot with his right hand."

My memory was now beginning to clear. "I remember seeing a blinding flash of light and falling backwards. There was a stinging sensation in my shoulder and I blacked out. Can you explain what happened?"

"We stopped time." Josh said. I wasn't sure I had heard him correctly as I stared wide-eyed. "We have the ability to freeze time—to essentially make time stop. Nick will explain about the buttons on your time-travel tool when you begin your training. One button can take you into the future, another, will send you back in time, and the third will stop or suspend time. There are other adjustments you will learn to use and it is also used as a weapon."

Leizal patted Josh on the arm. "Perhaps you're getting ahead Josh. We agreed to allow Nick the privilege of being Patrick's tutor. However, he might be curious to know what happened next, now that he knows he was shot."

"Whoa!" I stammered. "When was I shot?"

"Seconds before the blinding flash of light." Sherill said. I had almost forgotten she was in the room. "That's what caused the stinging sensation in your left shoulder, and why we took you back in time to be healed."

Visions once again shifted in my head. People in white linen hovering around me and the antiseptic smell of herbs mixed with a floral fragrance. "Where back in time did we go?"

"To Egypt—1350 BC, and the arrival period of our early relatives in Thebes," said Leizal, "Many of them were physicians to the pharaohs. Travel to Corvid would have taken too long and placed you in great danger with more stress than necessary. The healing talents of the ancient Egyptians came from Corvid. Some of their healing herbs are no longer available today.

"We couldn't treat you with any of the advanced methods from the future because they have not yet been invented for the present time and that would have caused too great a change.

"During the Amarna Period, Thebes was a city of almost 80,000 people. Akhenaten moved the capital city to his custom-built city, but his son Tutankhamun later returned the capital to Thebes once he took the throne. But I'm sure you know all of that history and you will visit there again in time."

I was stunned. "What happened to the wolves?" I was curious to learn everything.

"Nick," Leizal nodded in his direction.

"Those were demons, or warlocks under Kaleb's command. He must have found them without a master and brought them under his service. To humans they can be very dangerous, but we zapped them before they could cause any trouble."

I hadn't realized that Sherill was holding my hand. "In the meantime," she said, 'You need to eat, rest, exercise your shoulder, and you and I need to talk." The rest of the group smiled at her statement. "They already know," she said shaking her head with exasperation.

"Know what?" I asked.

Nick couldn't help but laugh out loud. "The bells man—the bells. I told you—you were hooked.

I gazed at Sherill, "Don't pay any attention to him. Let's take a walk—I've never visited the north rim of the Grand Canyon." They left the cabin hand in hand.

"Well Nick," Josh chuckled, "Looks like Patrick has found a new roommate."

Nick watched as they walked away from the cabin, "She'll be good for him, but I'm still going to be his tutor. How soon do we head for Sedona?"

"You'll have to do some fast training. We're due at the Vortex in two days."

Chapter
Eighteen

Nick began my training early the next morning. It was a cool crisp morning as the sun began to rise over the Grand Canyon. Muted shades of mauve, gray and blue faded into dazzling colors of amber, pink and gold as the canyon slipped on its formal dress for the day to greet the tourists. Echoes sounded and re-sounded bouncing off the canyon walls as humanity stirred to life.

"I know we haven't much time but you already know the basics, so start your travel tool as I instructed before." Nick was all business on such a beautiful morning.

"Now concentrate. The top button when touched will send you into the future—the bottom button takes you back in time and the middle button will stop or suspend time. None of them affect or hinder your movements."

"That sounds pretty basic." I said.

Circling the cylinder are three rings, by rotating these rings you can select the time period you wish to explore. However, people will not be able to see you. You were not there in the past, therefore you do not exist. You could get run over or injured. People can walk right through you…and let me tell you—that hurts. I speak from experience."

"You don't always need to use the rings if you can visualize the time and place you want to return to. Concentrate and just hold down the button until you arrive."

"Can you travel with me or do I have to go alone?" I said nervously.

"Don't worry, dude. You won't be traveling alone for a while. But we can make some trips back in history right here in the USA. Think about what you want to experience, even if you can't remember the year and date."

"The day that man took the first step on the moon." I said.

"Sorry, dude, we're not going to the moon."

"No, no—I want to be at NASA center… in the control room when Neil Armstrong took that first step on the moon."

"No problem, that's simple. I'll just hang on to your belt. Let's go."

~

Suddenly we were standing in the back of the room at the control center, watching the giant screen. I felt a little dizzy from the experience, but Nick assured me it would pass. People were scattered around the room all on their computers as Armstrong took that final step off the ladder. It was July 20th, 1969. A rush of adrenaline filled the room as the computer beeping silence of the moment was shattered by loud applause with hollering and celebration. No one saw us as we stood in the shadows. We weren't really there in person.

"Shall we return to the cabin?" Nick asked.

I pushed the top button and my thoughts of the north rim cabin and Sherill appeared in my brain. Suddenly we were standing in front of Sherill.

"Nick laughed, "Next time, think of the place and time—not the person."

"Oh! Hope we didn't frighten you," I apologized to Sherill.

"Not at all. I was expecting you both. If you're hungry, lunch is ready." She turned and entered the cabin as we followed.

"It's just the three of us. Mom and dad went ahead to Sedona, we'll see them tomorrow." She looked at Nick, "Dad said I should remind you to have your report ready, but he couldn't say how long you will need to be in Corvid."

I glanced at Nick, "So you won't be returning to Las Cruses with me?"

"I'll be back soon, but for now, Sherill is moving to New Mexico and will continue your basic training. Mom and dad already rented her a condo in our building. You're going to have plenty of company and several tutors who will offer instructions in specific areas and of course advanced ESP procedures."

"How soon do we leave for Sedona?

"Tomorrow morning. Time travel would be a lot faster but we can't leave the car here." Nicked chuckled. "We'll load up tonight so we can get an early start."

"Sounds like we're going to be neighbors," I said to Sherill.

"I think we are going to be more than just neighbors," she said with a twinkle in her eyes as tiny bells sounded in the distance.

~

The following morning we headed for Sedona, Arizona, and the hotel L'Auberge de Sedona on Oak Creek, where we would meet Leizal and Josh. The scenic drive took us through desert flatlands with giant buttes and rocky terrain, into the college town of Flagstaff at the base of the San Francisco Peaks, and down the winding road through the forested cliffs of Oak Creek Canyon and into the tourist bustling artistic town of Sedona.

After lunch with Leizal and Josh, we took a quick tour of the Chapel of the Holy Cross and Bell Rock. Their departure time was scheduled for 7:00 pm.

Nick reminded me that he would be leaving with his parents to make his report to the Council before returning to New Mexico. As we drove out to a remote area near the small airport, huge billowy clouds were starting to gather over the famous red rock formations in the late afternoon. It was the makings of a good old-fashion thunder storm.

"I think you missed the turn for the airport," I said. "Shouldn't we turn around?"

Nick smiled. "No problem, dude. We're taking the Corvid Express back home."

There was an open area just ahead as we pulled to the side of the road. Josh and Leizal were waiting for us in the clearing. "We'll say goodbyes for now, but look to see us again soon and take good care of Sherill," said Leizal giving us both a hug. We stepped back, as the wind began to spin and swirl around them.

My jaw dropped and I stood in awe, watching as Josh and Leizal began to rise on the currents of the wind. In the blink of an eye they had both transformed into large eagles, soring upwards—higher and higher, as they disappeared into the rolling cloud formations.

Nick chuckled as he watched my expression of amazement. "The clouds create a vision cover, or mirage for our transportation back to Corvid. As I explained before, a vision is a form of disguise. You'll learn how to see through a vision and how to recognize one when you see it. Until I return, Sherill will explain your training process and answer any questions you might have. And I'm sure there will be many.

"There is much to comprehend about time-travel and its effects on the human body. Your extrasensory perception has already improved at a rapid pace due to the transfusion you received, and you will be tutored in the art of transformation or shape-shifting if you prefer. I think you will make a great hawk to begin with, but the choice will of course be yours to make."

I listened carefully, determined not to miss a word that Nick was saying. There was much for my mind to absorb and attempt to understand. Sherill held my hand, giving it a gentle squeeze to let me know she was there for support.

Nick hugged us both as he stepped back in the swirling wind and began to rise off the ground. In a flash of light his body shifted into that of a large raven with black and iridescent green feathers glistening in a bright light shining from within the dark billowing clouds. His voice echoed to the ground below as he soared in slow circling motions, rising on the currents, "Remember, dude... whenever you see a raven, think of me until I return," he laughed.

I quickly shouted back, "There are thousands of ravens in New Mexico, dude. How will I know which one is you?"

I could hear his laughter. "You'll know," he answered. "You'll know," echoed his voice from the spiraling tunnel of the vortex as the raven disappeared into the billowing clouds. Moments later there was a flash of light and a loud clap of thunder.

As a gentle rain cooled the dry desert air, Sherill and I walked back to the SUV and headed to New Mexico with thoughts of more exciting adventures ahead.

About the Author—D.G. Heath

D.G. Heath is an author at 76, living in the Yucatan with John, his life-partner of 49 years. In his former life, he was an interior designer, private secretary, real estate broker, fashion model and CEO of his own company.

David and John owned and operated the Relais et Chateaux—Rancho de San Juan Country Inn, 38 miles northwest of Santa Fe, New Mexico for 22 years, receiving numerous awards in the hospitality industry.

Published Works

Adelaide Literary Magazine

The Cappuccino / No Time for Tears

Books

Tales from a Country Inn

D.G. Heath Mystery Collection—Volume I
Double Martini / Web of Intrigue / Codes and Confessions

D.G. Heath Mystery Collection—Volume II
A Person of Interest / Accent / Vortex

The Art of Imagination

David is busy writing, poetry, mysteries and a memoir series titled *Adventures in Life*. Fiction, fantasy, travel, humor, suspense and mystery are his tools.